D0227577

SNUFF FICTION

Robert Rankin

CORGI BOOKS

SNUFF FICTION
A CORGI BOOK : 0 552 14590 4

Originally published in Great Britain by Doubleday,
a division of Transworld Publishers

PRINTING HISTORY
Doubleday edition published 1999
Corgi edition published 1999

1 3 5 7 9 10 8 6 4 2

Set in 11/13pt Bembo by Falcon Oast Graphic Art

Corgi Books are published by Transworld Publishers,
61–63 Uxbridge Road, London W5 5SA,
a division of The Random House Group Ltd,
in Australia by Random House Australia (Pty) Ltd,
20 Alfred Street, Milsons Point, Sydney, NSW 2061, Australia,
in New Zealand by Random House New Zealand Ltd,
18 Poland Road, Glenfield, Auckland 10, New Zealand
and in South Africa by Random House (Pty) Ltd,
Endulini, 5a Jubilee Road, Parktown 2193, South Africa.

Reproduced, printed and bound in Great Britain by
Cox & Wyman Ltd, Reading, Berks.

For David Do 1, who takes life with a big pinch

And in memory of Peter Myers, with Love

SNUFF FICTION

1

The first man ever to be arrested for smoking was Rodrigo de Jerez, who sailed with Columbus on his first voyage. His fellow townsmen of Aymonte observed the smoke issuing from his mouth and nose and denounced him as a minion of the devil. He was imprisoned by the Inquisition. The year was 1504.

The school keeper's name was Mr Blot. Charles Henry Blot to be precise, although this was only ever revealed at his trial. To the children of Grange Junior School he was Mr Blot and you called him sir when you met him.

You met him unexpectedly. In the corridor, in the toilets, in the alleyway that ran down to where the dustbins were kept and you weren't supposed to be. He loomed at you, sniffed at you, muttered at you, then he was gone. Leaving behind him an odd smell in the air.

The source of Blot's smell was a matter for debate. A lad called Billy, who knew more than was healthy for one of his age, said that the smell was sulphur and that it came from certain glands situated close to Blot's arse. All male adults had these glands, according to Billy, and used them for marking their territory. Much in the manner of tom-cats.

And this was why Blot sniffed at you, to check whether you had developed your glands yet. And if you had, he would report you to the headmistress and she would make you see the school nurse and your parents would have to come up to the school and fill out a special form.

This particular disclosure led to a rather embarrassing incident, when I was caught by my mother in the bathroom, trousers around my ankles, bent double before the mirror, head between my legs and sniffing.

I lost a lot of faith in Billy after that.

Exactly what Mr Blot really did smell of was anybody's guess. He didn't smell like other grown-ups and other grown-ups smelled pretty strong. When Oscar Wilde wrote that youth is wasted on the young, he was only part of the way there. It's the senses that are really wasted, because nobody tells you that they're going to fade.

When you're a child, the world is a very colourful place. It's extremely noisy and it smells incredible. By the time you're a teenager you've lost nearly ten per cent of your sense of colour and sound and smell and you don't even notice.

It's probably something to do with your glands.

But Blot smelled odd and that was that.

Of course he looked odd too. School keepers always look odd. It's a tradition, or an old charter, or something. You don't get the job if you don't look odd. And Blot got the job and he kept it. He must have been well over six feet six. My father was a big man, but Blot loomed over him. Blot loomed and fairly dwindled. His head seemed the size of an onion and closely resembled one too. He wore a boiler suit of September grey with a matching cap and a blue woollen muffler, which made him look like an engine driver.

Billy explained to us that this had indeed once been Blot's profession. He had been the driver of the Trans-Siberian Express. A terrible incident had occurred which led to Blot fleeing Russia. His train had run into a snowdrift in midwinter a thousand miles from any-where. The crew had eventually been forced to dine upon the passengers, who were mostly peasants and used to that kind of thing. By the time the spring thaw came and the train could get moving again, Blot was the only survivor. Although the authorities were will-ing to forgive the consumption of passengers, as peasants had never been in short supply, they took a dim view of Blot having filled his stomach with trained railwaymen.

Billy said that down in Blot's lair amongst the heating pipes, he drank his tea from the stoker's skull-cap and sat upon an armchair upholstered in human skin.

As it turned out at the trial, Billy wasn't altogether wrong about the armchair.

But the trial was for the future and way back then, in the time that was our now, we hated Mr Blot. Hated his boiler suit and matching cap. Hated his woollen muffler and his onion head. Hated his looming and his sniffing and his smell.

The time that was our now was 1958 and we were nine years old and plenty of us. Post-war baby boomers, forty to a class. Weetabix and orange juice for breakfast, half a pint of milk at playtime with a straw.

Spam for lunch, and tea, if you were lucky. Bovril and Marmite and Ovaltine before you went to bed.

Our teacher was Mr Vaux. He wore a handlebar moustache that he referred to as a 'pussy-tickler' and a tweed sports jacket. In our youthful innocence we naturally assumed that pussy-tickling was some kind of exotic sport indulged in by gentlemen who wore tweed. We were right, in essence.

Mr Vaux was a gentleman; he had a posh accent and had flown Spitfires in the war. He had been shot down over France and the Gestapo had tortured him with a screwdriver. He had three medals in his desk drawer and these he wore on Empire Day.

Mr Vaux was something of a hero.

Mr Vaux and Mr Blot did not see eye to eye. In the winter it got very cold in class. We were allowed to wear our coats. Mr Vaux would turn up the radiators and Mr Blot would come in and turn them down again.

But it didn't seem to be winter that often. Mostly it seemed to be summer. Our classroom faced the west and on those summer afternoons the sunlight fell through the high Edwardian windows in long cathedral shafts, rich with floating golden motes, and put us all to sleep. Mr Vaux would try to rouse us with tales of his adventures behind enemy lines. But eventually he would give it up as a lost cause, open his silver cigarette case, take out a Capstan Full Strength and sit back, with his feet on the desk, awaiting the four o'clock bell.

It was Mr Vaux who got us into smoking really. Of course in those days everybody smoked. Film stars and politicians. Doctors and nurses. Priests in the pulpit and midwives on the job. Footballers all enjoyed a Wild Woodbine at half-time and marathon runners were rarely to be seen crossing the finishing lines without a fag in their faces.

And how well I recall those first pictures of Sir Edmund Hillary upon the summit of Everest sucking on a Senior Service.

Those indeed *were* the days.

But faraway days they are now. And in these present times, some fifty years later, in these post-technological days of heavy food rationing, riots and the new Reichstag, it is hard to imagine a golden epoch in the century before, when smoking was not only legal, but good for you.

And yet it is curious how, in so many ways, those times mirror our own. Then, as now, television was in black and white. Then, as now, there were only two stations and these run by the state. Then, as now, food was rationed. Then, as now, there was conscription. Then, as now, there were no computers.

But then, and unlike now, we were happy.

It is certainly true that the old often look back upon the days of their youth with an ill-deserved fondness. They harp on about 'the good old days, the good old days', whilst filling in the pock holes of hardship with the face cream of faulty recollection, and no doubt papering over the cracks of catastrophe with the heavily flocked and Paisley-patterned washable wallpaper of false memory syndrome. While this may be the case, some times are actually better than others. And most were better than ours.

As I write today, on 30 July 2008, a mere eight and a half years on from the great millennium computer crash, with the world gone down the pan and halfway round the old S bend, it is easy to breathe out a sigh for times gone by and wonder where they went.

Up in smoke is where they went, which brings me back to fags.

Mr Vaux, as I've said, smoked Capstan Full Strength, flavoursome and rich in health. As children, with our heightened nasal sensitivities, we had no difficulty in identifying any of the thirty or so leading brands of cigarettes, simply by taking a sniff or two of the smoke. Things could get tricky on long train journeys, as there were more than three hundred regional brands, not to mention imports and personal blends. But Capstan, Woodbine, Players and the other well-known names were easy.

Up north, where they were evidently more enlightened, junior-school children were allowed, indeed encouraged, to smoke in class. This was no doubt to prepare them for life down the pit, as in those days all men who lived north of the Wash worked in the coal mines. But in London, where I grew up, and in Brentford, where I went to school, you were not allowed to smoke in the classroom until after you'd passed your eleven plus and gone on to the Grammar.

So we did as all children did, and smoked in the toilets at playtime. The toilets were all equipped with fitted ashtrays next to the bog-roll holders and once a day the ashtray monitor would go around and empty them. Ashtray monitor was one of the better

14

monitoring jobs, as you could often collect up a good number of half-smoked cigarettes, crushed out hastily when the bell rang to end playtime, but still with a few fine puffs left in them.

There were monitors for everything back then. A milk monitor; a chalk monitor; an ink monitor; a window monitor, who got to use the big pole with the hook on the end; a monitor to give out the school books and another to collect them up again. There was the car monitor who cleaned the headmistress's Morris Minor; the shoe monitor who attended to the polishing of the teachers' footwear; and of course the special monitor who catered to the needs of the male teachers who favoured underage sex.

I was a window monitor myself, and if I had a pound now for every pane of glass I accidentally knocked out then and every caning I received in consequence, I would have enough money to employ a special monitor of my own to lessen the misery of my declining years.

But sadly I do not.

However, what I do have is a photographic memory whose film remains unfogged and it is with the aid of this that I shall endeavour to set down an accurate record of the way things were then. Of the folk that I knew, who would later play their parts in the misshaping of history. Good folk and bad, famous and not so. And of one in particular, whose unique talents, remarkable achievements and flamboyant lifestyle are now the stuff of legend. A man who has brought joy into the lives of millions with his nonpareil nose powder.

He is known today by many appellations. The tender blender with the blinder grinder. The master blaster with the louder powder. And the geezer with the sneezer that's a real crowd pleaser. And so on and so forth and suchlike.

Most will know him simply as the Sultan of Snuff.

I speak, of course, of Mr Doveston.

Those readers old enough to remember daily newspapers will recall with fondness the 'gutter press'. Tabloids, as were. These journals specialized in documenting the lives of the rich and famous. And during the final years of the twentieth century the name of Mr Doveston was often to be found writ in letters big and bold across their front pages.

He was both praised and demonized. His exploits were marvelled at, then damned to Hell. Saint, they said, then sinner. Guru, then Godless git. Many of the tales told about him were indeed true. He *did* have a passion for dynamite – the 'Big Aaah-choo!' as he called it. I can personally vouch for the authenticity of the infamous episode of the detonating dog. I witnessed it with my own two eyes. And I got a lot of it on me!

But that it was he who talked the late Pope into the canonization of Diana, Princess of Wales, is incorrect. The worship of Diana, Di-anity as it is now known, did not become a major world religion until after the Great Computer Crash. By which time Mr Doveston had fallen out with the ailing pontiff after an argument over which of them possessed the larger collection of erotically decorated Chinese snuff bottles.

The task I have set myself here is to tell the *real* story.

Give the facts and hold not back upon the guts and gore. There is love and joy and there is sorrow. There is madness, there is mayhem, there is magic, there is mystery.

There is snuff.

And where there's snuff, there's snot, the saying goes, and you shall have it all.

But let me explain from the outset that this is no ordinary biography. This book contains a series of personal recollections. I write only of the times that *I* spent with the Doveston.

I write of our childhood years together and of the meetings with his 'uncles'. Meetings that would shape our years ahead.

I write of the now legendary Puberty Party, of Brentstock, of the days at Castle Doveston and of the Great Millennial Ball. And I write, as I alone can, of his terrible end.

I can do no more than this.

And so, with that said, and well said too, let us begin our tale. The year is 1958, the month is good old flaming June. The sunlight falls through those high classroom windows, lighting up the head of Mr Vaux who's lighting up a fag. Outside, in the corridor, Blot looms above a startled child and sniffs and then is gone. And coming now across the quad, with shuffling gait, is a ragged lad, gum-chewing, with a whistle and a grin. His hair is tousled and nitty, and he does not wear his tie. His grubby hands are in his grubby pockets.

Can this urchin really be the boy who later, as the

man, will make so great a mark upon this world of ours?

It can.

Our tale begins.

2

At bull-baiting, bear-whipping and everywhere else, the English are constantly smoking the Nicotian weed, which in America is called 'tobaco'.

Paul Heutzner, 1598

The boy Doveston shuffled across the quadrangle. It was a definite shuffle he had, as opposed to, say, a waddle or a totter. There was the hint of a slouch to his gait and more than a little of the plod. There was trudge in it too, as a matter of fact, and a smidgen of amble as well.

But let it be set clear upon the record and right from the very start, there was no trace of sidle in that walk. And had he chosen, for reasons of his own, to increase the speed of his perambulation, there would have been no swagger, strut, or goose-step.

The boy Doveston moved with the honest and unprepossessing shuffle of the poor. Because he *was* poor, as indeed were we all.

That our school should be called the Grange was not without irony. For although the title conjures up an image of some well-bricked seat of learning, ivy-walled and gravelly-drived, this was not the case. The Grange was your bog-standard Edwardian day school, built by

19

the burghers of Brentford to educate the sons of the poor. Not educate them too much, of course, but just enough. Sufficient that they could spell their names and count their wages and learn to call their betters, sir.

And so it had for fifty years.

And done so rather well.

The boy Doveston had not been taught to shuffle. It came naturally to him. It was in his genes. Generations of Dovestons had shuffled on before him: few to glory and all to a pauper's grave. And while we did not suffer the wretched privations of our Irish counterparts, who plodded barefoot to school with a clod of turf under each arm and a potato clenched between their bottom cheeks, we were poor enough.

We suffered all the usual maladies of the impoverished: rickets, ringworm, scrofula and mange. As a typical child, the boy Doveston played host to a wide variety of vermin, from the aforementioned nits, to body lice, gut worm, trouser roach and plimsoll maggot. Blowflies feasted on the juices of his eyes and aphids dined upon his ear wax.

But this was the way of it. We knew no different. We were unconcerned and we were happy. The boy Doveston was happy. He grinned and he whistled – a popular tune of the day, breathed out in unrecognizable fragments, for it is almost impossible to grin and whistle at the same time.

The boy Doveston, having shuffled across the quadrangle, now shuffled under the veranda and into the school building. Our classroom was 4a and within it we were enjoying a history lesson. Mr Vaux stood before the blackboard, a piece of chalk in one hand and a

20

Capstan's Full Strength in the other, and spoke to us of Damiens' Bed of Steel.

Robert-François Damiens had in 1757 made an attempt upon the life of Louis XV. As a punishment for this and to discourage any other potential regicides, he had been brutally tortured to death. They had placed him upon an iron bedstead affair that was warmed to red hot. His right hand was roasted on a slow fire. Molten lead and wax were poured into wounds that were inflicted upon him by special pincers and he was eventually torn into pieces by four wild horses.

It was all very interesting and Mr Vaux evidently knew his subject well, judging by the graphic descriptions he gave of each particular torment. And it certainly served as an object lesson to any of us who harboured the ambition to become an assassin when we grew up: that we should plan our getaways with the utmost care!

The lesson was almost over by the time the boy Doveston entered the classroom, which was a shame because he had missed all the best bits. I know he would have enjoyed the part when Mr Vaux held his finger over a candle flame to demonstrate just how much pain a man can take before he screams really loud. I know I did. And while most of the soppy girls were quietly weeping and that softy Paul Mason had fainted, the boy Doveston would certainly have been the first to put up his hand when Mr Vaux asked who amongst us would like to sniff the burned flesh of his finger.

But as it was he missed it and as it was he entered without knocking first.

Mr Vaux swung around from the blackboard and pointed his charred digit at the boy. 'Out!' cried he, in outrage and in such a raised voice that Paul, awaking from his faint, was caused to faint once more.

The boy went out again and knocked. 'Come,' called Mr Vaux. The boy came in.

Our teacher laid his chalk aside and sought instead his slipper. He looked the boy both up and down and shook his head in sadness. And then he glanced up at the classroom clock and made tut-tutting sounds.

'Two-twenty-three,' said Mr Vaux. 'You have excelled yourself this time, Doveston.'

The boy scuffed his unpolished shoes on the floor. 'I'm truly sorry, sir,' he said.

'A laudable sentiment,' said Mr Vaux. 'And one which makes the violence I am about to visit upon your backside with my slipper purely symbolic. Kindly bend over the desk.'

'Ah,' said the boy. 'I think not.'

'*Think not?*' Mr Vaux's moustachios bristled as only moustachios can. 'Over the desk at once, my lad, and learn the errors of dissent.'

'The headmistress says that you are not to beat me for being late, sir.'

'Oh,' said our teacher, making a dramatic flourish with his slipper. 'You have received a dispensation from on high. Possibly you are to atone for your sins in some other fashion. Or is it a case of *venia necessitati datur*?'[1]

It was always a pleasure to hear Mr Vaux spout Latin. But as the subject was not taught in our school, we

---

[1]Pardon is granted to necessity.

never had the foggiest idea what he was on about.

'It is the case, sir, that I had to go to the police station.'

'O joyous day,' said Mr Vaux. 'And so at last you are to be taken off to Approved School and I shall be spared the onerous and thankless task of teaching you. Hasten then to clear your desk and take your leave at the hurry-up.'

'No, sir. I had to go to the police station because I witnessed a crime and helped to bring the criminal to justice.'

'Doveston,' said Mr Vaux, 'do you know the penalty for lying in this school?'

Doveston munched thoughtfully upon his chewing gum. 'I do, sir, yes,' he said at length. 'I do, sir, yes indeed.'

'That is good,' said Mr Vaux. 'For although the punishment falls somewhat short of that inflicted upon Damiens, it has always in the past proved itself to be a powerful deterrent in the fight against mendacity and falsehood.'

'Yes indeed,' said Doveston once more.

'So, with that firmly understood, perhaps you would care to share with us the details of your day?'

'I would, sir. Yes please.'

'Then do so.' Mr Vaux settled himself down at his desk, stubbed out his cigarette and put his hands behind his Brylcreemed head. 'The floor is yours,' he said, 'so say your piece.'

'Thank you, sir, I will.' The boy Doveston thrust his hands once more into the pockets of his shorts and sniffed away a runner from his nose. 'You see, sir,' he began, 'I left my house early, because I had to do an errand for my mum and I didn't want to be late for school. My mum had asked me to go to old Mr Hartnell's corner shop and buy her a packet of Duchess. Those are the new perfumed cigarettes from Carberry's of Holborn. The tobacco is a light mellow Virginia, flavoured with bergamot and sandalwood. And although I do not condemn the use of essential oils in the preparation of snuff, it is a different matter with cigarettes, tending to adulterate the taste of the tobacco rather than enhance it. I feel that with Duchess, as with Lady Grey's and Her Favourites, the application has been over-liberal. In my opinion, the perfuming of cigarettes is little more than an exotic blandishment, designed to lure gullible female smokers away from their regular brands.'

'An argument most eloquently put,' said Mr Vaux, his eyebrows raised. 'I had no idea that you were *au fait* with the subtleties of the tobacco-blender's craft.'

'Oh yes, sir. When I grow up I intend to go into the trade. I have certain ideas that I think will revolution-ize it.'

'Do you now? Well, I'm sure that they're all very interesting. But please confine yourself to the matter in hand.'

'Yes, sir. So I went into old Mr Hartnell's to purchase the cigarettes. Which, I might add, cost one and fourpence for ten, an outrageous sum. And there was a chap waiting to be served before me. He was dressed in the garb of a road-sweeper, but I chanced to notice that his shoes were highly polished. My sus-picions were further aroused when he asked to buy a packet of cigarettes.'

'Why?' asked Mr Vaux.

'Because he asked for a packet of Carroll's Golden Glories, a tipped cigarette smoked almost exclusively by the gentry. No road-sweeper would ever smoke a tipped cigarette, let alone a Carroll's. And then, sir, if this wasn't enough, he paid with a five-pound note.'

'Incredible,' said Mr Vaux.

'Incredible,' we all agreed.

And it was incredible. And as we listened and the boy Doveston spoke, the tale that unfolded was more than incredible.

It was exciting too.

He had followed the man from old Mr Hartnell's corner shop, down Moby Dick Terrace, along Abaddon Street to an empty house on the edge of the bomb site at the Half Acre. We knew all the empty houses in Brentford, but we'd never been able to get into this one because it was so well boarded up.

The man had entered the house through a hidden doorway at the back and the boy had followed him in.

Once inside, the boy had found himself in what looked to be a laboratory, with strange specimens suspended in tall preserving jars and much complicated apparatus of the electrical persuasion. He crouched down behind a work bench and watched as the man made a call on a tiny wireless set, speaking in a language that seemed to consist of squeaks and grunts. His call completed, he swung around, pistol in hand and demanded that Doveston show himself.

Grudgingly the boy complied.

'So,' said the man, 'you are an enterprising youth.'

'I'm lost, sir,' said the Doveston. 'Could you tell me the way to the railway station?'

'You are indeed lost,' said the man, in a voice that the boy described as chilling. 'But now *I* have found you.'

'Goodbye,' said the Doveston, turning to leave.

'The door is locked,' said the man. And it was.

'Please don't kill me,' the Doveston said.

The man smiled and put away his pistol. 'I have no wish to kill you,' he replied. 'On the contrary, when I have finished with you, you will be anything but dead. You will be more alive than you can possibly imagine.'

'I would rather just leave, if that's all right with you.'

'No,' said the man, 'it's not. Now listen carefully while I explain the situation to you and then, when I've finished, you can make up your own mind about what you do.'

'Do you mind if I smoke while I listen?'

'No, certainly, have one of mine.'

The boy Doveston grinned at Mr Vaux. 'I was hoping he'd say that,' he said, 'because I'd never tried a Carroll's before. I must say, however, that it was something of a let-down. The quality of the tobacco was good, but the watermarked paper has a slightly glossy feel and burns unevenly. I was impressed by the charcoal filter, but there is definite room for improvement there. Possibly the addition of a cork tip such as with Craven A. I—'

But this particular discourse was cut short by the sound of Mr Vaux's slipper striking his desk. 'Get on with it!' cried Mr Vaux.

The boy got on with it.

'The man told me that he was part of an élite group of scientists working for the government. They had created an electronic brain that was capable of predicting future developments in technology. It couldn't actually tell the future, because it couldn't access all the information required to do that. It worked on a mathematical principle. If you are asked to work out what two and two make, you will say: four. Which means that you have predicted the future. You have foretold what will happen when you add two and two. The electronic brain works something like that. He said that it had worked out that by the end of the century we would be almost completely reliant on machines like itself, computers, to run society. They would be linked into almost everything. Food production, military defence, telecommunications, transportation, hospitals, banking, whatever.

'But, he said, there would be an unavoidable design fault in the programming of these systems. Something to do with the little date-counters inside them. And this would mean that when they reached the year two thousand, many of them would break down. Society would then collapse, he said.'

Mr Vaux stroked at his moustachios. And if I'd had some to stroke, I'd have surely done the same. It was fascinating stuff. Radical stuff. Incredible stuff. And, curiously, it also seemed as if it were *familiar* stuff. I felt certain that I'd heard all this before. In fact, the more I thought about it, the more *absolutely certain* I felt that I'd heard all this before. Indeed that I'd *read* all this before.

In a comic book that the Doveston had recently lent to me.

27

I don't think Mr Vaux had read it though. I think he would have stopped the tale-telling sooner if he had. I think he quite enjoyed the bit when the boy refused to submit to the brain-implant operation that would have linked him to the electronic machine and the man pulled the lever that dropped him through the trapdoor into the cage beneath. It was here, of course, that the Doveston met the princess with the silver eyes, who had been kidnapped for use in some similar experiment. I don't know whether you can actually pick a padlock with a matchstick and whether there really is a maze of subterranean caverns beneath Brentford inhabited by dwarves with tattooed ears. I remain uncertain about the amount of firepower the Brentford constabulary were able to call upon when they surrounded the house. And I'm certain we would have heard the explosion when the man pressed the self-destruct button rather than be taken alive.

But it was a thrilling story and I do feel that it was really decent of Mr Vaux to let the Doveston finish.

Before he bent him over the desk.

Although we were never taught German at the Grange, we all knew the meaning of the word *Schadenfreude*. And we all enjoyed the beating. It was a suitably epic beating and at the end of it Mr Vaux had four of the injury monitors convey the unconscious Doveston to the school nurse to have his wounds dressed and the smelling bottle applied to his nostrils.

All in all it was a memorable afternoon and I include it here as I feel it offers the reader an insight into just what sort of a boy the Doveston was.

Imaginative. And daring.

At home-time we helped him out through the school gates. We were all for carrying him shoulder high, but his bottom, it seemed, was too tender. However, he was a hero, there was no mistake about that, and so we patted him gently upon what areas of his body remained uninjured and called him a jolly good fellow.

As we left the school our attention was drawn to a large black and shiny motor car, parked in the otherwise deserted street. On the bonnet of this leaned a man in a chauffeur's uniform and cap. At our rowdy approach he stepped forward. Not, however, to protect the car, but to hand the Doveston a bag of sweets.

We looked on in silence as the chauffeur returned to the car, climbed in and drove away at speed.

I have a lasting impression of that moment. Of the car turning the corner past old Mr Hartnell's shop. And of the passenger in the back seat, smiling and waving.

The passenger was a beautiful young woman.

A beautiful young woman with astounding silver eyes.

3

'Sir, will you be good enough to tell your friend that
my snuff box isn't an oyster.'

Beau Brummell (1778–1840)

Uncle Jon Peru Joans was no uncle of mine. And
neither was he one of the Doveston's. The boy had
adopted him.

He had adopted various adults in and around the
borough of Brentford and visited each on a regular basis.

There was an ancient called Old Pete, whose allotment patch he helped to tend. A tramp known as Two
Coats, with whom he went on foraging expeditions to
Gunnersbury Park. The lady librarian, who was apparently teaching him Tantric sexual techniques. And
there was Uncle Jon Peru Joans.

The boy's choice of adults had been scrupulous. Only
those possessed of useful knowledge qualified. Old Pete
was reckoned by most to be *the* man in the district when
it came to the growing of fruit and veg. Two Coats was
the man when it came to what we now call 'survivalism'.
The lady librarian was definitely *the woman* in most
respects. And then there was Uncle Jon Peru Joans.

'What exactly *does* he do?' I asked the Doveston, as

30

together we shuffled over the cobbles of the tree-lined drive that led to the historic Butts Estate.

The boy took to scratching his left armpit. There was currently a plague of pit weevil in the school and we were all most grievously afflicted.

'Come on,' I said, 'tell us.'

'He doesn't do much now,' said the Doveston. 'He is something of a recluse. But he served with the Royal Engineers and later the SAS. He knows all there is to know about dynamite.'

I kicked a bottle top into a drain. 'So it's blowing things up again, is it?' I asked.

'There's nothing wrong in blowing things up. It's a healthy boyish pursuit.'

'That's not what Vicar Berry says.'

'Vicar Berry is an old hypocrite,' said the Doveston, worrying now at his right armpit. 'He was an army chaplain and saw plenty of blowings-up. He merely wishes to deny the young the pleasures he himself enjoyed. You will find that's a common thing amongst adults.'

I couldn't deny this was true.

'Anyway,' said the Doveston, focusing attention on his groin, where an infestation of Y-front worm were gnawing at his nadgers. 'Uncle Jon Peru Joans doesn't only know all about dynamite. He knows all about orchids and hydro-dendrology.'

'Hydro-den-whatery?'

'Hydro-dendrology. It is the science of growing trees in water.'

I too gave my groin a thoughtful but much needed scratch.

'This is his house,' said the boy. And I looked up to see it.

The houses of the Butts Estate were of the Georgian ilk. Mellow pinky-bricked and proud-proportioned. The gardens were well tended and the folk who lived here were grand. A professor on the corner there and, deep amongst the trees, the Seamen's Mission. An old sea captain kept the place, but none of us had seen him. There was peace and quiet here and there was history.

We never got much in the way of local history at school. But we knew all the major stuff anyway. It had been passed down to us by our parents. 'That's where Julius Caesar crossed the Thames.' 'That's where King Balin fell during the famous Battle of Brentford.' 'That is the site of the coaching inn where Pocahontas stayed.' And, most interestingly of all, 'That is the house where P. P. Penrose was born.'

Prior to Mr Doveston, P. P. Penrose was undoubtedly Brentford's most famous son: author of the best-selling books of the twentieth century, the now legendary Lazlo Woodbine novels.

Throughout his life it was popularly believed that he had been born on the Lower East Side of New York. He affected a Brooklyn accent and always wore a fedora and trench coat. It was only after his tragic early death (in a freak accident involving handcuffs and a vacuum cleaner hose) that the truth finally came out (along with much of his lower bowel) – he had been born plain Peter Penrose in a house on Brentford's Butts Estate. He had never been to New York in his life.

They never put a blue plaque up, but we all knew

which house it was. The one with the blinds always drawn. In the summer, coachloads of American tourists would arrive to peer at those blinds. And our friend Billy, who knew more than was healthy for one of his age, would take his mum's vacuum cleaner along. The Americans would pay Billy to let them pose with it.

But I have nothing new to add on the subject of Penrose. And can do no more than recommend to the reader who wishes to delve further into the man, his work and his domestic habits, that they sample Sir John Rimmer's excellent biography: *Some Called Him Laz: The man who was Woodbine*.

Or the article on auto-erotic asphyxiation that was published in the last-ever issue of *Gagging for It!* magazine, December 1999.

'I'm gagging for a drink,' I said. 'Do you think that Uncle Jon Peru has lemonade?'

'He only drinks filtered water.' The boy Doveston reached out for the big brass knocker. 'Now remember what I told you to say,' he said in a serious voice.

'What was it you told me to say?' I asked, as I hadn't been listening at the time.

'That you are my brother Edwin and you share my interest in plants.'

'But you don't have a brother Edwin.'

The Doveston shook his scrofulous head. 'Do you want to see the monsters or not?'

'I do,' I said. And I did.

Normally, on a warm summer's evening like this, I would have been down at the canal, fishing for mud sharks. But the Doveston had promised me that if I gave him a shilling, he would take me to meet a man

33

who had monsters in his greenhouse and might even let me feed them, if I asked him nicely.

It was not the kind of offer a nine-year-old boy could refuse.

The Doveston tugged upon the big brass knocker. 'We'll have to wait for a bit,' he said. 'He has to check out the street.'

I made the face of puzzlement.

'Just wait,' said the boy. So we did.

After what seemed a considerable wait, during which thoughts began to enter my head that perhaps I didn't *really* want to see monsters at all and would rather have my shilling back, we heard the sounds of bolts being drawn and the big front door eased open a crack.

'Password,' came a whispered voice.

'Streptococcus,' said the Doveston, naming the Gram-positive spherical bacterium responsible for the outbreak of scarlet fever which had all but wiped out class three in the winter before.

'Enter, friend, and bring your brother.'

And so in we went.

When the front door closed it was rather dark and our host switched on the light. As I hadn't been expecting anything in particular, I was not at all surprised by what I saw. The hall was high and wide and rather grand. A patterned rug upon a polished floor. A jardinière with peacock plumes. A glimpse or two of splendid rooms. A bamboo stand with hats and coats, but very little more.

The sight of our host however, did surprise me. With the Doveston's talk of the Royal Engineers and

34

the SAS, I had at least been expecting a man who looked like an ex-soldier. But Uncle Jon Peru Joans was small and weedy. His cheekbones stuck out like a cyclist's elbows and his chin was that of Mr Punch. His baldy head was narrow and high and mottled as a pigeon's egg. His nose was slim as a paper dart, but his eyes were the very most worrying part.

Some months before I had sneaked in through the back door of the Odeon cinema in Northfields to see an X-certificate film called *Mondo Cane*. It was a documentary about curious customs around the world and included a lot of footage of bare-breasted native women jumping up and down. But the sequence that really stuck in my mind was the bit about a restaurant in China where they served monkeys' brains. Monkeys' brains from live monkeys. They had these special tables with little holes in the middle and the monkeys' heads were stuck up through these and held in place. And then, as coolly as you might peel an orange, the waiters would peel off the top of the monkeys' heads and the patrons would fish out the brains with little spoons and eat them.

It was the look in the eyes of those monkeys that I will never forget. The terror and the pain.

And Uncle Jon Peru Joans had eyes like that. They looked everywhere and nowhere and they put the wind up me.

'So this is your brother Edwin,' he said, his gaze darting over my head. 'Come to see my beautiful boys.'

I wished him a good evening and called him sir, because adults always respond to politeness. He reached forward to pat my head, but he must have noticed me flinching and so instead he just said, 'Can he keep our secret?'

'Oh yes, Uncle.' The Doveston grinned. 'He is my brother, after all.'

'Then I shall trust him as I trust you.'

The Doveston winked in my direction.

Uncle Jon Peru Joans led us down his hall. 'It has been a trying day,' he told us. 'The secret police have stepped up their campaign of harassment.'

'The secret police?' I asked.

'Oh yes,' said the weedy man. 'I am followed everywhere. They pose as passers-by, as window-cleaners and postmen, shopkeepers and mothers pushing prams. They know that I'm on to them and this makes them worse. Only this morning, when I went out to buy a packet of cigarettes—'

'Snowdon,' said the Doveston.

The uncle turned upon him, the wild eyes wilder yet.

'I can smell the smoke,' the boy explained. 'You've only just put one out. Snowdon is a menthol cigarette. It has a most distinctive smell.'

'Good boy,' said the uncle, patting the Doveston's shoulder. 'I change my brand every day to keep them guessing.'

'The secret policemen?' I asked.

'Exactly. And when I went into the shop there were two of them in there. Dressed up to look like old women with shopping bags. They were watching to see what I'd buy. They keep a record of everything I do. It all goes on file in the secret headquarters at Mornington Crescent.'

'Why do they do this?' I asked.

'Because of my work. Hasn't Charlie told you?'

'*Charlie?*'

'I thought it would be better coming from you,' said the Doveston.

'Good boy once more.' The weedy man led us into his kitchen, which smelled as bad as it looked. There were bags of rubbish piled up the walls and boxes and boxes of paper.

The uncle's eyes caught the look on my face, which was probably one of bewilderment. 'I throw nothing away,' he said. 'They go through my dustbins. I've seen them. They look like ordinary dustmen, but they don't fool me.'

I nodded and smiled and sniffed a little bit. There was a strange smell in this house. It wasn't the cigarettes and it wasn't all the rubbish. It was something else. A rich smell, heavy and pungent. And I knew where I had smelled it before. In the great glasshouses at Kew.

Uncle Jon Peru Joans lifted a chipped enamel bucket from the cluttered draining board and held it out in my direction. I took a peep inside and then a smart step backwards.

'It's only meat,' the uncle said.

'It's meat with bits of fur on.'

'They don't mind the fur, it's natural.'

I took the bucket, but I wasn't keen.

'Come on,' said the uncle. 'This way.'

He opened the outer kitchen door and the glasshouse smell rushed in. It literally fell over us. Engulfed us. Swallowed us up. It took the breath away. The heat smacked you right in the face and the

37

humidity brought sweat from every functioning pore.

'Hurry in,' said the uncle. 'We mustn't let the temperature drop.'

We hurried in and what I saw, to say the least, impressed me.

It was a Victorian conservatory.

I have always had a love for the Victorians. For their art and their invention and their architectural wonders. And while many purists sing the praises of the Georgians, for their classical designs, it seems to me that many of their buildings have the severity of maiden aunts. Those of the Victorian era, on the other hand, are big blowzy tarts. They rejoice in their being. They cry, 'Come and look at me, I'm gorgeous.'

The Victorians really knew how to build on a grand scale. When they constructed bridges and museums and piers and huge hotels, they simply went over the top. Wherever there was room for a flourish or a twiddly bit, they stuck it on.

The conservatory of Uncle Jon Peru Joans had more flourishes and twiddly bits than you could shake an ivory-handled Victorian swagger stick at. This wasn't just a blowzy tart, this was a music hall showgirl.

It swelled voluptuously from the rear of the house, all bulging bosoms of glass. The ornamental ironwork fanned and flounced, with decorative columns rising to swagged capitals. Like hymns in praise of pleasure, as Aubrey Beardsley wrote.

But if the conservatory itself was a marvel, the plants that grew within were something more. I had seen exotic blooms before at Kew. But nothing I had seen compared with these. This was exoticism taken to a wild extreme. The colours were too colourful, the bignesses too big.

I gawped at a monstrous flower that yawned up from a terracotta pot. You couldn't have a flower that big. You couldn't, surely.

'*Rafflesia arnoldii*,' said the uncle. 'The largest flower in the whole wide world. It comes from upper Sumatra, where the natives believe it is cross-pollinated by elephants.'

I leaned forward to have a good sniff.

'I wouldn't,' said the uncle.

But I had.

And 'Urrrrrrrrrgh!' I went, falling backwards and clutching at my hooter with my bucketless hand.

'Smells just like a rotten corpse,' said Uncle Jon Peru Joans. 'You'd best not sniff at anything unless you've asked me first.'

I sought to regain my composure. 'It wasn't too bad,' I lied.

'That's what Charlie said.' The uncle smiled a crooked smile. 'And there was me thinking that children had a more sensitive sense of smell.'

I fanned at my face. 'What is *that* called?' I asked, pointing to the nearest thing as if I gave a damn.

'Ah, this.' The uncle wrung his hands in pleasure and gazed lovingly upon a number of large fat white and frilly flowers that floated in a tub of oily water. 'This is called the Angel's Footstep.'

I wiped at the sweat that was dripping in my eyes. I was seriously leaking here. My vital fluids were oozing out all over the place. I'd been thirsty when I'd arrived, but now I was coming dangerously close to dehydration.

'The Angel's Footstep,' the uncle repeated. 'So named because it is said of angels that, like Christ, they can walk upon water. But only when the moon is full and only upon its reflection.'

'And the leaves are poisonous,' said the Doveston.

'Extremely,' the uncle agreed. 'Eat one of those and you'll join the angels. Oh my, yes indeed.'

'I think I might join the angels any minute if I don't have something to drink,' I said.

The uncle's eyes flicked over me. 'Put the bucket down,' he said kindly. 'There's a water tap over in the corner there and a metal cup on a chain. Don't touch anything else, or smell anything, all right?'

'All right, sir,' I said.

Being a resilient lad, who had already survived diphtheria and whooping cough and phossy jaw and Bengal rot, I wasn't going to let a bit of dehydration get me down too much. And so, having revived myself with a pint or two of Adam's ale, I was once more fit as a fiddle and fresh as a furtler's flute.

'All right now?' asked the uncle.

'Yes, thank you,' said I.

'Then let me show you these.'

The uncle drew my attention to a tub of plants. Deep green leaves they had, which spread in a flat rosette, interlaced with violet-tinged flowers. '*Mandragora officinarum*,' he said. 'The now legendary mandrake. Beneath the surface of the soil its root is the shape of a man. This is *the* witch plant, used in many magical ceremonies. It is said that when pulled from the ground it screams and that the scream will drive the hearer mad. Should we give it a little tug, do you think?'

I shook my head with vigour.

'No.' The uncle nodded. 'Best not, eh? The roots in fact contain a tropane alkaloid which taken in small doses can induce hallucinations and visions of paradise. In large doses however, they induce—'

'Death,' said the Doveston.

'Death,' said the uncle. 'It was very popular with Lucrezia Borgia. But three hundred years ago the Persians used it as a surgical anaesthetic.'

'They dried the root,' said the Doveston, 'ground it and mixed it with camphor, then boiled it in water. You sniffed the steam. The Romans originally brought it to England.'

'Your brother knows his stuff,' said the uncle, patting his prodigy's head and then examining his fingers for cooties.

I was given the full guided tour. Uncle Jon Peru Joans showed me his poppies. 'From which opium is distilled.' His *Cannabis sativa*. 'Indian hemp, beloved of beatniks.' His Menispermaceae. 'A member of the South American moonseed family, from which the arrow-head toxin, curare, is obtained.' And his *Lophophora williamsii*. 'Peyote. O wondrous peyote.'

We took in the monkshood and mugwort, the henbane and hellebores, samphire and the scurvy grass, toadflax and toxibelle. I didn't touch or smell anything.

It seemed clear to me that the uncle's collection consisted entirely of plants which either got you high or put you under. Or were capable of doing both, depending on the dose.

As I watched the weedy man with the weirdy eyes,

I wondered just how many of these narcotics he had personally sampled.

'And that's the lot,' he said finally. 'Except for the beautiful boys you've come to see and I'll show you those in a minute.'

I plucked distractedly at my shorts. My Y-fronts, ever crusty, were filling up with sweat and swelling to embarrassing proportions. 'It's all incredible, sir,' I said. 'But might I ask you a question?'

Uncle Jon Peru Joans inclined his pigeon-eggy head.

'Why exactly have you chosen to cultivate these particular varieties of plants?'

'For the Great Work,' said the Doveston.

'For the Great Work,' the uncle agreed.

I made the face that says 'eh?'

The uncle tapped his slender nose with a long and slender finger. 'Come', said he, 'and meet my boys, and I'll tell you all about it.'

A corner of the conservatory had been curtained off from the rest by a greasy damask tablecloth. The uncle stepped to this and flung it aside with a theatrical flourish.

'Wallah!' went he.

'Stone me,' said I, in the manner of Tony Hancock.

On a cast-iron pedestal stood an ancient aquarium and in this some of the queerest plants that I had ever seen.

I was not at first sure that they were plants. They had much of the reptile and some of the fish. They were scaly and shiny and all over odd and they made me feel most ill at ease.

As with all normal children, I harboured a healthy

fear of vegetables. Cabbage put the wind up me and I lived in terror of sprouts. Parental assurances that they were full of iron had been tested with a magnet and found to be naught but lies. Exactly why parents insisted upon piling vegetables onto their children's plates had been explained to me by Billy. Vegetables were cheaper than meat and times were ever hard. When, later in life, I briefly rubbed shoulders with folk of a higher social bracket, I was amazed to discover adults who ate nothing but vegetables. These folk, I learned, were called vegetarians and although they had enough money to buy meat, they actually *chose* not to do so.

As one known for his compassion, I naturally felt great pity for these sorry individuals, who clearly suffered some mental aberration that was beyond my power to cure. But ever philosophical, I looked upon the bright side. After all, the more vegetarians there are in the world, the more meat there is left to go round amongst us normal folk.

'My beautiful boys,' cried the uncle, startling me from my musings. 'Bring the bucket over here and we'll serve them up their supper.'

I hefted the bucket and cautiously approached. Scaly, shiny, reptile and fish and with more than a hint of the sprout: whatever they were, they were clearly alive, for they quivered and shivered and shook.

'Are they vegetables, sir?' was my question.

'Mostly,' said the uncle, peering in at his 'beautiful boys'. 'Mostly sprout, but partly basilisk.'

'Chimeras,' said the Doveston.

'Chimeras,' the uncle agreed.

'And they'll eat this meat in the bucket?'

Uncle Jon Peru Joans dug into his jacket and brought out a pair of long-handled tweezers. Passing these to me he said, 'Why don't you see for yourself?'

The Doveston nodded encouragingly. 'Go on,' he said, 'it's a big honour. Bung them a gobbet or two.'

I clicked the tweezers between my fingers. Sweat drip-dropped from my eyebrows and I felt far from well. But I *had* paid my shilling and this *was* what I'd come for, so I plucked some meat from the bucket.

'Arm's length,' the uncle advised, 'and don't get your fingers too near.'

I did as I was told and lowered a chunk of tweezered meat into the aquarium. It was as if I had dropped a dead sheep into a pool of piranhas. Nasty little hungry mouths all lined with pointy teeth came snap-snap-snapping. I fell back with big round eyes and a very wide mouth of my own.

'What do you think?' the Doveston asked.

'Brilliant!' said I and I meant it.

We took it in turns to feed the plants and we emptied the whole of the bucket. The uncle looked on, nodding his head and smiling, while his crazy eyes went every-which-way and his fingers danced with delight.

When we were done he said, 'There now then,' and closed the tablecloth curtain.

I handed the uncle his tweezers. 'Thank you very much, sir,' I said to him. 'That was jolly good fun.'

'Work can also be fun,' said the uncle. 'Even Great Work.'

'You were going to tell me all about that.'

'Maybe next time,' said the Doveston. 'We have to be off now, or we'll be late for Cubs.'

'Cubs?' I said.

'Yes, *Cubs*.' The Doveston gave me a meaningful look. Its meaning was lost upon me.

'I'm in no hurry,' I said.

'Good,' said the uncle.

The Doveston groaned.

'Are you all right, Charlie?'

'I am, Uncle, yes. Just a touch of King's Evil, that's all.'

'I've a root that will cure that.'

'I'm sure that you have.'

'Am I missing something?' I asked.

The uncle shook his little bald head. 'I think Charlie has a girlfriend,' he said. 'And is eager to practise upon her the skills he has learned from the lady librarian.'

The Doveston sniffed and shuffled his feet.

I made the 'eh?' face again.

'The Great Work,' said the uncle, striking a dignified pose. 'The work that will earn for me a place in the history books. But *they* know that I stand poised upon the threshold and that is why they watch my every move.'

'The secret policemen?'

'The secret police. They have powerful telescopes trained upon us even now. Which is why I keep my boys behind the curtain. The secret police want to know about my work and steal it for their masters at Mornington Crescent. But they won't, oh my word no.'

'I'm very pleased to hear that.'

'What I'm doing here,' said the uncle, 'is for all mankind. Not just a favoured few. What I am doing here will bring about world peace. You asked why I chose to cultivate these particular varieties of plant, didn't you?'

I nodded that I did.

'It is because of the drugs that can be distilled from them. Powerful hallucinogens, which, when blended correctly and taken in careful doses, allow me to enter an altered state of consciousness. Whilst in this state it is possible for me to communicate directly with the vegetable kingdom. As Dr Doolittle talked to the animals, so I can talk to the trees.'

I glanced across at the Doveston, who made a pained expression.

'What do the trees have to say?' I asked.

'Too much,' said the uncle, 'too much. They witter like dowagers. Moaning about the squirrels and the sparrows, the traffic and the noise. If I hear that old oak by the Seamen's Mission go on one more time about how civilized the world used to be, I'm sure I'll lose my mind.'

I ignored the Doveston's rolling eyes. 'Do all trees talk?' I asked.

'As far as I know,' said the uncle. 'Although of course I can only understand the English ones. I've no idea what the Dutch elms and Spanish firs are saying.'

'Perhaps you could take a language course.'

'I've no time for that, I'm afraid.'

I nodded moistly and plucked once more at my groin. 'So the secret police want to talk to trees too, do they?' I asked.

'Their masters do. You can imagine the potential for espionage.'

I couldn't really, so I said as much.

The uncle waved his hands about. 'For spying. You wouldn't need to risk human spies, if plants could do it for you. Just think what the potted plants in the Russian embassy have overheard. They'd be prepared to tell you, if you asked them nicely.'

'I see,' I said, and I did. 'But you'd have to learn how to speak Russian.'

'Yes, yes, but you get the point?'

'I *do* get the point,' I said. 'So *that* is the Great Work.'

'It's a part of it.'

'You mean there's more?'

'Much more.' The uncle preened at his lapels. 'Communicating with plants was only the first part. You see I wanted to know just what it was that plants wanted out of life and so I asked them. The ones in this conservatory grow so well because they tell me what they want and I give it to them. How much heat, how much light and so on. But there's one thing that all plants really want, and do you know what that is?'

'Love?' I said.

'*Love?*' said the Doveston.

'Sorry,' I said. 'Not love then?'

'They want to get about,' said the uncle. 'Move about like people do. They get really fed up spending all their lives stuck in one place in the ground. They want to uproot and get on the move.'

'And that's why you've bred the chimeras.'

'Exactly. They are the first of a new species. The

47

plant/animal hybrid. My beautiful boys are a different order of being.'

'They're rather fierce,' said I.

'Well, you need to be fierce when you go into battle.'

'Cubs,' said the Doveston. 'Time for the Cubs.'

'No,' I said. 'What battle, sir?'

'The final conflict,' said the uncle, rising on his toes. 'The battle of good against evil, as foretold in the Book of Revelation. This will come in the year two thousand and I shall be ready for it.'

'Are you digging a fallout shelter then?'

'No fallout shelter for me, lad. I shall be leading the charge. I intend to seed the entire globe with my chimeras. They will grow in any climate. They will grow big and fierce and when the call to arms comes, I shall give the signal and they will rise up in their millions, their hundreds of millions, and slay the oppressors. They will march across the lands, a mighty mutant army, destroying all before them, answering to only me. Only *me*, do you hear, *only me!*'

That was the last time I saw the uncle. I didn't go calling on him again. About a month after that some other folk came knocking at his door. Policemen they were, accompanied by others in white coats. There had been some complaints about missing cats and dogs and apparently a number of blood-stained collars were found in a bag beneath his sink.

My friend Billy, who was leading a party of American tourists around the Butts, said that he saw the uncle being hauled away, dressed in a long-sleeved jacket that buckled down the back. There was foam coming out of his mouth and the tourists stopped to take pictures.

On the following day a fire broke out. The house itself was hardly touched, but the beautiful conservatory burned to the ground.

Nobody knew how the fire had started.

Nobody seemed to care.

Nobody but for the Doveston. And he was clearly upset. He had been very fond of his 'adopted' uncle and was greatly miffed at his hauling away. I did what I could to console him, of course, such as buying him sweeties and sharing my fags. I think that we must have grown rather close, because he began to call me Edwin and I began to understand that he had 'adopted' me also.

One lunchtime during the following school term he took me aside in the playground.

'I believe that I have it in me to make my name famous,' he said. 'And I wish you to become my amanuensis and biographer. You will be a Boswell to my Johnson, a Watson to my Sherlock Holmes. It will be your job to chronicle my words and deeds for posterity. What say you to this offer?'

I pondered upon the Doveston's words.

'Will there be money and long-legged women?'

'Plenty of both,' he replied.

'Then count me in,' I said and we shook hands.

And there have indeed been plenty of both. Plenty of both and then some. But before we close the page upon Uncle Jon Peru Joans, one thing remains to be mentioned.

And that is the matter of his 'beautiful boys'.

With the destruction of his conservatory, it was my conviction that I had seen the last of those fierce fellows and so it came as a horrid surprise when four decades later I saw them again. No longer small and enclosed by glass, but wandering large on a country estate.

Called Castle Doveston.

4

Tobacco, divine, rare, superexcellent tobacco, which goes far beyond all their panaceas, potable gold and philosophers' stones, a sovereign remedy for all diseases.

Richard Burton (1577–1640)

We were rarely afraid of anything much – although there was plenty to fear. These were, after all, the 1950s and we were living in the shadow of *the Bomb*.

Our parents worried a lot about *the Bomb*, but we had been given our pamphlets at school and knew that as long as you shielded your eyes from the big flash with a sweet wrapper and remembered to 'duck and cover', you'd come out of the holocaust unscathed. What fears we had, we saved for more tangible dangers. There were things you had to know in order to survive childhood and we were pretty sure we knew them all.

Snakes you had to be careful of. Snakes and the beetles that bite.

Of snakes there was much common lore, which was passed mouth to ear in the playground. All snakes were deadly and all snakes must die, it was get them before they got you.

Gunnersbury Park was the best place for snakes, or the *worst place*, perhaps I should say. It was well understood that the park fairly heaved with the buggers. They dangled from the trees, great anacondas and pythons, lurking camouflaged amongst the leaves, eager to take the heads off foolish children who dawdled underneath. The ornamental pond and boating lake were homes to water vipers, slim as hair and fast as Stirling Moss.

It was well known that if you took a piddle in the boating lake, they would swim up the stream of pee and enter your knob. Once inside they blocked the passage and you filled up with pee and died. The only cure was a terrible one: they had to cut off your willy.

Snakes loved to get inside you by whatever means they could. A boy from Hanwell, it was said, had taken a nap in the park and slept with his mouth open. An adder had slipped down his throat and taken up residence in his stomach. The boy, unaware of this, had eventually woken up and gone home. He was soon taken poorly, however. No matter how much food he now ate he remained all sickly and thin and complained of great churnings in the gut. His worried mother took him to the doctor, who placed his hand upon the boy's stomach and realized the awful truth.

This boy was lucky, for he didn't die. The doctor starved him for two days, then wedged his mouth open and hung a piece of raw meat above it. The hungry adder smelled the meat and came up for a bite. The doctor was able to drag it out of the boy's mouth and kill it.

The snake was now preserved in a jar and many claimed to have seen it.

My friend Billy (who knew more than was healthy for one of his age) said that the story was palpable nonsense. In his opinion the boy would have choked to death had the adder been lured out of his throat.

Billy said that it came out of his bum.

But the threat was real enough and no-one napped in Gunnersbury Park.

I do have to say that although I spent a great deal of my childhood in that park, I never actually saw a snake myself.

Which was very lucky for me.

The other great danger was beetles that bite. Earwigs were the most common, for, as everybody knows, these crawl into your ear at night and lay their eggs in your brain. Our local loony bin, St Bernard's, was well stocked with incurable victims of the earwig. Their horrible howls could be heard in the night, as these cranial parasites drove them to distraction with their gnawings and scurryings.

Stag beetles were deadly and could take your finger off.

Red ants could strip a grown man down to the bone in less time than it would take his wife to boil a kettle of water.

Various spiders lived beneath the toilet seat, ever anxious to scuttle up your bottom and more than three bee stings would kill you for sure.

What with the snakes and the beetles that bit, it was a miracle that any of us lived to see our teens. But most of us somehow did and this was probably down to either good fortune in avoiding the snakes and the beetles, or to our good health, which was down to our diet.

We were smitten by disease and by personal vermin that bit like the very devil himself, but although the occasional epidemic wiped out a class or two here and there, our year survived all but unscathed.

And this was down to our diet.

It was not down to the diet our parents provided, the cabbage and sprouts and the rest. It was down to the extras we fed to ourselves. It was all down to the sweeties.

Now, it is no coincidence that we lose our taste for sweeties upon reaching puberty.[1] This is the time when we lose that ten per cent of our sense of colour and sound and smell without our even noticing. This is the time of the stirring loins, when sweeties lose their attraction.

You see, our bodies always know what they need and childhood bodies need sweeties. It is a 'bodily instinct', quite removed from the brain. If our child-hood bodies need extra sugar, they send a message to our childhood brains. 'Give me sweets,' is this message. It is a message that must be heeded. Upon reaching puberty, needs change. Extra starches and proteins are required. 'Give me beer,' calls the body to the brain. But, you will observe, it rarely calls this message to a six-year-old.

Our bodies know what they want and what they need. And woe unto those who deny this.

[1] Well, some of us do!

Sweeties kept us healthy. We are living proof of this.

Although we didn't actually know that we *needed* sweeties, we knew that we *wanted* them and curiously much common lore existed regarding the curative properties of certain brands of confectionery.[1]

A popular nursery rhyme of the day may serve to illustrate this.

> Billy's got a blister.
> Sally's got a sore.
> Wally's got a willy wound
> That weeps upon the floor.
>
> Molly's got the mange rot.
> Ginny's got the gout.
> Take 'em down the sweet shop.
> That'll sort 'em out.

And how true those words are, even today.

As children, we instinctively knew that the sweetie shop held more in the way of medicine than any branch of Boots. And any qualified chemist who knows anything about the history of his (or her) trade will tell you that most sweeties began life as cures for one complaint or another.

Liquorice was originally a laxative. Peppermint was good for the sinuses. Aniseed helped dispel internal gas. Hum (one of the principal ingredients in humbugs) staved off dropsy, and chocolate, lightly heated and

---

[1] As has now been scientifically proven. See Hugo Rune: *Sherbert Lemons: Their part in the Making of Man*.

then smeared over the naked body of a consenting adult, perks up a dull Sunday afternoon no end.

And how true *those* words are, even today.

Our local sweetie shop was run by old Mr Hartnell. His son Norman (not to be confused with the other Norman Hartnell) was in our class and a popular boy was he. Norman was a born confectioner. At the age of five his father had given him a little brown shop-keeper's coat of his own and, when not in school uniform, Norman was rarely to be seen wearing anything other than this.

Norman lived and breathed (and ate) sweeties. He was to sweeties what the Doveston would later be to tobacco, although he would never achieve the same fame. He would, in later life, receive acclaim for his scientific endeavours, which have been written of in several books and indeed will be written of here.

The Doveston and I befriended Norman. Not that he lacked for friends, you understand. He attracted friendship in the way that poo does flies. But, in the Doveston's opinion, these were just friends of the fair-weather persuasion. Good-time Charlies and Johnny-come-latelys, buddying up with the shop-keeper's son for naught but the hope of free sweeties.

'What that Norman really needs,' declared the Doveston, one July morning, during P.E., 'is the guiding hand of a mentor.'

'But where might such a hand be found?' I asked.

The Doveston showed me one of his own. 'On the end of my arm,' said he.

I examined the item in question. It was grubby as usual and black at the nails, with traces of jam on the thumb. If this was indeed the hand of a mentor, then I possessed two of my own.

'What exactly *is* a mentor?' was my next enquiry.

'A wise and trusted adviser or guide.'

'And you think Norman needs one?'

'Just look at him', the Doveston said, 'and tell me what *you* think.'

I glanced along at Norman. We were all lined up in the big hall, mentally, if not physically, preparing ourselves for the horrors of the vaulting horse. Norman had, as ever, been thrust to the head of the line by his 'friends'.

He was a stocky, well-set lad, all big knees and podgy palms. And being the son of a confectioner, there was much of the sweetie about him. His skin was as pink as Turkish delight and his cheeks as red as cherry drops. He had lollipop lips and a marzipan chin, butterscotch hair and a mole on his left shoulder that resembled a Pontefract cake.

Norman stood in his vest and pants, having forgotten to bring his games kit. Mr Vaux, all tweed and cravat, blew his whistle. Norman made the sign of the cross, ambled forward, gathered speed, jumped and plunged headfirst into the horse.

The mighty leathern four-legged beasty took it with scarcely a shudder. Norman stiffened, did that comedy stagger which in cartoons is always accompanied by small birds circling the head, and then collapsed unconscious on the parquet floor.

There were no great cries of horror and no runnings forward to help. After all, we'd seen this happen many times and if you ran to help without permission, you got walloped with the slipper.

Mr Vaux called for injury monitors and we all put up our hands, for it was well known that Norman always kept a few toffees hidden in his underpants.

Our teacher did a 'you and you' and Norman was gathered up and stretchered from the hall.

'What that lad needs is a mentor,' I said.

The Doveston nodded. 'You're not wrong there.'

On this particular occasion Norman's concussion was sufficiently severe to merit a sending home early and so, after school, the Doveston and I went around to his daddy's shop to offer our best wishes and hopes for a speedy recovery.

It was Wednesday afternoon and the shop was early-closed. We knocked and waited and while we waited we gazed longingly through the front window.

This week it was dominated by a display for a new brand of American cigarette: Strontium Nineties. There were large cardboard cut-outs of fresh-faced college boys and girls, flat-topped and ponytailed, grinning and puffing. Speech bubbles issued from their toothy mouths, with phrases such as 'Gee whiz, they sure taste good' and 'Radiating pleasure, yes siree' printed upon them.

'What do you think about those?' I asked.

The Doveston shook his head. 'I've read a lot about them in the trade press,' he said. 'They're supposedly impregnated with a radioactive element which makes them glow in the dark. The Americans irradiate everything nowadays, it's supposed to be very good for the health.'

'They irradiate Coca-Cola, don't they?'

'Allegedly,' said the Doveston. 'Allegedly.'

He knocked again and we waited some more. I knew that the Doveston's attempts to adopt old Mr Hartnell had met with no success and I must confess that I did not believe that his intention to become Norman's mentor was altogether altruistic. But the lure of free sweeties and possibly fags was too much for me to ignore.

The Doveston squinted through the shop-door glass. 'Someone's coming,' he said.

Norman's face appeared before us, somewhat grey and mournful. 'Piss off,' it said.

'Hello, Norman,' said the Doveston. 'Is your dad at home?'

'He's gone to the wholesalers. Same as he does every Wednesday afternoon and he told me not to let any kids in. Same as he does every Wednesday afternoon.'

'Very wise too,' said the Doveston. 'So, are you coming out, or what?'

'I'm ill,' said Norman. 'I've got a headache.'

'We're going to the fair.'

'What fair?' asked Norman.

'What fair?' I asked too.

'The one on the Common, of course.'

Norman shook his aching head. 'It doesn't open until Saturday. Everyone knows that.'

'It opens for me,' said the Doveston. 'I have an uncle who runs one of the attractions.'

Norman's eyes widened behind the door glass. 'You have?' he said slowly. 'Which one?'

'His name is Professor Merlin. He runs the Freak Show.'

My eyes too widened somewhat at this. The Freak Show was always a *big* attraction. Last year there had been an eight-legged lamb and a mermaid. Both had admittedly been stuffed, but there were live exhibits too. Giants and dwarves, a bearded lady and an alligator man.

'You're lying,' said Norman. 'Piss off.'

'Please yourself,' said the Doveston, 'but we're going. I just thought you might like to see the dog-faced boy. They say that he bites the heads off live chickens.'

'I'll get my coat,' said Norman.

'We'll come inside and wait for you.'

'No you bloody won't.'

Norman fetched his brown shopcoat, the new one he'd been given for his ninth birthday. He closed the shop door and, under the disguised scrutiny of the Doveston, locked it with his own set of keys. And then the three of us shuffled off towards the Common.

I did have my doubts about this. We all stayed well clear of the fair until it officially opened. The gypsies there had very large dogs and no love for casual callers.

'Are you sure this is wise?' I asked the Doveston as we approached the circle of caravans.

The Doveston sshed me to silence. He had been explaining to Norman about another uncle he had who was a lama in Tibet. This particular uncle was skilled in the art of levitation, an art that could prove useful in all manner of activities. The vaulting of gymnasium horses, for example. The Doveston felt certain that his lamaic uncle might be persuaded to pass on the secrets of this invaluable art to Norman, in exchange for nothing more than a carton of Strontium Nineties.

'Piss off,' said Norman.

Some very large dogs were beginning to bark and between the high-sided caravans we could make out the figures of Romany types. Big-boned burly bods were these, with walrus moustaches and rings through their ears. Tattooed and terrible, hairy and horrid.

The menfolk looked no better.

'Just wait here while I have a word,' said the Doveston, hurrying off.

We scuffed our shoes about on the grass and waited. Norman fished a jujube from his pocket and popped it into his mouth. I hoped he'd offer me one, but he didn't.

'Gypsies eat their young, you know,' said he.

'They never do.'

'They do.' Norman nodded. 'My dad told me. There's only ever nine hundred and ninety-nine gypsies ever alive at one time. It's because they have magical powers, like being able to tell the future and knowing where to find hidden gold. The magic is only strong enough to go round between the nine hundred and ninety-nine of them. One more and they'd lose it. So a new gypsy isn't allowed to be born before an old one dies. If one is, they kill it and eat it.'

'How horrible,' I said.

'That's nothing compared to other things they get up to. My dad's told me all about them.'

'Your dad certainly knows a lot about gypsies.'

'He should,' said Norman. 'My mum ran off with one.'

The Doveston returned and said, 'Come on, it's safe, you can follow me.'

We shuffled after him in between the high caravans and into the great circle where the attractions and rides were being assembled. The tattooed moustachioed women toiled away, singing songs in their native Esperanto as they hoisted the sections of the Pelt the Puppy stalls and Sniff the Cheese stands into place.

The menfolk lazed on their portable verandas. Dollied up in floral frocks and sling-back shoes, they sipped their Martinis and arranged cut flowers into pleasing compositions.

'That's the life for me,' said Norman.

And who could argue with that?

5

They do not just eat their own young. As if that wasn't
bad enough, they grind up all the small bones and
produce a kind of snuff, which they snort up their
noses through bigger bones all hollowed out. The
skullcaps of the murdered infants are fashioned into
ashtrays that they hawk on their stalls to good
Christian folk like us.

Gyppo bastards!

Norman's dad

I have never, before nor since, seen a man quite like
Professor Merlin. He wore a purple periwig upon a
head so slim it made you shiver. His nose was the beak
of a fabulous bird and his eyes were turquoise studs.
Above a smiling mouth, which glittered with a treasury
of golden teeth, sprang slender waxed moustachios.
And beneath this mouth was a chin so long that, when
the merry lips were closed, it all but touched his
hooter.

He was dressed in the style of a Regency blade, with
a high starched collar and white silk cravat. His waistcoat
was red and a-twinkle with watch-chains. His tailcoat
was green, with embroidered lapels. He was old and tall
and skinny. He was weird and wonderful.

At our approach he extended a long, thin, pale and manicured hand to shake the grubby mitt belonging to the Doveston.

'My dear little Berty,' he said.

'Berty?' I whispered.

'And this would be your brother?'

'Edwin,' said the Doveston. 'And this is my good friend Norman.'

'Berty?' said Norman. 'Edwin?'

'Norman is the son of Brentford's pre-eminent purveyor of tobacco and confectionery.'

'Fiddle dee, fiddle dum,' went the professor. 'I am honoured indeed.' He fished into his waistcoat pocket and brought to light a marvellous snuffbox, silver and shaped like a coffin. This he offered in Norman's direction. 'Would you care to partake?' he enquired.

Norman shook his tousled head, which in profile resembled a pear drop. 'No thanks,' said he. 'I find that stuff makes me sneeze.'

'As you will.' The professor now grinned goldenly upon the Doveston. 'Would you like a pinch?' he asked.

'Yes please, uncle,' said the boy.

Professor Merlin leaned forward. 'Then you shall have one,' he said and pinched him hard upon the ear.

The Doveston howled and clutched at his lug-hole. Norman dissolved into foolish mirth and I just stood there, boggle-eyed and gaping.

'Fairground humour,' explained the professor. 'What do you think of it?'

'Most amusing,' said I.

'And what say you, Berty?'

The Doveston wiped away tears from his eyes and managed a lop-sided smirk. 'Most amusing,' he agreed. 'I must remember that one.'

'Good boy.' Professor Merlin handed him the snuff-box. 'Then take a little sample and tell me what you think.'

The boy gave the lid three solemn taps before he flipped it open.

'Why do you do that?' I asked.

'Tradition,' the Doveston told me. 'For Father, Son and Holy Ghost.'

'Born to the art,' said the professor.

The boy took snuff and pinched it to his nose. He inhaled deeply through his nostrils and then made a thoughtful and satisfied face.

Professor Merlin cocked his head. 'Let us see if he can identify the blend. A florin says he will not.'

The Doveston's nose went twitch twitch twitch and I awaited the inevitable explosion. But none came. Instead he just smiled, before reciting a curious verse.

'Thai [went he,] and light as nutmeg.
One part sassafras, one part sage.
Strawberry seasoned, blueberry blended.
Crad from the stock of the Munich Mage.
Daintily dusted, finely ground.
Bought in Bradford, two quid a pound.'

'Remarkable,' said the professor.

'Rather too fussy for my taste,' said the boy. 'And more a winter blend, I would have thought. Would you like me to name both brand and supplier?'

Professor Merlin nodded.

'Crawford's Imperial, from Cox's Tobacco Emporium, High Street, Bradford.'

'Incredible.' Professor Merlin wrung his slender hands. 'Even down to the hint of Crad. The boy is a genius.'

'Poo,' said Norman, who wasn't impressed.

'It was rather clever,' I said, 'and in a poem too.'

'Poems are poofy,' said Norman.

I noticed now that the professor's snuffbox was sliding into the Doveston's pocket. The professor noticed this too and snatched it back. 'Thank you,' he said.

The Doveston grinned. 'That's a florin you owe me.'

The professor made mystical motions with his hands and produced a coin from thin air. The Doveston took it, bit it, examined it, slipped it in his pocket and grinned a little more.

'Fiddle dee fiddle dum.' Professor Merlin bowed. 'You have impressed me as ever, my boy. So what have you come to see?'

'Norman would like a look at the dog-faced boy.'

'I would,' said Norman. 'I want to see him biting the heads off live chickens.'

'Well you can't,' said the professor. 'Doggart has been taken to the vet's.'

'As if,' said Norman.

'No, he truly has. And you're wrong about the description, Berty. He's not a dog-faced boy. He's a boy-faced dog.'

'As if,' said Norman once more.

'I kid thee not.' Professor Merlin crossed his heart.

'The body of an Alsatian dog and the head of a boy. I purchased him several months ago in this very borough, from a chap called Jon Peru Joans.'

I looked at the Doveston.

And he looked back at me.

'So why's he at the vet's?' asked Norman.

'Ah,' said the professor. 'An embarrassing incident occurred today. We had been invited to lunch by the lady mayoress, who'd expressed a desire to meet Doggart. We arrived at her house somewhat early and her secretary informed us that she was still upstairs taking a shower. We were sent to wait in the lounge, but Doggart somehow got off his lead and ran upstairs. The bathroom door had been left open and the lady mayoress was still in the shower. She was just bending down to pick up the soap when Doggart entered. He must have misunderstood the situation, because the next thing you know he—'

'No!' said Norman. 'He never did!'

'He did. It's the nature of dogs, you see. He couldn't help himself. The lady mayoress demanded that Doggart be taken off to the vet.'

'To be destroyed?'

'No,' said the professor. 'To have his paw-nails clipped. We've been invited back again for supper.'

We all looked at each other and then began to laugh. These were, after all, the 1950s and Political Correctness was still many years away.

No-one, of course, would dare to tell a joke like that nowadays.

'So, what *have* you got?' asked Norman. 'Anything worth seeing?'

Professor Merlin golden-grinned. 'You really are a very rude little boy, aren't you?' he said.

Norman nodded. 'Very. That's one of the benefits of having a dad who runs a sweetie shop.'

'Ah, privilege.' Professor Merlin made a wistful face. 'So, what can I show you? Ah yes, indeedy-do. I know just the very thing.'

And with that said he turned upon a merry heel and led us across the great circle towards his caravan. We shuffled after the curious gent, the Doveston whistling and grinning away, Norman secretively unwrapping Gooble's Gob Gums in the pocket of his brown shop-keeper's coat and sneaking them into his mouth and me scratching at the family of ticks that had recently made their nest in my navel.

Perhaps this had me thinking about families, because I chanced to wonder whether one of the straining hirsute gypsy women might be Norman's wayward mum.

'Here we go,' said the professor as we approached a particularly grand caravan. It was a glorious antique affair, its sides decorated with the swirls and flourishes of the Romany persuasion in golds and silvers and pearly pastels. The words 'PROFESSOR MERLIN'S GREATEST SHOW OFF EARTH' were writ in letters big, and elephants and ostriches and dancing girls and jugglers were painted on in rich and dashing fashion.

'Gaudy,' said Norman, munching on a sweetie.

'Inside now, come on.' We pressed together up the steps and I pushed open the door. As I looked inside, I recalled the words of Howard Carter, who, having chiselled a little hole into the tomb of the boy king and shone his torch through it, was asked what he could see. 'Wonderful things,' said Howard. 'I see wonderful things.'

We bundled into the professor's caravan.

'Sit down. Sit down.' And we sat.

On the walls were many posters of circuses and sideshows. Adverts for incredible performances and impossible feats. But these were not the wonderful things. The wonderful things were brass contraptions. Inexplicable Victorian mechanisms consisting of whirling ball governors and clicking chains, each purring and turning and moving and busily doing something or other, although just what, it was impossible to say.

'What's all this old toot?' asked Norman.

'The work of another age,' smiled the professor. 'A distant technology.'

'Yeah, but what do they do?'

'They don't *do* anything, Norman. They don't *do*, they simply *are*.'

Norman shrugged and munched some more.

'Refreshments,' said the professor, pouring lemonade into tall green glasses. 'And fags too. Name your favourites.'

'You won't have them,' said Norman.

Professor Merlin handed out the lemonade. 'Try me,' he said.

'MacGuffin's Extra Longs.'

'Easy,' said Professor Merlin, producing one from thin air.

Norman took and examined it. 'Good trick,' he said, sulkily.

69

'Edwin?'

'I'm easy,' I said. 'Anything.'

'Make it hard.'

'All right.' I thought for a moment. 'I'd like to try a Byzantium.'

'Yeah, me too,' said the Doveston. 'Except you can only buy them in Greece.'

'One each then.' The professor snapped his fingers and we took the cigarettes. They were the genuine article and we hastened to light them up.

'I'd like one of those as well,' said Norman.

'Well, you can't have one. But' – Professor Merlin reached over to a nifty little side table, crafted from an elephant's foot, and took up a small and dainty box – 'I've something else I think *you* will like.'

Norman puffed upon his cigarette.

'Sweeties,' said the professor, turning the box towards him. 'This is a very special little box with very special sweeties.'

'Give us them,' said Norman.

Professor Merlin glittered out another grin. 'It's a very beautiful box, isn't it? The tanned hide has been so perfectly prepared. The craftsmanship is exquisite.'

'What about the sweeties?' Norman asked.

'You hold on to the box and help yourself and while you do, I will recount to you a tale that I hope will make your visit worth while.'

'I'd rather have seen the dog-boy.' Norman wrestled the lid from the box and got stuck into the sweeties.

'I have been in the showman's trade for many many years,' said Professor Merlin, settling himself back into a throne-like chair all wrought from bones and buckles.

'And I think I can say that, if it's there to be seen, I've seen it. I have travelled all over this world of ours and visited many strange places. If I have heard rumours of some remarkable performer or human oddity, I have followed up these rumours. Tracked these rumours to their source. And I am proud to say that I have exhibited some of the greatest artistes of this or any age.

'But, and it is a big but, every showman dreams that one day he will find THE BIG ONE. The most exotic, the most wonderful, the biggest greatest crowd-puller that there has ever been. Barnum found it with General Tom Thumb, but for most of us the search goes on.'

'These sweeties aren't too bad,' said Norman. 'They taste almost meaty.'

'Shut up!' said the Doveston, elbowing Norman. 'Please continue, uncle.'

'Thank you, Berty. As I say, we search and search, but mostly in vain. And maybe that is for the best. Maybe it is better to search than actually to find.'

'How can that be?' the Doveston asked. 'If you want something, it's better to get it than to not get it.'

'You may be right, but I have not found this to be the case. Quite the reverse, in fact. You see, I found what I was looking for and I wish that I never had.'

The old showman paused, drew out his snuffbox and favoured his nostrils with Crawford's Imperial. 'I travelled with the carnival in India,' he continued, 'where I hoped to encounter a fakir who had mastered the now legendary rope trick. But I found something more wonderful than this. Something that I wanted, wanted more than I have ever wanted anything. Some*thing*, did I say? Some*one*. She was a temple

71

dancer, so beautiful and perfect as to overwhelm the heart. She moved with such grace that it made you weep to watch her and when she sang it was with the tongue of an angel.

'I knew at once that if I could persuade this beautiful creature to travel with me and perform around the world, my fortune would be made. The men of the West would fall at her feet. There would be fame and there would be fortune.'

'And was there?' asked Norman.

'I'll thump you,' said the Doveston.

'Fame?' said the professor. 'Infamy, more like. I sought out the guardians of this girl. The villagers were not eager to tell me, but I bribed a few with strong liquor and the hut was pointed out to me. A rude dwelling it was, nothing more than mud and reeds, filthy and wretched. I knocked and entered and there found an ancient fellow sucking upon a narghile. This old body spoke no English and so I conversed with him in his own tongue. I speak more than forty languages and I was able to make myself understood.

'I informed him that I was an emissary sent by Queen Victoria, the Empress of India, who wished to honour the beautiful dancer of whom she had heard so much.'

'You lied to him,' said Norman.

'Yes, Norman, I lied. I said that the Queen of England wished to meet her in person. I was greedy for this girl. I would have said anything. The old man wept greatly. He said that the girl was his granddaughter and that she was one favoured by the Gods. I agreed that she was very beautiful, but he said that this was not what he meant. She had been chosen by the Gods. He said that, as a girl, she had been sleeping beneath a sacred bodhi tree and she had been bitten by a king cobra.'

'I hate snakes,' said Norman. 'There was this boy in Hanwell who slept in the park with his mouth open and—'

Smack went the Doveston's hand.

'Ouch, you bastard,' went Norman.

'The bite of the king cobra is fatal,' said the professor. 'But the girl did not die. The people of the village took this to be a sign that she was one blessed of the Gods. Possibly even a Goddess herself. Naturally, as a civilized Englishman, I scorned such nonsense, but I told the old man that Queen Victoria too was a Goddess and that she wished to meet one of her own. The old man could not bear to see the girl go, he pleaded and pleaded and I lied and lied. The girl would soon return, I said, with great riches, bestowed upon her by the Goddess Queen. He did perk up a bit at this. But he said that the girl must be returned to him before six months were up, because she was to sing at some religious festival or another. I readily agreed.

'And so I took the girl from him. Her name was Naja and I determined that I would make that name world famous. We toured up through Persia to Asia, from Greece into Europe, and everywhere she sang and danced the crowds went wild. We played before crowned heads and were entertained in palaces and by the time we reached the shores of England I had no doubt at all that she would actually meet with Queen Victoria.'

'And did she?' Norman asked.

'No, Norman, she did not. Five months had passed and Naja wanted to return home. I told her that she should soon meet the great Queen and that then I would take her back to her people. But of course I had no intention of doing that. You see, I had fallen hopelessly in love with her. I desired her. I wanted to possess her totally. Naja began to pine. She grew pale and drawn and would not eat. She would lock herself in her caravan and refuse to come out and she grew sicker with each passing day. I tended to her as best I could, but I watched with growing horror as her beautiful face drained of its beauty, as lines formed about her wonderful eyes and the voice that had been so, so sweet became a cracked whisper.

'I called for physicians to aid her back to health, but these learned men examined her and shook their heads. There was nothing that could be done.'

'So, she snuffed it, did she?' said Norman.

'No, Norman, she did not snuff it. She went home.'

'That's a pretty crappy story,' said Norman. 'And a pretty cop-out ending.'

'Oh, it's not the end.' Professor Merlin shook his ancient head. 'It's not the end at all. I sat beside her bed and watched helplessly as she slipped away from me. I watched as that faultless skin began to wrinkle up and lose its colour and those eyes grow dim. She begged me to leave her alone, but I refused. I realized what I had done; how, in my greed, I had brought her to this. And then one night it happened.'

'She *did* die,' Norman said.

'She *screamed*!' cried the professor, making Norman

74

all but wet himself. 'She screamed and she began to writhe about on the bed. She tore the covers from her and she tore away her nightdress. I tried to hold her down, but as I did so she fought free of my grip and it happened. Her skin began to come apart; right before my eyes, it fell away. She rose up before me on the bed and shed her skin. It fell in a crumpled heap and she stepped from it, beautiful, renewed and naked. I staggered from the shock and fainted dead away and when I awoke the next morning she was gone. She had left a note for me and when I read it I truly realized the evil thing that I had done in taking her away from her village.

'You see, she was sworn to the Gods. When as a child she had been bitten by the king cobra her mother had prayed to Shiva, offering her own life in exchange for that of her daughter. The Most High must have heard her prayers and taken pity upon her. The mother died, but the child survived. But the child was now the property of the Gods and from that day on she never aged. Each year she shed her skin and emerged new born. The old man in the village was not her grandfather, he was her younger brother.

'She had taken all the money I had made from displaying her and bought a passage back to India. I made no attempt to follow her. For all I know, she is probably to this day still in her village. Still as beautiful and young as ever. I will never return there and I pray that no other Westerner will.'

We lads had finished our cigarettes and sat there struck dumb by this incredible tale.

Norman, however, was not struck dumb for long.

'That's quite a story,' he said. 'It's a pity you can't prove any of it.'

'But you have your proof,' said the professor.

'What? That the story is true because you say it is?'

'What more proof should you need?'

'You could show us the skin.'

'But I have.'

'No you haven't,' said Norman.

'Oh indeed, my boy, I have. I had the skin tanned and made into a box. The one you've been eating the sweeties from.'

I had never seen projectile vomiting before and I do have to tell you that I was impressed. Norman staggered grey-faced from the caravan and fled across the fairground.

Several very large dogs gave chase, but Norman out-ran them with ease.

The professor stared at the mess upon his floor. 'If he made such a fuss about the box,' he said, 'it's a good thing I didn't tell him what the sweeties were made out of.'

'What exactly *were* the sweeties made out of?' I asked the Doveston as, a few weeks later, we sat night-fishing for mud sharks.

'Beetles that bite, I believe.'

I tossed a few maggots into the canal. 'I don't think I want to meet any more of your so-called uncles,' I told the lad. 'They're all a bunch of weirdos and they give me bad dreams.'

The Doveston laughed. 'The professor is all right,'

he said. 'He has the largest collection of erotically decorated Chinese snuff bottles that I have ever seen.'

'Good for him. But what about that tale he told us? Do you believe it was true?'

The Doveston shook his head. 'No,' said he. 'But it had the desired effect upon Norman, didn't it? He's a much nicer fellow now.'

And it was true. Norman was a much nicer fellow. In fact he had become our bestest friend and looked upon the Doveston as something of a mentor. Whether this had anything to do with the professor's story is anyone's guess. I suspect that it had more to do with what happened a day or two later.

It seems that during Norman's flight from the professor's caravan he somehow dropped his keys. Someone had picked them up and that someone had let themselves into Mr Hartnell's corner shop during the hours of night and made away with several cartons of American cigarettes, leaving the keys behind them on the counter.

Norman, who had not told his father either about losing his keys or visiting the fair, seemed likely to have had the truth beaten out of him had not the Doveston intervened on his behalf.

The boy Doveston told the elder Hartnell a most convincing tale about how young Norman had saved an old lady from being robbed in the street, only to be set upon and robbed himself.

When pressed for a description of the villain, he could only say that the man wore a mask, but had 'much of the gypsy about him'.

Looking back now across the space of fifty years, it

seems to me that the professor's tale was not told for Norman's benefit at all. Its message was meant for the Doveston. The professor was right when he said that 'Maybe it is better to search than actually to find.'

The Doveston searched for fame and fortune all his life; he found both, but was never content. But the search itself was an adventure and I am glad that I shared in it. Much of it was fearful stuff. As fearful as were snakes and beetles that bit, but there were great times and long-legged women and I wouldn't have missed them for the world.

'All's well that ends well, then,' I said to the Doveston as I took out my fags.

'It's not a bad old life,' said the lad. 'But here, don't smoke those, try one of mine. They're new and they glow in the dark.'

6

When I was young, I kissed my first woman and smoked my first cigarette on the same day. Believe me, never since have I wasted any more time on tobacco.

Arturo Toscanini (1867–1957)

I awoke one morning to find that I had lost nearly ten per cent of my sense of colour, sound and smell. The wallpaper seemed to have faded overnight and the noise of the day appeared duller. The normally rich and wholesome tang of frying lard, rising through the cracks in the kitchen ceiling to enter my bedroom between the bare boards, had lost its fragrant edge. But I noticed another smell, creeping out from under my sheets. The brimstone reek of sulphur.

I stumbled from my bed and blinked into the wall mirror. My ruddy if disease-scarred countenance looked pale and drawn and eerie. Fuzzy whiskers fringed my upper lip and large red spots had blossomed on my chin.

My attention became drawn to my pyjama bottoms. They were sticking out oddly at the front. I undid the knotted string and let them fall.

And beheld the erection!

Shafts of sunlight fell upon it. Up on high the angels sang.

'My God,' I said. 'I've reached puberty.'

Well, I had to try it out and so I did.

Five minutes later I went down for breakfast.

My mother eyed me strangely. 'Have you been playing with yourself?' she asked.

'Certainly not!' I replied. 'Whatever gave you that idea?'

My father looked up from his *Sporting Life*. 'I think it was the loud shouts of "I've come! I've come!" that gave it away,' he said kindly.

'I'll bear that in mind for the future,' I said, tucking into the lard on my plate.

'By the way,' said my father. 'President Kennedy's been shot.'

'President who?'

'Kennedy. The President of the United States. He's been assassinated.'

'My God,' I said, for the second time that day.

'It's a bit of a shock, eh?'

'It certainly is.' I ran my fingers through my hair. 'I didn't even know they had a president. I thought America was still a British colony.'

My father shook his head. Rather sadly, I thought. 'You're getting lard all over your barnet,' he observed. 'You really must learn to use a knife and fork.

'And a condom,' he added.

I set off to school a bit late. I thought I'd give puberty another go before I went. This time without the shouting. My mother banged on the bathroom door. 'Stop jumping up and down in there,' she told me.

School for me was now St Argent of the Tiny Nose, a dour establishment run by an order of Holy Brothers chosen for the smallness of their hooters. It was an all-boys school, very hot on discipline and nasal training. Smoking was forbidden in class, but the taking of snuff was encouraged.

I had somehow failed my eleven plus and so while the Doveston, Billy, Norman and just about everybody else in my class had gone on to the Grammar, I had been packed off to St Argent's with the duffers of the parish.

I didn't feel too bad about this. I had accepted early in life that I was unlikely to make anything of myself and I soon made new friends amongst the Chicanos and Hispanics of Brentford's Mexican quarter who became my new classmates.

There was Chico Valdez, leader of the Crads, a rock'n'roll outlaw of a boy who would sadly meet an early end in a freak accident involving gunfire and cocaine. 'Fits' Caraldo, leader of the Wobblers, an epileptic psychopath, whose end would be as sudden. Juan Toramera, leader of the Screamin' Greebos, whose life also came to a premature conclusion. And José de Farrington-Smythe, who left after the first year and went on to theological college.

He later became a priest.

And was shot dead by a jealous husband.

Our school reunions were very quiet affairs.

I was greatly taken with Chico. He had tattooed legs and armpit hair and told me that at junior school he had actually had sex with his teacher. 'Never again,' said Chico. 'It made my bottom far too sore.'

Chico initiated me into the Crads. I don't recall too much about the actual ceremony, only that it involved Chico and me going into a shed on the allotment and drinking a great deal of colourless liquid from an un-labelled bottle.

I know I couldn't ride my bike for about a week afterwards. But you can make of that what you will.

The Crads were not the largest teenage gang in Brentford. But, as Chico assured me, they *were* the most exclusive. There was Chico, the leader, there was me, and there would no doubt be others in time.

Once we had 'gained a reputation'.

Gaining a reputation was everything. It mattered far more than algebra and history and learning how to spell. Gaining a reputation made you *somebody*.

Exactly how you gained a reputation seemed un-certain. When questioned on the subject, Chico was vague in his replies. It apparently involved gunfire and cocaine.

I arrived in school as Brother Michael, our teacher, was calling the register. He had been scoring lines through the names of those boys slain in last night's drive-bys and seemed quite pleased to see me.

I received the standard thrashing for lateness, nothing flashy, just five of the Cat, put my shirt back on and took my seat.

'Chico,' I whispered from behind my hand, 'have you heard the news?'

'That your mother caught you whacking off in the bathroom?'

'No, not that. President Kennedy's been shot.'

'President who?' whispered Chico.

'That's what I said. He was the President of the United States.'

'Just another dead gringo,' said Chico and he thumbed his teeth.

And that was the end of that.

We got stuck into our first lesson. It was, as ever, the history of the True Church and I think we'd got up to the Borgia Pope. We had not been at it for more than ten minutes, however, before the classroom door opened and Father Durante the headmaster entered.

We rose quickly to our feet. 'Bless you, Holy Father,' we all said.

'Bless you, boys,' said he, 'and please sit down.'

Father Durante approached Brother Michael and whispered several words into his ear.

'President who?' said Brother Michael.

Father Durante whispered some more.

'Oh,' said Brother Michael, 'and was he a Catholic?'

Further whispered words went on and then the Father left.

'Oh dear, oh dear,' said Brother Michael, addressing the class. 'Apparently President Kennedy, who is, before you ask, the President of the United States, has been assassinated. Normally this kind of thing would not concern us. But it appears that President Kennedy was a Roman Catholic and so we should all express our sorrow at his passing.'

Chico stuck his hand up. 'Holy sir,' said he.

'Yes, what is it, Chico?'

'Holy sir, this gringo who got snuffed. Was he the leader of a gang?'

'He was the leader of a mighty nation.'

'Whoa!' went Chico. 'Kiss my ass.'

'Not here,' said Brother Michael. 'Was there anything specific you wished to know about the president?'

'*El presidente*, huh? How did the motherf—'

But he didn't get to finish his no doubt most pertinent question.

'You can all take the rest of the day off,' said Brother Michael. 'Spend it in quiet contemplation. Pray for the soul of our departed brother and write me a five-hundred-word essay on the subject: *What I would do if I became the President of the United States.*'

'I'd get a better bodyguard,' said Chico.

'Go with God,' said Brother Michael.

So we did.

I caught up with Chico at the school gates, next to the barbed-wire perimeter fence. He had learned to swagger whilst still young, but I was yet a shuffler.

'Where are you off to now?' I asked.

Chico flipped a coin into the air and then he stooped to pick it up. 'I think I'll go and hang out at the Laundromat,' he said. 'I love to watch the socks go round and round together with the soap-suds. Don't you get a kick outa that?'

'Yeah,' I said. Not really, I thought.

'So, what you gonna do?'

'Well,' I said. 'As I've just reached puberty this morning, I was hoping to have sex with a long-legged woman.'

Chico looked me up and down. 'You want I introduce you to my mother?'

'That's very kind, but she is a bit old.'

'You feelthy peeg, I cut your throat.' Chico sought his flick knife, but he'd left it in his other shorts.

'Don't get upset,' I said. 'I'm sure your mother's a very nice woman.'

Chico laughed. 'You never met my mother then. But you get the wrong idea. It's OK. I don't mean you have my mother. I mean my mother get you a girl.'

'Why would she do that for me?'

'Because that's what she do. She run the whorehouse.'

'Chico,' I said, 'your mother is a *whole*saler. She runs a *ware*house.'

'Curse this dyslexia,' said Chico.

The sun went behind a cloud and a dog howled in the distance.

'I tell you what,' said Chico, perking up. 'I take you to my aunty's place. She runs the House of Correction and don't tell me that ain't no whorehouse.'

The House of Correction was a proper whorehouse. Well kept and properly run. You had to take your shoes off when you went in and you weren't allowed to jump on the furniture or tease the cat.

The House of Correction was semi-detached in a leafy Brentford side street. Those who remember the final shaming of America's last president would recognize it from the pictures posted on the internet at the time.

Chico's aunty, who ran it throughout the 1960s, was

one of those big-bosomed Margaret Dumont kind of bodies, the like of which sadly we won't see again.

The front door was open and Chico took me in. His aunty was seated in what was appropriately named the sitting room. She was on the telephone.

I thought I caught the words 'President who?' but given the law of diminishing returns this was probably not the case.

I was greatly impressed by the scale of Chico's aunty and by just how so much flesh could be contained within so little clothes. She glanced down at our stockinged feet and then up at our stockinged faces.

'Why are you wearing those?' she asked.

Chico shrugged. 'It was the gringo's idea,' he said.

'You lying bastard.' I pulled off my stocking. 'You said we had to come in disguise.'

'Only if you're famous,' said Chico's aunty. 'Are you famous?'

I shook my head.

'Don't get nits on my carpet.'

'Sorry.'

'And you've got lard in your hair.'

'The gringo wants a long-legged woman,' said Chico.

'I've just reached puberty this morning,' I explained. 'I don't want to waste any time.'

Chico's aunty smiled the kind of smile that you normally see only on the face of a road-kill. 'Can't wait to try out your pecker,' said she. 'Think that the entire female species is nothing more than walking pussy, gagging for you to ram it right in.'

'I wouldn't put it quite that way,' I said.

'But, in essence, I'm correct?'

'Oh yeah. In essence.'

'You'd better open an account then. How much money have you got?'

I dug about in my shorts. 'About half a crown,' I said.

Chico's aunty tut-tut-tutted. 'You won't get much for half a crown,' she said between the tuts. 'Let me have a look at the tariff.' She took up a clipboard and examined it with care. I noticed how her finger ran from top down to the bottom. 'Chicken,' she said, finally. 'For half a crown, a chicken.'

'A *chicken*?' I said in horror.

'It's not just any old chicken. It's a Swedish chicken. Specially trained in those arts which amuse men.'

'I don't want to have it away with a chicken,' I said. 'And anyway, I've heard that joke.'

'What joke is this?'

'The one where the bloke walks into a brothel and he doesn't have much money and the fellow in charge talks him into having it away with a chicken and the bloke is desperate and so he does, but the next day he's walking along the street and he thinks, Hang about, I've been done here, I could have got a chicken cheaper in Sainsbury's. So he goes back to complain and the fellow says to him, "All right, I'll let you have something for free to make up," and he's shown to this darkened room where there's all these other blokes looking through a one-way mirror at this incredible orgy going on. And he has a good look too and then he says to this other bloke there, "That was incredible, wasn't it?" And the other bloke says, "If you think that was incredible you should have been here yesterday——" '

'There was a bloke in there with a chicken,' said Chico's aunty.

'Oh, you've heard it too.'

'No, I was only guessing.'

'Well, I'm *not* having sex with a chicken,' I said. 'And that's that.'

Chico's aunty grinned another cadaverous grin and set her clipboard aside. 'I was only testing,' she said. 'Just to see whether there was any decency in you. I'm pleased to see that there is. Would you care for a cup of tea?'

'That would be very nice, thank you.'

Chico's aunty called for tea and this was presently brought. I was quite amazed by the teapot. All sheathed in leather it was, with spikes on the handle and studs all round the top.

'For very special clients,' she explained.

Chico swaggered off to the Laundromat to watch the socks go round and I spent a pleasant hour in his aunty's company. She told me a lot about women and put me right on a great many things. Women are not sex objects, she told me. They are people too and must be respected. *No* does not mean *yes*, even if you've had ten pints of beer. You should never fart in front of women. Always wait until they've had their turn.[1] And countless other things, which I must say have helped me a lot over the years in what dealings I've had with the opposite sex. I do not believe that I've ever been a selfish lover, nor have I ever been disloyal. I have not elevated women,

[1]Humour (although hardly appropriate).

but neither have I degraded them. I have treated them as people and I have Chico's aunt to thank for that.

She charged me half a crown for the consultation and I considered it cheap at the price. She kissed me on the cheek and I left the House of Correction never to return.

I lounged about outside for a while, wondering just how I would spend the balance of the day. I had just made up my mind that I would go and join Chico and watch the socks go round and round when the door of his aunty's opened and the Doveston came out.

'Hello,' I said, 'what have you been up to?'

'Business.' The Doveston winked.

'Business with a woman?'

'Yep,' said the Doveston, straightening his tie.

I sighed and looked him up and down. 'What are all those feathers on your trousers there?' I asked.

7

What a blessing this smoking is! Perhaps the greatest
that we owe to America.

Arthur Helps (1813–75)

The Doveston did not say 'President who?' He knew
all about America. It was his ambition to own a tobacco
plantation in Virginia. An ambition he would one day
realize.

'It was probably the secret police who killed him,'
was the Doveston's opinion.

'The secret who?' I asked.

'The secret police. Don't you remember that time I
took you to visit my uncle Jon Peru Joans? He said the
secret police were after *him*.'

'But he was a stone bonker.'

'Maybe. But I was never able to find out what
happened to him. They supposedly took him off to St
Bernard's and banged him up with the earwig victims.
But I couldn't get in to visit him and you're not going
to tell me that it was just a coincidence that his
conservatory burned to the ground.'

'So you think there's some kind of world-wide organization of secret policemen who do this kind of stuff?'

'Bound to be. It's what's called a conspiracy theory. There's a great deal more going on in this world than we get to read about in the papers. There are secrets everywhere.'

'Did you really have sex with a chicken?' I asked.

But the Doveston didn't reply.

We shuffled down Brentford High Street, pausing now and then to admire the beautiful displays of fruit and veg and viands that filled the shop windows and spilled onto the pavement in baskets and barrels and buckets. We were greatly taken with the meat at Mr Beefheart's.

'That butcher really knows his stuff,' said the Doveston, pointing to this cut, that cut and the other. 'Wildebeest, I see's on special offer.'

'And the wild boar.'

'And the wolverine.'

'And the white tiger too.'

'I might buy some of those wallaby burgers, I'm having a party on Friday.'

'A party?' I said, much impressed. 'But I thought only rich toffs had parties.'

'Things have changed,' said the Doveston, eyeing up the walrus steaks. 'We're in the Sixties now. No more ration books and powdered egg. The Prime Minister says that we've never had it so good.'

'I've never had it at all.'

'Well, you must come to my party. You never know your luck. Oh, and bring your friend Lopez, I want to have a little word with him.

'Lopez isn't with us any more. He pulled a knife and someone shot him dead.'

The Doveston shook his head and viewed the rack of water buffalo. 'You know, if this keeps up,' he said, 'the Chicanos are going to blast themselves to extinction and then Brentford won't have a Mexican quarter any more.'

'I find that rather hard to believe. Brentford's always had a Mexican quarter.'

'Mark well my words, my friend. It's happened before. Do you remember the Street of the August Moon?'

'No,' I said. 'I don't.'

'That's because it's now called Moby Dick Terrace. It used to be Chinatown. But they all wiped themselves out during the great Brentford tong wars of 'fifty-three.'

'I think my dad once mentioned those.'

'And when did you last see a pygmy around here?'

'I don't think I ever have.'

'Well, there used to be a whole tribe of them living in Mafeking Avenue until they fell out with the Zulus of Sprite Street. And you know the Memorial Park?'

'Of course I do.'

'That was once an Indian reservation. The Navajo lived there for hundreds of years until they fell out with the council, back in Victorian times.'

'Why was that?'

'The council wanted to put up a slide and some swings. The Navajo said that the land was sacred to their ancestors.'

'So what happened?'

'The council sent some chaps to parley with the chief. Heated words were exchanged and scalps were taken.'

'Blimey,' I said.

'The council called in the cavalry. The Third Brentford Mounted Foot. They made short work of the Redskins.'

'I've never seen that in a history book.'

'And you won't. A shameful hour in Brentford's noble history. Kept secret, you see. The only reason I know about it is because my great-grandfather was there.'

'Did he kill many Indians?'

'Er, no,' said the Doveston. 'He wasn't fighting on that side.'

I opened my mouth to ask further questions, but the Doveston drew my attention to a display of wolf-cub sausages. 'I'll get some of those for my party,' he said.

We shuffled away from the butcher's and passed the Laundromat just in time to see Chico being forcibly ejected.

'You sons of bitches,' cried the ganglord from the gutter. 'Since when is sniffing socks against the law?'

'Bring *him*,' said the Doveston. 'He sounds like fun.'

We left Chico to it and shuffled off to the Plume Café. Here the Doveston talked me into borrowing half a crown from him to buy two frothy coffees so that we could sit in the window with them and look cool.

'So what's this party all about?' I asked as I spooned in sugar.

'It's a coming-of-age thing really. To celebrate puberty.'

'I've done that twice already. And you've er . . .' I made chicken motions with my elbows.

93

'You'll get a smack,' the Doveston said, 'if you ever mention that again.'

'So are there going to be balloons at this party and jelly and games?'

'You haven't quite got to grips with puberty yet, have you? And do you *really* still fancy jelly?'

I thought about this. 'No, I don't. I *really* fancy beer.'

'Then you're getting there.'

'Are you going to have girls at this party?'

'Girls and beer and a record player.'

'A record player?' I whistled. 'But I thought only rich toffs—'

The Doveston raised his eyebrows to me.

'Sorry,' I said. 'The Sixties, I know.'

'And it's going to be a fancy dress party, so you'll have to come in a costume. Make it something trendy and don't come as a policeman.'

The Doveston brought out cigarettes and we sat, taking smoke and sipping froth and watching as the Brentford day went by.

About an hour after his forcible ejection, Chico returned at the wheel of a stolen Morris Minor in the company of several Pachucos. This he drove through the Laundromat's front window.

The Laundromat staff were Ashanti and they replied to the assault upon their premises with the hurling of assegais. It seems clear that they must have had some long-standing feud with the Kalahari Bushmen next door who owned the dry cleaner's, because these lads were soon out on the street and siding up with the wetbacks.

With all this fuss and bother going on, it wasn't long

before the volatile Incas from the chemist shop were in it, lobbing soap at the Spaniards who ran the haberdasher's next to the Mongolian cheese boutique.

The Doveston took a stick of dynamite from his pocket and placed it on the table before me. 'Now should I, or shouldn't I?' he asked.

I don't think he should have really. But on this particular occasion it seemed to have the desired effect. The mob had been turning rather ugly and the explosion certainly calmed them all down. We felt it prudent to take our leave before the bomb smoke cleared and the appliances arrived to battle the fires that were starting up.

We had done our good deed for the day and did not need any pats upon the back.

I record this incident only because it was one of the rare occasions when the Doveston's dynamite brought peace instead of mayhem. I mentioned in the opening chapter his love for what he called the 'Big Aaah-choo!'. But, other than for a brief allusion to the infamous episode of the detonating dog, I took the matter no further. This is not because I fear the consequences that disclosure of his childhood bombings might incur. After all, most of the buildings that went up in smoke have long since been rebuilt and all the survivors rehoused.

The way I see it is this. We all make mistakes when we're young and do things we later regret. Children behave badly, they shouldn't but they do, and it is far better just to forgive and forget.

Of course what they get up to when they're older is another matter and I have no hesitation whatsoever in putting that down upon paper.

Especially as it was my bloody dog that he blew up. Bastard!

We parted company at the allotment gates and the Doveston shuffled off to see how his tobacco crop was coming along on his 'uncle' Old Pete's plot.

I went shuffling homeward bound, my head already full of plans for the costume I might wear to impress the girls at the party. Something trendy, the Doveston had said, and *not* a policeman. *Not* a policeman narrowed it down quite a bit. Whatever could you dress up as that wasn't a policeman? A pirate, perhaps, or a parrot at a push. Or a parsnip, or a pimple, or Parnell.

I've always had a great deal of respect for Parnell. Charles Stewart Parnell (1846–91), that is, who led the Irish Home Rule movement in Parliament with his calculated policy of obstruction. He won Gladstone over in the end, but his career was sadly ruined through the scandal of his adultery with Mrs O'Shea.

Still, these things happen and Parnell was probably too obvious a choice. And I didn't want to make myself look silly by turning up as Parnell to find three other Parnells already there and only one Mrs O'Shea to go round between the four of us.

I had plans for something clever. Clever and trendy with it.

The next day at school I told Chico all about the party and asked him if he wanted to come. Chico looked a might battered and somewhat charred about the edges. I had to speak quite loudly to him, as he said that one

of his eardrums had been perforated due to an unexpected explosion. What did he think he would come
as? I asked him.

I awaited the inevitable reply and was actually quite
surprised when he passed over Parnell in favour of a
chap called Che Guevara who was some kind of
revolutionary, of all things. Outrageous!

Chico asked whether it would be all right for him to
bring along a couple of new gang members. I said I felt
sure that it would be, as long as he promised that they
wouldn't shoot anybody. Since it wasn't my party.

He agreed to this and then asked whether there
would be balloons at this party and jelly and games.

Kids, eh!

By the time Friday evening came around, there
seemed to be quite a big buzz in the neighbourhood.
Everyone was talking about the Doveston's party. Everyone seemed to be going.

I must say that I was really looking forward to it. For
one thing I had quite lost touch with all my old friends
from the Grange. When they went on to the Grammar
and I went on to St Argent's, it was almost as if they
hadn't wanted to speak to me any more, although I
can't imagine why that would have been. The only one
who remained close to me was the Doveston. But then
he *was* my bestest friend and I was to be his biographer.

One thing about the party did have me baffled and
that was how everyone was going to fit into the
Doveston's house. It was, after all, just a bog-standard
two up and two down terraced affair, with an outdoor
privy and six feet of yard. It was six doors down

from my own, on the sunny side of the street.

Still, I was confident that he knew what he was doing.

And, of course, he did.

Looking back now, across the wide expanse of years, it seems incredible to me that I did not see what was coming. All the clues were there. The unexpected envelope, delivered to my parents, containing two free tickets for the *Black and White Minstrel Show* on Friday night, along with vouchers for a steak dinner at a Piccadilly restaurant. The fact that the Doveston had borrowed the keys to our shed, to 'store a few crates of beer'. The 'printer's error' on the invitations he was giving out, which had the number of *my* house down as where the party was to be held.

These were all significant clues, but they somehow slipped by me.

At six o'clock on the Friday night my parents went off to the show. They told me not to wait up for them, as they wouldn't be home before midnight. We bade our farewells and I went up to my room to proceed with getting ready. Five minutes later the front-door bell rang.

I shuffled downstairs to see who was there. It was the Doveston.

He looked pretty dapper. His hair was combed and parted down the middle and he wore a clean Ben Sherman shirt with a button-down collar and slim leather tie. His suit was of the Tonic persuasion, narrow at the shoulders and high at the lapels. His boots were fine substantial things and polished on the toe-caps.

I smiled him hello and he offered me in return a look of unutterable woe.

'Whatever is the matter?' I asked.

'Something terrible has happened. May I come inside?'

'Please do.'

I led him into our front sitting room and he flung himself down on our ragged settee. 'It's awful,' he said, burying his face in his hands.

'What is?'

'My mum and dad. The doctor's just been round. They've come down with Lugwiler's Itch.'

'My God!' I said, for what I believe was the first time that day. 'Not Lugwiler's Itch.'

'Lugwiler's Itch,' said the Doveston.

I made the face that says 'hang about here'. 'But surely,' said my mouth, 'Lugwiler's Itch is a fictitious affliction out of a Jack Vance book.'

'Precisely,' said the Doveston.

'Oh,' said I.

'So the party's off.'

'*Off?* The party can't be off. I've been working on my costume. It's really trendy and everything.'

'I was going to dress up as Parnell. But it's all off now, there's nothing I can do about it.'

'What a bummer,' I said. 'What a bummer.'

The Doveston nodded sadly. 'It's the loss of face that hurts me most. I mean, having a party really *gains you a reputation*. If you know what I mean.'

'I do,' I said. 'Gaining a reputation is everything.'

'Well, I've blown it now. I shall become the butt of bitter jokes. All that kudos that could have been mine is gone for ever. I wish the ground would just open and swallow me up.'

'Surely there must be some way round it,' I said. 'Couldn't you hold the party somewhere else?'

'If only.' The Doveston dabbed at his nose. 'If only I had some trusted friend whose house was available for the evening. I wouldn't mind that he earned all the kudos and gained the reputation. At least I wouldn't have let everybody down. Let all those beautiful girls down. The ones who would be putty in the hands of the party-giver.'

There followed what is called a pregnant pause.

8

Cigareets and wuskey and wild wild women.
They'll drive you crazy. They'll drive you insane.

Trad.

Yes, all right, I know it *now*.

But what else could I say? It just seemed the perfect solution. Well, it *was* the perfect solution.

'The church hall,' I said to the Doveston. 'You could hire the church hall.'

If only I *had* said that. But I didn't.

'Hold the party *here*?' said the Doveston. 'In *your* house?'

'The perfect solution,' I said.

'We ought to ask your parents first.'

'They've gone out and they won't be back before twelve.'

'That's settled then.' The Doveston rose from the settee, shook me by the hand, marched to the front door, opened it and whistled. Then all at once a number of young men I'd never seen before came bustling into my house carrying crates of brown ale, cardboard boxes full of food and a real record player and records.

101

In and out and round about they went, like some well-drilled task force. The Doveston introduced me to them as they breezed by.

'This is Jim Pooley,' he said. 'And this is John Omally and this is Archroy and this is Small Dave.'

'Where?' I asked.

'Down here,' said Small Dave.

'Oh, hello. They're not in fancy dress,' I whispered to the Doveston.

'Well, nor are you.'

This was true. And this was a problem. If the party was going to be held at my house, how was I going to make the big dramatic entrance in my costume?

'Hadn't you better get changed?' the Doveston asked.

'Yes, I . . . But—'

'Listen,' the Doveston said. 'You are the host of this party and I think you should have the chance to make a big dramatic entrance in your costume.'

'That's what I was thinking.'

'Then you go up to your bedroom and get ready, I'll take care of things down here and when everybody has arrived, I'll come and get you and you can make a *really* big dramatic entrance. How's that?'

'Wonderful,' I said. 'You're a real pal.'

'I know.' The Doveston pushed past me. 'I want those cartons of cigarettes stacked in the kitchen,' he told one of his task force. 'That's where I will be setting up my shop.'

So I went up to my bedroom.

It didn't take me too long to get ready and having posed a good few times before the wall mirror, I sat down upon my bed and listened to all the comings and goings beneath.

The sounds of music drifted up to me as platter-waxings of the latest rockin' teenage combos went round and round on the real record player at forty-five revolutions per minute.

And although I didn't know it then, I was about to make history. You see, during the 1950s there had never been such a thing as a teenage party. Lads were conscripted into the armed forces on their thirteenth birthday and not set free upon society until they reached twenty. At which time they were considered to be responsible citizens.

My generation, the post-war baby boomers, missed conscription by a year and what with us never having had it so good and everything, we literally invented the teenage party.

And what I didn't know then was that the party in my house would be the *first ever* teenage party. The one that would set the standard against which all future teenage parties would be judged.

So I suppose, in this respect, I have much to thank the Doveston for. And although he did blow up my dog, he did apologize afterwards.

I sat there upon my bed, getting all excited.

An hour or so later, I began to fret. My bedroom was hazing with cigarette smoke rising from the kitchen, the merry sounds of partying were growing ever louder and the Doveston had not yet come to get me.

I reasoned that he was waiting for the right moment. Indeed waiting until the gang were all here.

At around about nine my doubts set in. Waiting for the right moment was all very well, but I was missing my own party and I was quite sure that I had heard one or two breaking sounds. As if things were getting smashed. I really couldn't wait much longer.

It was nearly ten before a knock came at my door. My bedroom was now so full of smoke that I could hardly see across it. I stumbled to my door and flung it open.

On the landing stood John Omally, his arm around the shoulder of a teenage girl. I smiled heartily. Omally was dressed as Parnell, the girl as Mrs O'Shea.

I must have created quite an impression, what with all the smoke bursting out around me and everything. The girl shrieked and Omally fell back, crossing at himself.

'Where's the Doveston?' I asked.

Omally made dumb pointings in a kitchenish direction.

I shrugged. I couldn't wait any longer. I was going down now and that was that.

It was quite a struggle getting down. The stairs were crowded with couples and these couples were snogging. I stepped over and between them going 'Sorry, sorry' and 'Excuse me, please'. There were so many people in our little hall that I had to push with all my might. The front door was open and I glimpsed a great deal more party folk outside in the garden and the street. I fought my way to the front sitter where all the dancing was going on and tried without success to make myself heard. The record player was on much too loud and nobody was paying me the slightest bit of notice.

I must confess that I was fed up. Really fed up at all this. I shouted '*Oi!*' at the top of my voice and at that very moment, the record that was playing finished and I found that I had the attention of everybody in the room.

They turned and they stared and then they screamed. Well, the girls all screamed. The blokes kind of gasped. That softy Paul Mason, who used to be in my class at the Grange, and who I was unimpressed to see had come dressed as a pimple, simply fainted. And then there was a lot of pushing and shoving and shouting and a good deal of backing away.

I hadn't noticed that the Doveston was there. His costume was so convincing that I wouldn't have recognized him anyway. He hadn't come as Parnell at all. He had come as Lazlo Woodbine, private eye. Trench coat, fedora and vacuum-cleaner nozzle. He stepped forward and looked me up and down. I smiled back at him and said, 'What do you think?'

The Doveston extended a finger, ran it down my cheek, put it to his nose and sniffed.

'It's tomato ketchup,' he said. Then, turning to the starers and the gaspers, he said, 'It's all right, it's only tomato ketchup.' And then he turned back to me and he glared. 'What the fuck do you think you're up to?' he asked. 'Coming down here with your head all covered in tomato ketchup and frightening the shit out of my guests?'

'But you said I was to come as something trendy.'

'So you came as a tomato ketchup bottle?'

'No,' I said. 'I've come as President Kennedy.'

Now what happened next made me angry. In fact it

made me very angry. It was all so undignified. The Doveston grabbed me by the scruff of the neck and dragged me from the room. He frogmarched me into the kitchen, rammed my head into the sink and turned on the taps. Once he had washed all the ketchup from my hair and face he straightened me up, thrust a tea towel into my hands and called me a twat.

'What?' I said. '*What?*'

'Coming as a dead bloke, you twat.'

'But you've come as a dead bloke.' I dabbed at myself. 'And that John Omally has come as Parnell, he's a dead bloke and—'

The Doveston cut me short. 'I was going to say, coming as a dead bloke before I had a chance to introduce you properly. I knew you'd come as Kennedy, I saw you nick the ketchup bottle from the Plume Café and I put two and two together. I was going to play "The Star-spangled Banner" on the record player and pretend to shoot you as you came down the stairs. But you've screwed it all up now.'

'Oh,' I said. 'I'm sorry.'

'And so you should be. Would you care for a beer?'

'Yes I would.'

My first beer. I will never forget that. It tasted horrible. Why do we bother with the stuff, eh? Whatever is the attraction? I didn't like my first beer at all; I thought it was foul. But I felt that as beer was so popular and all adult males drank it, I'd better see the thing through. I finished my first beer with difficulty and belched.

'Have another,' said the Doveston.

'I don't mind if I do.'

The second tasted not so bad. The third tasted better.

I swigged down my fourth beer, went 'Aaaah', and smacked my lips.

'It grows on you, doesn't it?' said the Doveston.

'Pardon?' I replied.

'I said *it grows on you.*'

'*Oh, yeah.*' I shouted too, as the music was now very loud indeed and the hustling and bustling in the crowded kitchen made it almost impossible to talk.

'*Go and dance,*' the Doveston shouted. '*Enjoy the party.*'

'*Yes. Right.*' And I thought I would. After all, it was *my* party and there seemed to be an awful lot of girls. I pushed my way back into the hall, rubbing up against as many as I could. There were girls here dressed up as princesses, page boys, panel-beaters and Pankhursts – mostly as Emmeline Pankhurst (1858–1928) the English suffragette leader, who founded the militant Women's Social and Political Union in 1903.

I squeezed by a girl who was dressed as a parachute and elbowed my way into the front sitter. The joint was a-rockin' and I was impressed. There were popes here and pilots and pit lads and pastry chefs. Even a couple of Pushkins. Whoever Pushkin was.

I was about to get in there and boogie when someone tapped me on the shoulder.

'Hey, homes,' a voice shouted in my ear.

I turned. It was Chico.

'I'm not Sherlock Holmes,' I shouted. 'I'm President Kennedy.'

'President who, homes?'

'Eh?'

'Forget it.'

I looked Chico up and down and all around. He had a bath towel over his head, held in place by a fan belt. He was robed in chintzy curtains, secured at the waist by a dressing-gown cord. His face was boot-blackened and he wore upon his chin a false goatee fashioned from what looked like (and indeed turned out to be) a pussycat's tail.

'Who are you supposed to be?' I shouted.

'Che Guevara,' he shouted back.

The light of realization dawned.

'Chico,' I shouted. 'That's *Che* Guevara, not *Sheik* Guevara.'

'Curse this dyslexia.'

Oh how we laughed.

Chico had brought the new gang members and he hauled me outside into the street to make the introductions.

'Your costumes are great,' I told them. 'You look just like Kalahari Bushmen.'

'But we *are* Kalahari Bushmen.'

Oh how we laughed again.

Chico winked in my direction. 'I also brought one of my sisters.'

'Not the one with the moustache?'

We would no doubt have laughed again, but Chico chose instead to hit me. As he helped me back to my feet he whispered, 'Just for the benefit of the new guys, no offence meant.'

'None taken, I assure you.'

And then there was a bit of a crash as someone

flew out through the front sitter window.

'Neat,' said Chico. 'Where's the booze?'

I gaped in horror at all the blood and broken glass.

My parents wouldn't be happy about this.

The Doveston appeared in the front doorway. He came over and handed me another beer. 'Don't worry about the damage,' he said.

'But—'

'Here,' said the Doveston. 'Have this too.'

He handed me a large fat cigarette. It was all twisted up at one end.

'What is that?' I asked.

'It's a joint.'

My first joint. I will never forget that. It tasted . . . W O N D E R F U L

I drifted back towards the house and was met by two girls dressed as pixies who were patting at a big and soppy Labrador.

'Is this your dog?' one of them asked.

I nodded dreamily.

'What's its name?'

'Well,' I said. 'When I got it I thought it was a boy dog and so I named it Dr Evil.'

'Oh,' said one of the pixies.

'But it turned out to be a girl dog, so my mum said I had to call it something else.'

'So what's its name?'

'Biscuit,' I said.

The pixies laughed. Rather prettily, I thought. And I was aware of the pale pink auras that surrounded them and so I smiled some more and swigged upon my beer and sucked again at my joint. 'Try some of this,' I said.

I suppose things really got into full swing around eleven o'clock. Up until then only one person had been thrown out through the front window and he had got off lightly, with nothing more than minor scarring for life. The bloke who'd climbed up onto the roof wasn't quite so lucky.

I didn't actually see him as he plunged past my parents' bedroom window onto the spiked railings beneath. I was in the double bed with one of the pixies.

We were having a go at puberty together.

My first sex. Now I really *do* wish I could remember *that*!

I do have a vague recollection of a lot of people piling into the bedroom and saying that I had to come downstairs because there had been an accident. And I think I recall stumbling down the stairs naked and wondering why the walls had been spray-painted so many different colours. I don't remember slipping over in the pool of vomit on the hall carpet, although apparently this got quite a laugh. As did the look on my face when I saw that the front sitter was on fire.

I have absolutely no idea who took the fridge and the cooker, and, as I told the magistrate, if I had known that there was a gang bang going on in my back parlour and being filmed by students from the art school, I would have done something about it.

What I do recall clearly, and this will be forever

tattooed on my memory cells, is Biscuit.

Biscuit, coming up to me as I stood in the open front doorway, staring out at the police cars and fire appliances. Biscuit, licking my hand and gazing up at me with her big brown eyes.

And me, looking down at Biscuit and wondering what that strange firework fizzing was, coming from under her tail.

9

Snout: British prison slang for tobacco.

I awoke naked and covered in Biscuit.

Now, you know that panicky feeling you get when you wake up after a really heavy night of drink and drugs and know, just *know*, that you've done something that you shouldn't have?

Well, I felt like that.

I did a lot of blinking and gagging and groping about and I wondered how come my bedroom ceiling was suddenly all tiled over.

Now, you know that panicky feeling you get when you wake up after a really heavy night of drink and drugs and find yourself naked in a police cell?

No?

Well, it really sucks, I can tell you.

I screamed. Screamed really loud. And I wiped at myself with my fingers and I gaped at the guts and the dark clotted blood.

'Biscuit,' I screamed. 'Biscuit.'

A little metal hatch in the large metal door snapped open. 'You won't get a biscuit here, you bastard,' called a voice.

'Help,' I called back. 'Let me out. Let me out.'

But they didn't let me out. They kept me locked away in there all day, with only a plate of cornflakes and a cup of tea to keep me going. And at about three o'clock in the afternoon the door swung open and Brother Michael from St Argent's sauntered in.

Now, as you don't know the panicky feeling you get from waking up naked in a police cell, you probably won't know the *really* panicky feeling you get when you find yourself naked in a police cell and locked in with a pederastic monk.

It's a real bummer and I kid you not.

Brother Michael shook his tonsured head and then sat down beside me on the nasty little cot. I shifted up a bit and crossed my legs. Brother Michael placed a hand upon my knee. 'This is a very bad business,' he said.

I began to snivel. 'Somebody blew up my Biscuit,' I blubbered.

'Blew up your biscuit, eh?' The monk smiled warmly. 'That's not so bad. I remember the first time someone blew up my biscuit. I was just a choirboy at St Damien of Hirst's and—'

'Stop right there,' I told him. 'I am talking about my dog, Biscuit.'

'Somebody blew up your dog biscuit?'

I turned a bitter eye upon the monk. 'My dog's *name* was Biscuit. Someone blew her up.'

'I am becoming confused,' said Brother Michael, giving my knee a little squeeze. 'But I think we should turn our attention to the matter of your defence. Due to the large quantity of Class A drugs seized on your premises, you will have to put your hands up to the dealing charges. But I feel we can get you off with manslaughter if—'

'What?' I went. 'What what *what*?'

'Was the chap you pushed to his death another drug-dealer? Is this a Mafia thing? I wouldn't want to get directly involved without the permission of the mob. I mean I *am* a Roman Catholic monk, so obviously I *am* in the Mafia, but I know which side my communion wafer is buttered. If you know what I mean and I'm sure that you do.'

'*What?*' I went. '*WHAT?*'

'The other charges are no big deal. Soliciting minors, running an unruly house. Don't you just love that phrase?'

'*WHAT?*' I went once again.

'You're looking at ten years,' said Brother Michael, squeezing a bit more at my knee. 'But you'll only end up serving eight with good behaviour. You'll still be a young man when you come out, with your whole life ahead of you. Of course, with the stigma of a prison sentence attached to you, you'll probably end up swabbing toilets for a living. But that's not so bad. You meet all kinds of interesting people in toilets.'

'Wah,' I wept. 'Wah and boo hoo hoo.'

'It's such a pity that you're not a monk.'

'Wah,' I went and, 'What?'

'Well, if you were a monk, you wouldn't have to worry. We monks have theological immunity, we do not have to answer to Common Law.'

'You don't?'

'Of course we don't. We answer only to a higher power.'

'God?'

'God. And the Pope. And the Mafia, of course. If you were a monk, you could walk right out of here.'

'How could I do that?'

'Because if you were a monk, you could hardly be guilty of a crime, could you? Whoever heard of a bad monk?'

'There was Rasputin,' I said.

'Precisely.'

'Eh?'

'Well, anyway. If you were a monk, you'd get off scot-free.'

'Is that Sir George Gilbert Scott (1811 to 1878), the English architect so prominent in the Gothic revival, who restored many churches and cathedrals and designed the Albert Memorial?'

'No,' said Brother Michael. 'Why do you ask?'

'Oh, no reason.' I sighed deeply. 'I wish I was a monk,' I said.

Brother Michael made a thoughtful face. 'There is a way,' he said. 'But, no.'

'No what? What do you mean?'

'Well, I could make you a monk and then you would walk free of all the charges and not have to go to prison.'

'Then do it,' I said. 'Do it.'

'It's not strictly orthodox. It should really be done in a vestry.'

'Do it,' I begged. 'Do it now. Do it here.'

'Oh all right. You've talked me into it. The actual

115

initiation won't take too long, but you might find it a bit uncomfortable. You'd better drink this.' He produced a bottle of colourless liquid. 'Drink it down and find yourself something to bite on.'

And it was *that* close.

If the cell door hadn't opened at that very minute and a policeman come in to tell me that I could go straight home, because no-one was pressing any charges, what with me still being a minor and everything and nobody being badly hurt.

It was *that* close.

I almost became a monk.

My parents were waiting outside with a change of clothes for me. I went meekly, accepting that I was in big big trouble.

But the trouble never came. Instead my mother hugged and kissed me and my father told me that I was very brave.

It turned out that the Doveston had spoken with them and explained everything.

He had told them how he and I had been at my house giving the place a good spring clean to surprise my parents when they got back from the show. And how the evil big boys had broken into the house and wreaked terrible havoc.

And how they had blown up my Biscuit.

When pressed for descriptions, the Doveston could only say that they all wore disguise, but 'had much of the gypsy about them'.

10

Don't Bogart that joint, my friend.
                                    Trad.

Personally, I had a great deal of time for the 1960s. I know that a lot of old bunkum has been talked about them. All that 'if you can remember the Sixties, you weren't there' rubbish. But there was a lot more to those years than simply sex and drugs and rock'n'roll (as if this mighty trio was not in itself sufficient).

Yes, there was free love, for the Secret Government of the World had yet to invent AIDS. Yes, there were drugs, and many a young mind was blown and expanded. And yes, indeed to goodness yes, there was good old rock'n'roll. Or rather good *new* rock'n'roll.

But there was more, so much more.

For one thing, there were yo-yos.

You might remember yo-yos, they enjoyed a brief renaissance back in the late 1990s, and possibly you have one, gathering radioactive dust in a corner of your fallout shelter. But I bet you can't remember how to work it, and I'll also bet that you don't know that the yo-yo was invented in Brentford.

Oh yes it was.

Norman Hartnell[1] invented the yo-yo. It was his very first invention. It is true to say that he did not invent it with the intention of it becoming a toy. He invented the yo-yo as a means to power his Vespa motor scooter.

Norman had this thing about alternative sources of power and it remained with him throughout his life. His search was for the free energy motor. That holy grail of science, perpetual motion. How the idea originally came into his head seems uncertain. But my money would be on the Doveston putting it there.

By 1967, the year of which I now write, the Doveston had firmly established himself as Norman's mentor.

Norman now ran the family business, his father having met a tragic early death in a freak accident involving handcuffs, concrete and canal water. The exact circumstances remain a mystery to this day and although the police questioned the Sicilians who ran the off licence next door, no arrests were made. Why the police should have suspected foul play in the first place is quite beyond me. And if they were thinking of fitting up the Sicilians, their evil schemes were soon thwarted.

For the Sicilians were all wiped out, a week after the death of Norman's dad, in another freak accident. This one involving their letter box and a stick of dynamite.

They were the last Sicilians in Brentford and, in the words of Flann, I do not think that their like will ever be seen here again.

---

[1] Still not to be confused with the other Norman Hartnell.

Now, 1967 is remembered with great fondness for being the Summer of Love. Nineteen sixty-seven *was* the Summer of Love. There were other seasons, of course, and these too had their names. There was the Winter of Downheartedness, the Spring of Utter Misery and the Autumn of Such Dire Gloom that it made you want to open your wrists with a razor. But for some unknown reason, people only remember the summer.

I remember that summer well. For it was the summer of yo-yos and Brentstock.

Ah, Brentstock. The now legendary three-day festival of Love and Peace and Music. I was there, you know, I saw it all. Allow me to tell you about it.

For me it began one spring morning. I was feeling utterly miserable, although I have no idea why. I'd left school the previous July and gone from one job to another. They had all been menial and underpaid and I had been sacked from each of them. This, of course, presented no problem. There was full employment in the Sixties and no sooner were you sacked from one place than you could begin work at another. Sure, they were all crap jobs, but hey, it was better than being unemployed.

But in that spring I had a new job and one with prospects. I was employed by the Doveston. My job description was *Overseer of the Plantation* and I got to wear a special uniform with boots and carry a riding crop. It was a doddle. All I had to do was stride about, clouting migrant workers with my crop and telling them to get a move on.

It was the kind of job you only dream about.

So I'm still not sure why I was so miserable.

The Doveston used to have a catchphrase, which was; 'Tomorrow belongs to those who can see it coming'. He was certainly one of the *those*. I remember him telling me that one day there would be no Mexican quarter in Brentford and I remember how I scorned the idea at the time. But he'd been quite right; by 1967 all the Pachucos had blown each other away and all the remaining Mexicans, mostly old women and little girls, lived in the shanty town of huts and sheds on the edge of the plantation and worked for the Doveston.

I should perhaps say something now about where the plantation was located. After all, it was the site of Brentstock.

It was located upon Brentford's St Mary's allotments.

Up until the middle Sixties there had been many allotment holders, each with their own little plot of land, rented from the council and yielding up its yearly crop of fruit and veg. But one by one the old boys who dug the soil died off and one by one their plots became available.

And one by one the Doveston acquired them.

And now he had them all but one. That one belonged to his 'uncle', Old Pete, and that remained untouched. As for all the rest, they were ploughed over and the great square of land, sloping gently to the River Thames, became a tobacco plantation.

I had scratched my head a lot about this. I'd always thought that it was illegal to grow tobacco without some kind of government licence. But apparently this was not true in Brentford. In Brentford it didn't apply.

It was a tradition, or an old charter, or something.

So I got the job as Overseer. Uniform and boots and riding crop and all.

'Sixty-seven brought in the first big harvest. And everything had to be done just as the Doveston wished it. Years of work had gone into this. Tobacco does not grow happily in a London suburb and this particular strain had been genetically modified.

The Doveston possessed many pages of notes penned by a certain Jon Peru Joans and with the aid of Old Pete he had created a fast-growing tobacco plant that was resistant to native pests and thrived on English weather. It was quite an achievement and those who were allowed through the guarded gate of the high barbed-wire perimeter fence marvelled at the beauty of the plants. Although not for too long, or they got a whack from my crop.

On the spring morning in question, the first harvesting had begun. Female workers toiled away and the Doveston and I lazed in raised chairs, toking on newly rolled cigars[1] and swigging colourless liquid from un-labelled bottles.

The Doveston dug into the hip-pocket of his fashionable kaftan and brought out something to show me. 'I bet you've never seen anything like this before,' he said, handing it to me.

I examined the object: two slim cylinders of wood joined by a narrow wooden dowel to which was attached a length of string. 'You're right there,' I said. 'I haven't. What is it?'

[1]Rolled upon the thigh of a dusky maiden.

'It's a down-and-upsy-down-again.'

'That's easy for you to say,' I said. 'But what does it do?'

'It goes down and upsy down again. Look, I'll show you.' He took the item from me, looped the end of the string about his middle finger and let the item drop from his hand. When it had reached the end of the string he gave it a little jerk. It rose again and he caught it.

'Incredible,' I said. 'That is one of the most amazing things I have ever seen.'

'Are you being sarcastic?' the Doveston asked.

I thought about this. 'Possibly,' I said. 'But how does it work? Is there a little engine inside it? Or is it, as one might reasonably suppose, the work of some demonic agency?'

The Doveston reached over and took away my bottle. 'You've drunk quite enough of this, I think,' said he.

I shook my head. 'It's not the booze. Although it might well be the tab of acid I had for my breakfast.'

'Well, I can forgive you that. After all, these *are* the 1960s.'

'So how *does* it work? It appears to defy gravity.'

'That is what Norman originally thought. But sadly it doesn't. It works by momentum, with a little help from your wrist.'

'As do many things,' said I. 'Or at least one I can think of. So what is it for? Or isn't it for anything?'

'It must be for something.' The Doveston turned the item on his palm. 'Everything must be for something. You can do tricks with it.'

'I can't, you know.'

'All right. I mean, *I* can do tricks with it.'

'Go on then, show me.'

The Doveston showed me. He sent the thing scurrying down again, but this time let it skim across the ground before jerking it up once more. 'I call that one "walking the dog".'

I clapped.

He then performed another trick, this one involving some intricate string-work. 'That one's called "rocking the baby".'

I clapped some more.

He ran right through his repertoire. He had given a name to each trick. There was 'spanking the monkey', 'worrying the pussy', 'splitting the beaver' and one called 'taking tea with the parson', which involved such complicated manoeuvres that sweat broke out on his forehead.

'You know what you've got yourself there?' I said, when he was finally done.

'No, what?'

'Two bits of wood on the end of a string. Throw the stupid thing away before someone sees you with it.'

But somebody *had* seen him with it. In fact everyone working on the plantation had seen him with it. They were all standing and staring and now, to my amazement, they were clapping too.

The Doveston eyed his appreciative audience and I eyed the Doveston. He hadn't given his permission for them to stop working and I felt it likely that he would give me the order to shoot a couple of the old ones as an example.

But he didn't. Because now the workers were falling

123

to their knees. They were bowing to the Doveston.

'Yo Yo,' cried one of them. Then, 'Yo Yo,' cried the rest.

'What are they doing?' the Doveston asked.

I shook my head in wonder. 'They're worshipping you. They think that you are Yo Yo.'

'And who in the name of Virginian Gold is Yo Yo?'

'Ah,' I said. 'You don't know about Yo Yo, because you didn't go to St Argent's, like me. The Mexicans may be Roman Catholics on the surface, but they also worship their Old Gods. Yo Yo is one of those. He screwed up in some way in Heaven and was sent down to Earth. Here he did good work amongst the farmers and ascended to Heaven again. Where he screwed up again and was sent down again, where—'

'He did more good works and went up again.'

'That's it. Up again and down again and up again again. Just like your down-and-upsy-down-again.'

The Doveston smiled a most Godly smile. 'Just like my *yo-yo*, you mean.'

The harvest came in right on time that year. And it didn't cost the Doveston a penny. He had me go straight round to Norman's with a small bale of tobacco. This I exchanged for one hundred yo-yos, which the shopkeeper knocked out on his lathe in less than an hour. The Doveston paid off his workers with these and they were well pleased, bearing the sacred objects away to their huts with much bowing and tugging at forelocks. Or whatever the female equivalent of a forelock is. A forelock, probably.

And so the yo-yo craze was born. It soon spread

across the borough and Norman, had he had the foresight to patent the thing, would probably have made a fortune selling them.

The patent was, however, taken out by a certain Mr Crad, who sold it on to a leading toy manufacturer for an undisclosed sum and a royalty deal.

It was many years later that I discovered Mr Crad and Mr Doveston to be one and the same person.

The yo-yo craze was born and how it spread. The case was, as it has so often been, today Brentford, tomorrow the world. There was trouble, of course. The Archbishop of Canterbury condemned it as 'an evil pagan cult', which increased sales no end. Mary Whitehouse called for questions to be asked in the Houses of Parliament and questions *were* asked. A member of the Cabinet gave an interview on the lawn before the Palace of Westminster, stating that yo-yos were in no way harmful and his own daughter was filmed by the news teams playing with one.

There were the inevitable scare stories in the gutter press about yo-yo deaths and suicides. There was an epidemic of yo-yo finger, caused by overtight strings cutting off the circulation and this had Mrs Whitehouse back on the phone, demanding that government health warnings be put on the things.

This, in turn, had the Cabinet Minister back on the lawn, but this time unaccompanied by his daughter, who was apparently in hospital.

'YO-YO MADNESS', as the tabloids were now calling it, eventually died a natural death. These things just do. Crazes come and crazes go and few, if any, know the reasons why. They are here today and gone tomorrow.

And tomorrow belongs to those who can see it coming.

But what about Brentstock, I hear you ask.

Well, what about Brentstock indeed.

11

If music be the food of love, then I don't know
what a cigar is.

Nimrod Tombs

'I'm thinking of giving something back.'

So said the Doveston.

We sat outside the Flying Swan. It was a warm late
spring evening and I still felt utterly miserable. Mind
you, with summer on the way, I was beginning to feel
a bit more loving.

The sun was just going down behind the gasometer,
its final rays glinting upon our pints of Large, and
glittering in our eyes of baby-blue.

'Giving something back?' I said.

'Giving something back.'

'Well, I don't know what you've taken, but I'll have
it back if you're giving it.'

'Not to *you*,' the Doveston said. 'To the borough, as
a whole.'

'I quite like the borough,' I said. 'I don't think you
should call it a hole.'

The Doveston lightly cuffed me in the ear. 'Whole,'
he said, 'with a W.'

I picked myself up from the ground. 'I fear you have lost me on this one,' I said.

'I've had a good year so far.' The Doveston finished his pint and gazed into its empty bottom. 'My harvest is in early. Soon the tobacco will be ready for packing and soon after that, cigars and cigarettes and snuff, bearing the distinctive Doveston logo, will be rolling off the production lines. Also, I am worshipped as a God, which is no small thing in itself. And I've had a bit of luck in one or two other directions.' He took his yo-yo from his pocket and buffed it on his sleeve.

'So you're thinking of giving something back?'

'To the borough, yes.'

'And what did you have in mind? Not something revolutionary, like paying your workers a living wage?'

'Beware the fist that falleth on your ear. My workers have gone their way, to toil in the Crad fields of Chiswick. I was thinking that I'd like to organize some kind of celebration.'

'A party?'

'Something like that.'

'Well not in my house, mate!'

'Something bigger than that.'

'Well, you can't hire the scout hut again. They know it was you who blew off the roof.'

'Aaah-choo!' said the Doveston. 'By the way, did you ever buy yourself another dog?'

'No, I didn't and I'll thank you not to mention it again.'

'I said I was sorry.'

'But you didn't mean it.'

'Meaning it is not the point. It's saying it that matters.'

I finished up my pint. 'You can buy me another of these,' I said. 'And I've said *that*, so it matters.'

'Do I look like I'm made of money?'

'Actually you do. And if you really are intending to give something back to the borough, you might as well start right away.'

The Doveston got us in two more pints. 'Listen,' he said, cupping a hand to his ear. 'Tell me what you hear.'

I listened. 'Is it God already praising you for your generosity?'

'No. It's the jukebox.'

'Ah yes,' I said. 'The jukebox that has only three records on it, these three being privately produced pressings made by the landlord's son and his band.'

'Precisely.'

I sipped at my beer.

'Aren't you going to make some fatuous remark?'

I shook my head, spilling beer down my front.

'That will do for me,' said the Doveston. 'What would you say if I told you that I was going to put on a rock festival?'

'Firstly I would ask you who was going to play at it. Then, once you'd told me, and if I was keen to see whoever it was, I would ask you how much the tickets were. And then, once you'd told me *that*, I would fall back in horror and say something like, "You must be frigging joking, mate!" That's what I'd say.'

'I was thinking of organizing a *free* festival.'

'You must be frigging joking, mate!'

'I'm serious. We could hold it on the plantation. We could get a thousand people on there easily – two thousand, at a push.'

'Tramping all over your crops?'

'The crops are up. The land is lying fallow. This would be a golden opportunity to earn a little extra from it.'

'I thought I heard you say it was going to be a *free* festival.'

'It would be free to get in. But people have to eat, don't they? And buy their cigarettes and beer. We would set up stalls to cater to their every need.'

'Exactly who is this *we* you keep talking about?'

'Well, naturally *you* will want to get involved. After all, you *are* my biographer and amanuensis, are you not?'

'Oh yes,' I said. 'I keep a careful record of everything *you* get up to.'

'Then there is nothing more to be said. I'll leave all the booking of the bands with you. Get somebody big, the Beatles, or the Rolling Stones, or someone.'

I looked at the Doveston.

And the Doveston looked at me.

'Shall I see if I can get the landlord's son?' I asked.

Actually things went a great deal better regarding the booking of bands than I might reasonably have expected. As the summer came on, bands who would normally have charged a royal ransom for their services began to come over all lovey-dovey and start playing gigs for free.

We now had a telephone in our house and one morning in July, I replaced the receiver after taking a long-distance call from foreign parts.

'Captain Beefheart's coming,' I told my mum.

'Captain who?' she replied.

'Beefheart,' said my father. 'Otherwise known as Don Van Vliet, an avant-garde musician with a four-octave vocal range, whose seminal album *Trout Mask Replica* is still hailed today as being one of the most original pieces of work ever produced in the rock canon.'

I took my dad quietly aside. 'Just one or two small details,' I said. 'Firstly *Trout Mask* is a double album. And secondly it doesn't come out until 1969. I think these things probably matter.'

My father nodded thoughtfully. 'Captain *who*?' he said.

Actually the good captain was unable to make it, but the Jimi Hendrix Experience and Big Brother and the Holding Company were still up for the gig.

'Mark well my words, my friend,' said the Doveston, when I told him, 'Jimi Hendrix and Janis Joplin will both be dead from drugs in a few years from now.'

I shook my head. 'You might have been right about the Mexican quarter,' I said, 'but that is quite absurd.'

I must confess that I was rather miffed when, a month before the festival, both Jimi and Janis had to pull out for unspecified reasons. I would no doubt have sunk into a state of utter misery, had I not been feeling so full of love.

'About your boy and his band,' I said to the landlord of the Flying Swan.

*

131

With just three weeks to go, the Doveston called a special meeting of the festival committee at his flat. I had been to the Doveston's flat many times before. In fact I had helped him move in, being given responsibility for many of the heavier pieces of furniture. It was a pretty fab flat and I offer a description of it now to set the scene for what was to become one of those 'moments in history'.

The Doveston's flat occupied the entire top floor of Hawtrey House, one of the six new flat-blocks that had been built on the site of the old ethnic quarters. Each of these flat-blocks had been named after some titan of the British silver screen. There was Hawtrey, James, Windsor, Williams, Sims and McMurdo. McMurdo was a bit of a mystery and I couldn't think of any famous actor of that name. The only McMurdo I knew was Councillor McMurdo, head of the town-planning committee.

So it obviously wasn't him!

When the old streets were demolished to make way for the new flat-blocks, their residents had been rehoused elsewhere. It was intended that they would all get new flats as soon as the building work was completed. But I suppose there must have been some clerical error, or the council must have mislaid their new addresses, or something, because none of the original residents of that area ever came back to Brentford to live in the flat-blocks. Young, smart, out-borough types, who wore suits and had 'jobs in the City' moved in.

The Doveston moved in also.

He was very lucky, as it happened. The top floor of

Hawtrey House should have been divided into three separate flats. But it seemed that the council must have run out of money, or something, because the dividing walls were never put in and the Doveston got to rent the entire floor for the price of a single flat. He told Norman that an uncle of his had put him on to it. Norman told me that he couldn't remember this uncle's name, but he thought it had a Scottish ring to it.

It certainly was a pretty fab flat.

Its décor was all of the modern style. Lava lamps, bean bags and curtains of bead. Colourful rugs lay all scattered about. The floor was gloss-painted, the blinds were of reed.

By now the Doveston had accumulated an extensive collection of books dedicated to the subject of tobacco. Many of these bore the distinctive stamp of the Memorial Library upon them, but I did not comment on this.

There were, however, a number of items in the flat which I did comment on. There was a most exquisite jardinière, which I had first seen in the conservatory of Jon Peru Joans. A leather-bound and studded teapot, from which tea had once been poured for me in the House of Correction. And a beautiful box, wrought from skin, that I felt certain was the very one Professor Merlin had shown to us in his caravan, nearly a decade before.

When I asked about the provenance of these *objets d'art*, the Doveston was vague in his replies.

The sheer spaciousness of the flat gave it an air of grandeur. Its broad windows overlooked the borough, offering romantic vistas. The smell of joss sticks (the Doveston created his own) filled the air with heady fragrances and the sounds of sitar music, issuing from the Doveston's new hi-fi, added that certain something.

I would have been quite sick with jealousy, had my mother not taught me that 'jealous boys all go to Hell, where they have to look at Heaven all day through the wrong end of a telescope'.

The Free Festival Committee consisted of myself, Norman and Chico. Chico had survived a recent shooting and now worked full time as the Doveston's chauffeur. The Doveston's first car was a battered Morris Minor that Chico had converted into a low-rider. Since then the Doveston has owned a great many cars, but he never learned to drive himself.

We sat upon bean bags, smoking the cigars we were offered, and spoke about how things were going. The festival was to take place on the weekend of the twenty-seventh of July, which, by coincidence, was the Doveston's birthday.

'Speak to me of bands,' said the Doveston.

'Right,' said I. 'Bands, yes indeed.'

'So?'

'Yes, right.' I cleared my throat. 'Right, yes, absolutely.'

'You have actually booked some bands, haven't you?'

'Oh yes. Well, not actually booked, as such. Which is to say that there's nothing down on paper. No contracts or anything. But I—'

'But you what?'

'Chico just punched me in the ear,' I complained.

'Bands,' said the Doveston.

'Yes.' I rooted a crumpled list from my kaftan pocket. 'Well, I couldn't get any big names. They were all too busy, going on their holidays and stuff like that, and a lot of them seem to have buggered off to San Francisco.'

'So who have you got?'

I read from my list. 'Astro Lazer and the Flying Starfish from Uranus. Rosebud Lovejuice. The Seven Smells of Susan. Wompochumbassa. The Chocolate T-Shirts and Bob Dylan.'

'Bob Dylan?' said the Doveston. 'You got Bob Dylan?'

'Yes, his dad said he could have the Saturday off.'

'Bob Dylan's dad?'

'Johnny Dylan, owns the delicatessens in the High Street. Bob usually does the cheese round on Saturdays. But his dad said it would be OK for him to have the time off so he could do his juggling in front of a live audience.'

'Bob Dylan is a juggler.'

'Of course he is, what did you think he was?'

The Doveston shook his head. 'Anyone else?'

'Sonny and Cher,' I said.

'*Sonny and Cher?*'

'Sonny Watson and Cher O'Riley. They manage a pub in Kew.'

The Doveston raised his hand. 'And they juggle too, I suppose.'

'No, they tap dance.'

'Perfect. And do you have a uni-cycling plumber

135

from Chiswick who goes by the name of Elvis Presley?'

I checked my list. 'No,' I said. 'Do you want me to put him on?'

Chico smote my ear once more.

'Stop doing that,' I told him.

'So,' said the Doveston, taking out his yo-yo and 'chasing the dragon'. 'We have a bunch of completely unknown bands and three—'

'Ringers,' said Chico. 'Are you thinking what I'm thinking, boss?'

'That we might just elevate Bob, Sonny and Cher to the top of the bill?'

'It should bring in a lot of punters.'

I scratched at my head. It was a far less scabby head now, though I still had plenty of dandruff. 'I don't get this,' I said. 'Bob, Sonny and Cher aren't all *that* good. I thought they might just fill in between the bands.'

'Trust me,' said the Doveston. 'I know what I'm doing.'

And of course he did. But then, so did I. Because I was not completely stupid. I knew perfectly well who the real Bob Dylan and the real Sonny and Cher were. But I wasn't going to let on. The way I saw it was this. If I'd just given the Doveston a list of complete unknowns, he would probably have had Chico throw me out of the window. This way it gave him the opportunity to do one of the things that he enjoyed doing most.

Getting one over on people.

And the way I also saw it was this. If the duped crowd turned ugly and ripped the festival's organizer limb from limb, it was hardly my business. And it

136

would serve him right for blowing up my Biscuit.

'So that's settled then,' said the Doveston. 'Will you see to the posters?'

'Oh yes please,' I said. 'I'll draw them myself. How do you spell Dylan? It's D-I-L-L-O-N, isn't it?'

'Perhaps you had better leave the posters to me.'

'All right. If you think that's best.'

'Now, we need a good name for this festival.'

'I've got one,' I said. 'It's Brentford's Ultimate Music Festival of Love and Peace. BUMFLAP for short.'

'I like it,' said Chico.

'*I* don't,' said the Doveston.

'Nor do I,' said Chico. 'I don't like it at all.'

'You're becoming a right little yes-man, Chico,' I told him.

'No I'm not.'

'Yes you are.'

'No I'm not.'

'Yes you are.'

'Chico,' said the Doveston. 'Get us all a beer.'

'Yes, man,' said Chico.

Oh how we laughed.

Once we had all got our beers and the laughter had died down, the Doveston said, 'We are going to call this festival Brentstock.'

'I like that,' said Chico.

'I don't,' I said. 'What does it mean?'

'It means quality and taste at a price you can afford.'

'I knew that,' said Chico.

'Oh no you didn't.'

'Oh yes I did.'

'Oh no—'

137

'Excuse me,' said Norman. 'But Brentstock does mean quality and taste at a price you can afford. Because Brentstock is the name of Mr Doveston's exclusive Brentford Reserve Stock Cigarettes, which will be on sale to the public for the very first time ever during the festival.'

'I knew that too,' said Chico.

'Oh no you didn't.'

'Oh yes I did.'

'Oh no you—'

Chico drew a gun on me and aimed it at my ribs. 'Listen,' I said. 'If you say you did, then you did.'

'So,' said the Doveston, 'rimming the rooster' with his yo-yo. 'We have the bands, we have the name. So what about the drugs?'

'*The drugs?*' I ducked as the yo-yo whirled in my direction.

'Drugs!' The Doveston 'rogered the rabbit'. 'I do not want my festival ruined by a lot of out-borough drug-pushers selling bad dope to the crowd.'

'Damn right,' said Chico. 'They can buy their bad dope from us.'

'That is *not* what I meant. I don't want there to be any dope at all at this festival. Do you understand?'

'Oh yeah, right, man.' Chico winked.

'No,' said the Doveston. 'I'm deadly serious. No dope at all.'

'But this is the Sixties, man. You're always saying this is the Sixties.'

'No dope,' said the Doveston. 'I want everyone to enjoy themselves. Norman will be organizing all the stalls, won't you, Norman?'

'Oh yes.' The shopkeeper nodded. 'The cigarette stands, the T-shirt stalls and, of course, the beer tent.'

'And the food?'

'All taken care of. Hot dogs, ices, macrobiotic brown rice and felafel. I've rented out the pitches and we take a percentage on sales.' Norman patted the top pocket of his Paisley-patterned shopcoat. 'I have all the figures written down.'

'Then perfect. The punters can eat and drink and rock to the music.'

'And purchase Brentstock cigarettes with the money they would otherwise be wasting on dope?' I suggested.

'They might.' The Doveston performed a trick with his yo-yo that left him all but breathless. '"Straining the greens",' he explained. 'But trust me on this. There will be secret policemen mingling amongst the crowd. I don't want people getting busted. I want this festival to run like a well-oiled—'

'Penis?' said Chico.

'Machine,' said the Doveston.

'Curse this dyslexia.'

'Eh?'

Brentstock did *not* run like a well-oiled machine, nor even a well-oiled penis. It ran, if anything, more like a painted turnip through a field of eager toothbrushes. Or at least it did for me. I can't speak for anybody else. Most of those who actually survived it were in no fit condition to say anything to anyone for a number of weeks afterwards. Some even took vows of silence and never spoke again.

Sitting there that evening in the Doveston's flat, none of us could possibly ever have predicted what would happen.

I'm not saying that it was *all* the Doveston's fault. Some of it undoubtedly was. I will say that none of it was *my* fault. I am innocent of all charges.

I told the magistrate, 'It wasn't me.'

But did he listen?

Did he bugger!

He said that in all his long years at the bench, he had never heard of such appalling stuff and that he was having to undergo counselling to help him get over the nightmares.

Which is probably why he handed down such a heavy sentence.

But I am getting ahead of myself. Nineteen sixty-seven, the Summer of Love and Brentstock.

Ah Brentstock.

I was there, you know.

It all began on the Friday night.

12

A custom loathsome to the eye, hateful to the nose, harmful to the brain, dangerous to the lungs, and in the black stinking fumes thereof, nearest resembling the horrible Stygian smoke of the pit that is bottomless.

James I (1566–1625), A Counterblast to Tobacco

Brentstock, Brentstock. Get your Brentstock cigarettes, they're luverly.

Norman Hartnell[1]

They came in their thousands. Gentle people, with flowers in their hair. They wore beads and they wore bells and they wore sandals. They also wore flares, but as these were the 1960s, they could be forgiven.

They were colourful and beautiful and the plain folk of Brentford looked on. Mothers stood upon their doorsteps, cradling their infants. Fogeys leaned on walking sticks and sucked upon their briars. Shopkeepers came out to gawp and pussycats on window sills raised their furry heads and gazed and purred.

[1]Don't look down here, I'm not going to mention it again.

Old Pete lounged in the doorway of his allotment hut. 'Pack of pansies,' he said as he observed the arrivals. 'They could all do with a dose of National Service.'

'Peace and love not really your thing?' I said.

'Don't get me wrong, boy. I'm all for free love.'

'You are?'

'Damn right. I'm fed up with having to pay for it.'

I smiled politely. 'Well, I have to be off,' I said. 'I have to make sure that the stage is all set up and everything.'

'Huh,' sniffed Old Pete. 'Oh, and when you see the Doveston, tell him I want those drums of chemicals moving from out of my hut. The fumes make my knees go wobbly.'

'Drums of chemicals?' I asked.

'Fungicide. The stuff we used on the crop. Some American rubbish that's all the rage in Vietnam. Can't be having with it myself. I told the Doveston, but did he listen?'

'Did he bugger!'

Old Pete spat into the water butt. 'Precisely,' he said, 'so bugger off.'

I buggered off. I had a great deal to do. I had to make sure that the stage was OK and the lighting *and* the PA system. Oh yes, we'd got all that. The whole shebang. Hired it from a local prop house called Fudgepacker's Emporium that supplied stuff to the film and TV industries. There's not much you can't get in Brentford, if you know where to look.

I'd had to pay for it all with my Post Office savings,

but the Doveston had promised that I would be reimbursed.

I climbed up onto the stage and stared out over the hairy heads of the growing multitude. And then I did something that I've always wanted to do. I took hold of the nearest microphone and went 'One two, one two' into it.

It was something of a disappointment, really.

I turned to one of Fudgepacker's men, who was carrying cable about. 'This microphone isn't switched on,' I said.

'Nothing's switched on, mate. We can't find anywhere to plug the power cables in.'

It was one of those very special moments. You know the ones. The ones that separate the men from the boys, the heroes from the woosies, the captains of industry from the shovellers of—

'Shit,' I said, going weak at the bladder. 'Nowhere to plug the power in.'

'What time are you expecting the generator van?'

I smiled in a manner which I felt might inspire confidence. 'What is a generator van?' I enquired.

The Fudgepacker man nudged a companion. 'Did you hear that?' he asked.

His companion smirked. 'Perhaps he just wants us to plug it into someone's house.'

I used the voice of quiet authority that always gains respect from common types. 'That is *exactly* what I want you to do, my good man,' I told him. 'I can't be having with generator trucks. My own house backs on to the allotments, we can run the cable through the kitchen window and plug it into the socket we use for the electric kettle.'

By the way that their jaws dropped open, it was clear I had gained not only their respect, but also their admiration.

'Electric kettle socket,' said one of them, softly.

'That's right,' I nodded. 'We *do* have an electric kettle. These *are* the 1960s, you know.'

'Right,' they both went. 'Yeah, right.'

It took a lot of cable, but we finally reached my back wall. I shinned over, climbed through the kitchen window, pulled out the kettle lead and plugged in Brentstock.

I was rather pleased with myself and as I walked back to the stage (you will note that I walked and did not shuffle) I ignored the foolish titters and behind-the-hand remarks. These fellows knew they were dealing with a natural superior and I'm sure that it must have irked them greatly.

Peasants!

On my return to the stage, I was glad to find the first band already setting up. This was Astro Lazer and the Flying Starfish from Uranus. Chico had recommended them to me. They were a mariachi band.

They looked very smart in their national costume: sleeveless denim jackets, headbands and tattoos. I watched them as they tuned their trumpets, flugelhorns, ophicleides, cornets and euphoniums. I wondered whether it would be a good idea for me to go out in front and do a couple of one twos into the mic. just to get things started. And then it occurred to me that someone should really be introducing this festival.

And that someone should be the Doveston.

I found him around by the mixing desk and I must say that he looked the business. He wore a long flowing white robe that reached to his ankles and, what with his lengthy hair that was parted down the middle and his wavy little beard, he put me in mind of—

'Christ!' went the Doveston. 'What do *you* want?'

'Karl Marx,' I said.

'What?'

'You put me in mind of Karl Marx, 1818 to 1883, the German founder of modern communism in England from . . . oh . . .'

My running gag was cruelly cut short as I spied out the floral-haired hippy chick who was kneeling down before the Doveston and giving him a—

'Blow!' went the Doveston. 'Scram! Clear off!'

'But I thought you'd want to go on stage and officially open the festival. It is *your* festival, after all.'

'Hm. A very sound idea.' He waved away the hippy chick. 'You can finish adjusting my yo-yo later.'

I viewed the Doveston's yo-yo. 'You'd better put that away before you go on stage,' was my advice.

'What?'

'Well, you don't want to trip over the string.'

I must say that the Doveston's opening speech was a blinder.

The style of his oration owed a lot to that of another famous German. The one who had given all those stirring pep talks to the Aryan nation at Nuremberg before the last war. There was much cupping of the hands over the groin area, stepping back to let a point sink in, beating the heart with a fist and so on and so forth and suchlike.

I couldn't help thinking that the little Führer might well have enjoyed an even greater success had he been able to adopt the Doveston's technique of spicing up his speeches with a yo-yo trick or two.

The Doveston spoke of love and peace and music and how it was our duty to make the very most of every minute. And when he broke off suddenly to light a cigarette and 'enjoy a Brentstock moment', I realized that I was truly in the presence of greatness.

He left the stage to thunderous applause and joined me back at the mixing desk. 'What did you think?' he asked.

'Brilliant,' I said. 'It will be worth at least three paragraphs in the biography. Although I do have one criticism.'

'Oh yes, what?'

'You didn't go one two, one two into the mic. before you started.'

Friday evening was a gas. The bands played and the beautiful people danced. And they ate and they drank and they bought Brentstock cigarettes. Chico and some of his buddies moved amongst the crowd, targeting any out-borough pushers and teaching them the error of their ways. The sun sank low behind the mighty oaks that lined the riverside and I felt sure that this was going to be a weekend to remember.

It was.

I was rudely awoken from my bed rather early on the Saturday morning. I rolled over, expecting to see the beautiful face of the young woman I'd met the previous evening. The one with the blond hair and the colourful bikini top, who had been sitting on the shoulders of a bloke right near the front of the audience. Her name was Litany.

But Litany wasn't there. Because Litany had told me to piss off.

'Wake up,' shouted Norman. 'We've got troubles and they all begin with P.'

I groaned. 'Troubles always begin with P. Remember my Party, everyone came as something that began with a P.'

'Really?' said Norman. 'How interesting. But this lot all begin with P. Private Property, Public order offences, Police Prosecutions and Poo Poo.'

I took to groaning some more. 'Go on then,' I said with a sigh. 'Tell me all about them.'

Norman took a deep breath. 'Urgh,' he said. 'You've farted.'

'All men fart first thing in the morning. Tell me about the bloody troubles.'

'Right, yes. Well, firstly no-one got permission to hold the festival on the allotments. They're private property, the council owns them. Then there's all the noise. Most of the nearby residents have complained and so the police have come to close the festival down. And then there's the poo poo.'

'Tell me about the poo poo.'

'Well, there's two thousand people camping out there and most of them need to take a dump. Would it be all right if they used your outside loo?'

I scratched at my tousled head. 'I don't know,'

I said. 'I expect so. I'll have to ask my mum.'

'That's all right then.'

I leapt from my bed. 'No it's bloody not!' I shouted. 'What are we going to do?'

'I thought I might just run away and hide somewhere.'

'We can't do that. We can't let the Doveston down.'

'Why not?' Norman asked.

I gave this some thought. 'Where would be a good place to hide, do you think?'

'How about South America?'

I shook my head. 'We can't do it. We can't let all those people down. We can't disappoint them.'

'What, all those people who've come to see Bob Dylan and Sonny and Cher?'

'What's the weather like in South America?'

'Very favourable.'

The Doveston now entered my bedroom.

'The weather's looking favourable,' he said.

Norman and I nodded our heads. 'Very favourable,' we agreed.

'So,' said the Doveston. 'Any chance of some breakfast? I've spent half the night bonking away with a bird called Litany and I've worked up quite an appetite.'

'There are one or two problems,' said Norman, carefully.

'What, not enough eggs? Never mind, I'll just have some bacon.'

'The police are surrounding the allotments. They're going to close down the festival.'

It was another one of those special moments. The

ones that separate the men from the boys, the knights of honour from the ne'er-do-wells, the lion-hearted from the lily-livered, the bulldog breed from the—

'Bollocks,' said the Doveston. 'I think I'd best pass on the bacon.'

He rose to the challenge, though, left my house, shinned over the back wall and marched out to meet the policemen. The Doveston had long since ceased to shuffle and as he moved through the crowd, now all sitting down and many with their legs crossed, they cheered him and rose to their feet. It was quite stirring stuff really – almost, dare I say this, Biblical.

At the gates, which someone had had the foresight to close and bolt from the inside, he paused and stared eye to eye at the gathered policemen. 'Who is in charge here?' he asked.

A big broad-shouldered chap stepped forward, the uniform of a chief constable straining to contain a mass of corded muscle. 'Hello, Doveston,' he said. 'I see you've got Norman with you and who's that twat skulking there in the pyjamas?'

I waved feebly.

'Don't you recognize *me*, then?'

The Doveston viewed the amply sized upholder of the law. 'Mason,' he said. 'It's that softy Paul Mason from the Grange.'

'Softy no longer. And it's Chief Constable Mason to you, you hippy turd.'

'Oooooooooooooooooh,' went the crowd and some-one muttered, 'Pig.'

'I've come to read the riot act,' said Chief Constable Mason.

'But there's no riot here.'

'No, but there will be once my lads have started to lay about your lot with their truncheons.'

'Ooooooooooooooooh,' went the crowd once more and someone muttered, 'Nasty pig.'

'I suppose you have us bang to rights,' said the Doveston.

'Certainly I do.'

'Show us your warrant, then.'

'My what?'

'Your warrant. You do have a warrant, don't you?'

'I don't need any warrant, lad. I have the evidence of my own eyes. I can see two thousand people trespassing on council property.'

The Doveston glanced around. 'Everyone sit down again,' he shouted.

Everyone sat down.

'Now what do you see?'

'Two thousand people sitting down on council property.'

'Almost,' said the Doveston. 'What you are actually seeing is two thousand people *squatting* on council property. We claim squatters' rights and we demand that this land be returned to its rightful owners, the Navajo nation.'

'Crap,' said the Chief Constable. 'This land never belonged to the Navajo nation, that was the Memorial Park. And I should know, my great-grandfather fought in the battle.'

'Did he kill many Indians?'

'He wasn't actually fighting on that side. But that has

nothing to do with it. The Navajo nation never owned this land.'

'Oh yes they did.'

'Oh no they didn't.'

'Oh yes they did. You can look it up in the library.'

'What?'

'Look it up in the land charter at the Memorial Library. And if I'm wrong, I promise I'll give myself up and everyone else will walk away quietly without any fuss.'

'You promise?'

'Cross my heart.'

'Right,' said the Chief Constable. 'It's a deal.' He turned away to take his leave. And then he paused a moment, shook his head and turned back. 'You must think I'm really stupid,' he said.

'Excuse me?' said the Doveston.

'You think I'm so stupid that I'm going to go round to the library now and look up the land charter?'

'Why not?' the Doveston asked.

'Because the library is closed on Saturdays. It doesn't open until Monday morning.'

'Damn!' said the Doveston. 'You're right.'

'I *am* right. So who's the stupid one now?'

'I suppose I am.'

'You are,' said Chief Constable Mason. 'So you know what this means?'

'No.'

'It means that you'll all have to stay here until Monday morning, when I can get this sorted out.'

'Oh,' said the Doveston. 'I suppose it does.'

'It does, my lad, it does.' And with that said the

Chief Constable marched away to his squad car.

I nudged at the Doveston. 'I cannot believe you actually got away with that,' I said.

'I haven't, yet.'

The Chief Constable had just reached his car when he shook his head again, threw up his hands, turned right around and marched back to the gate.

'Hold on, hold on, hold on,' he said in a very raised voice. 'You must think I'm really really stupid.'

The Doveston shrugged.

'You think that I'm just going to drive away and leave you lot here for the whole weekend?'

The Doveston shrugged again.

'No way, my lad, no way.'

'No way?' asked the Doveston.

'No way. I'm going to put a guard on this gate to see that none of you sneak off. You'll all have to stay inside for the entire weekend, eating and drinking whatever you have in there.'

'You're a tough man to deal with,' said the Doveston. 'Firm, but fair though, I'll bet.'

'None firmer and fairer.'

'That's what I thought. So would you mind if I asked you a favour?'

'Ask away.'

'Would it be all right if we played some music? Just to keep everyone entertained while we're waiting?'

'Fair enough. But try and keep the noise down after midnight.'

'No problem. I'll see you on Monday morning then.'

'You certainly will, *stupid*!'

With that said, the Chief Constable stationed a policeman at the gate and then drove away. Chuckling to himself.

The Doveston had saved the day and a mighty cheer went up. He was carried shoulder-high to the stage, where he blew the crowd many kisses and enjoyed another Brentstock moment.

I enjoyed one too. I'd acquired a few free packets from Norman and although I can't say that they were a great smoke, they did have something special about them.

The Doveston left the stage to a standing ovation and I found him back at the mixing desk, where a goodly number of females had gathered, all eager to adjust his yo-yo. As I have never been too proud to bathe in a bit of reflected glory, I introduced myself all round and enquired suavely as to the chances of getting a shag.

And did I get one?

Did I bugger!

Saturday afternoon was a gas. More bands played and the beautiful people continued to dance. The bands had no difficulty getting into the festival, because the constable on guard had only been ordered to stop people getting out.

I dwelt a bit upon all that business with the Chief Constable. I mean, the whole thing was ludicrous really. Totally far-fetched, absurd and beyond belief. I mean, only *one* constable on duty at the gate.

You'd have needed at least *two*, surely?

It was just around the five o'clock mark when I became fully aware that things weren't altogether right with me. It seemed that throughout the afternoon I had been slowly acquiring a number of mystical powers. The power to see sounds in colour, for instance, and also the power to hear smells.

I found that I was becoming just a little bit confused by what was going on around me and this was not helped at all by the curious sense of detachment I was experiencing.

Every time I took a couple of steps forward, I had to stop to let myself catch up.

'I feel distinctly odd,' I said to Humphrey.

'You're tripping, man, that's all.' His words emerged as purple stars that floated off into the sky.

'I can't be tripping. I haven't done any acid.'

'Go with the flow, man. Go with the flow.'

Purple stars and little yellow patches.

Someone tapped me on the shoulder and I turned around very slowly, to keep my consciousness inside my head.

'What are you doing?' asked the Doveston.

'I'm talking to Humphrey. He says that I'm tripping. But I can't be, I haven't done any acid.'

'Don't take any notice of Humphrey,' said the Doveston. 'He can't be trusted.'

'Oh yes I can,' said Humphrey.

'Oh no you can't.'

'Oh yes I can.'

'Why can't he be trusted?' I asked.

'Because Humphrey is an oak tree,' said the Doveston.

13

Tobacco hic,
If a man be well it will make him sick.
John Ray, 1627–1705

We shared a Brentstock moment.

There was a band playing up on the stage. The band was called the Seven Smells of Susan: five small dwarves with very tall heads and a rangy fellow in tweeds. The Seven Smells played 'coffee-table music', the 1960s precursor of Ambient. They only ever released one album and this, I believe, was produced by Brian Eno. It was called *Music for Teapots*. I don't have a copy myself.

I was no great fan of the Smells, their music was far too commercial for me, but on this day they were magic. The sounds of the duelling ocarinas and the semi-tribal rhythms of the yoghurt-pot maracas[1] issued from the speakers in Argus-eyed polychromatic fulgurations, which were both pellucid and dioptric, daedal and achromatic, simultaneously. It was as if I were actually viewing the trans-perambulation of pseudo-cosmic anti-matter, without having recourse to an inter-rositor.

[1] *Blue Peter.*

Nice.

But good as the band were, nobody seemed to be listening. The centre of attention was no longer the stage. The crowd had withdrawn to the riverside end of the allotments, to re-form in a number of Olympic Ring-like interlocking circles, each of which centred on one of the ancient oaks. Most of the folk were sitting cross-legged, but I noticed some were kneeling with their hands together in prayer.

'The trees,' I said to the Doveston. 'They're *all* talking to the trees.'

My words were tiny green transparent spheres which burst all over his forehead, but he didn't seem to notice, or perhaps he was being polite. 'What the fuck is going on?' I heard and saw him say.

'Everybody's tripping. *Everyone*. Someone must have dropped acid into the water supply, or something.'

'Or something.'

'So what are you going to do?' My question was orange, with small yellow stars.

'I'll get Chico on to it.' Red diamonds and fairy-lights.

'He might be stoned as well.' Pink umbrellas.

'He'd better not be.' Golden handbags and grated cheese guitars.

'I can't handle this,' I said, in a mellowy-yellowy-celery way. 'I'm going home to bed.'

I stumbled across the tobacco-stubbled waste, pausing now and then to let myself catch up, climbed carefully over the back garden fence and in through the kitchen window. The Smells' music was really beginning to do my head in and I was quite pleased when,

157

at the exact moment that I plugged in the electric kettle to brew a cup of tea, they apparently finished their set.

Obviously there were some who were not so pleased as I, because I heard the sounds of shouting and of blows being exchanged. But it was hardly any of my business, so I just sat there waiting for the kettle to boil.

It took an age. It took a lifetime. It took an aeon.

Did you ever see that documentary about the scientist Christopher Mayhew? It was made by the BBC in the 1950s. Old Chris takes mescalin and attempts to describe the on-going experience to this terribly proper BBC commentator-chappie. There is one classic moment when he stares briefly into space and then announces that he has just returned from 'years and years of Heavenly bliss'. The bit that sticks with me is the part at the end. After the effects of the drug have worn off, he is asked what he has learned from his experience. Mr Mayhew concludes, 'There is no absolute time, no absolute space.'

As I sat and waited for that kettle to boil, I knew just what he meant. At that moment I stepped outside of time. It was as if the part of me that kept me forever only in the present had been removed or switched off. All times were instantly accessible. The past, the present and the future. I had no wish to revisit the past. I'd been there and done it and not been there and done it very well. But the future, oh the future. I saw it all and it terrified me. I saw what I was going to do and I knew why I would have to do it.

I saw myself a prisoner. A prisoner of time, perhaps? Shut away for years and years and then released to wander on a lonely moor. And then I saw bright lights and London town, and then myself, a man of property. I wore fine clothes and drove a snazzy car. And then, upon a bleak horizon, loomed a mighty house, a Gothic pile, and there, within, debauchery and drugs and long-legged women. I enjoyed this part considerably and lingered in my time-travelling to dwell upon the details and the depths of my depravity. And very nice it was.

But then came tragedy. A death that seemed to shake the world and shortly after, a great and wonderful party, which, for some reason that I could not understand, I did not enjoy at all. And then the world went mad. It was the end of the world as we knew it. Nuclear war. Then wastelands and scattered communities.

This part was all pretty crap. Like some cheap *Mad Max* imitation, so I skipped through it as quickly as I could. But I was drawn up short by a really nasty episode that made me feel sick in my stomach.

I was in a tiny underground room beneath ruins, with an old frail man who sat in a chair. And this old man was ranting at me, and I really hated him, and suddenly I was killing him. My hands were about his wrinkly throat and I was squeezing the life from his body.

And I could see myself here, today, in the year 2008, writing these words. Remembering then what I remember now, remembering.

So to speak.

I feel certain that I would have been able to see well beyond the extent of my own brief lifetime and off into eternity, had I not been quite so rudely interrupted. I don't know who it was who came crashing in through my kitchen window and ripped the kettle plug out of the wall and started beating me over the head with the kettle. He looked a bit tweedy and rangy to me, but as I was soon very unconscious, I really couldn't be sure.

Now, you know that panicky feeling you get when you wake up after a really heavy night of drink and drugs to find that you can't move and then it slowly dawns on you that someone has glued your head to the floor and then it slowly dawns on you that no they haven't, you've just chucked up in your sleep and the vomit has dried and stuck your face to the lino and—

No. You don't know that feeling, do you.

Well, it's almost as bad as the police cell one. Almost, but not quite.

I tried to lever myself up, but I didn't make too much progress. Luckily I happened upon a spatula I'd dropped a couple of weeks previously, which had somehow got kicked under the cooker, and was able to ease it between the floor and my face and gently prise myself free. It was a horrible experience, I can tell you, and I got all breathless and flustered and desperately in need of a nice cup of tea.

I really won't bore you with what happened after I plugged the electric kettle in again.

But what happened might well have saved my life, or at least my sanity. If I hadn't taken that second beating and if the ambulance hadn't been called to whisk me off to the cottage hospital, I would certainly have gone back to the festival and what happened to all those innocent people would undoubtedly have happened to me. Whoever beat me back into oblivion spared me from all that.

But spared me for what?

And for why?

That I should go forward through my life knowing what was to come and yet be powerless to prevent it?

That I should be some kind of helpless puppet doomed to a terrible fate?

That the grinning purple kaftan of truth should shed its wings and eat the flaccid ashtray of tomorrow?

The latter was a puzzle and that was for sure!

But hey, these were the 1960s after all.

I have pieced together what happened that day from conversations I had at the hospital and later with Norman and others, through secret police documents that came into my possession, and suppressed film footage. The real story has never before been told.

I tell it here.

To begin, let us examine the statement given by the ambulance-driver Mick Loaf.

'Oh yeah, right, is the tape rolling? OK. So, yeah, we got the call-out at about ten on the Sunday morning. I'd just come on shift. I'd been away for a couple of days, visiting my aunt. What? Pardon? Tell the truth? I am telling the truth. What, the machine says I'm not? OK. Yeah, well, it wasn't my aunt, but does that matter? Yeah, right, I'll just tell you what I saw. We had the call-out, house a couple of streets away from the hospital. The caller said that a chap called Edwin had been beaten up by some gypsy-looking types and was bleeding to death in his kitchen. So we drove over, OK?

'Well, you have to pass right by the allotments and I didn't know there was some kind of festival going on and as we're driving by we see all these thousands of people sort of swaying to the music. All in time, very impressive it was. But it was warm, see, and I had my window open, and I couldn't hear any music. So I says to my mate, Chalky, "Chalky," I say, "look at all those mad hippy bastards dancing to no music." And Chalky says, "Look at the stage." And we stopped the ambulance and looked at the stage and there wasn't a band up there, there was just a whole load of potted plants with microphones set up around them, as if these plants were the band. Weird shit, eh?

'What? The chemicals? Oh, you want to know about the chemicals. Well, there's not much to tell. I gave my statement to the police. When we got to the house the front door was open. We went inside, but we had to come out again and get the respirators because of the smell. There were all these drums of chemicals stacked up in the hall. American army stuff – someone told me that they use it in Vietnam, but I don't know what for. Smelled bloody awful though, made me go wobbly at the knees.

'Anyway, we found the Edwin bloke in the kitchen. He was in a right old state. We got him back to the hospital and they gave him a transfusion. Saved his life.

'That's all I know. I missed what happened later. Bloody glad I did.'

Councillor McMurdo, head of the town-planning committee, gave only one interview to the press. This he did by telephone from his villa in Benidorm.

'The allotments' water supply is separate from that of the rest of the borough. It is supplied from an Artesian well beneath the allotments themselves. If toxic chemicals were used on the allotments, there is every likelihood that they would contaminate this supply. There is only one tap on the allotments. This is situated next to the plot owned by a person known locally as Old Pete. It is my understanding that stall-holders who had the food franchises at this festival used this tap. The council can in no way be held responsible for the tragedy that occurred.'

All becoming clear? A big picture starting to form?

But what exactly did happen? What was the tragedy?

Let us hear it all from Norman Hartnell, as he told it at the trial.

'I went home early on the Saturday afternoon, before things began to turn strange. I'd completely sold out of Brentstock cigarettes, didn't even get to try a packet myself. I thought I'd go home for tea and grab an early night. I wanted to be up bright and fresh on the Sunday and get a good place down at the front by the stage. I was really looking forward to seeing Bob Dylan and Sonny and Cher.

'I brought a flask of tea with me on the Sunday, just as I had done the day before, but even though I got there really early, I couldn't get near the stage. In fact, I couldn't even see the stage, because all this silent dancing was going on. I don't dance a lot myself, do the Twist a bit at weddings, that's about all. But as a lot of the girls there had taken all their clothes off, I thought I'd join in, just to be sociable.

'So, I was sort of jigging about with this very nice girl who had the most amazing pair of Charlies—'

At this point the magistrate interrupts Norman to enquire what 'Charlies' are.

'Breasts, your honour. Fifth generation Brentford rhyming slang. Charles Fort rhymes with *haute*. *Haute cuisine* rhymes with queen. Queen of the May rhymes with hay, and hay and barley rhymes with Charlie.'

The magistrate thanks Norman for this explanation and asks him to continue.

'So,' continues Norman. 'We're dancing away and I'm saying to her that not only does she have a most amazing pair of Charlies, she has a really stunning Holman—'

Once more Norman is asked to explain.

'Holman Hunt, 1827 to 1910,' says Norman. 'English painter and one of the founders of the Pre-Raphaelite Brotherhood in 1848. He painted a lot of women in the nude. But some of them didn't like that, so he used to put his trousers back on. He always wore a headband.'

The magistrate then asks Norman whether a Holman Hunt is a type of headband. Norman says no. 'It's a tattoo of a giraffe.'

The magistrate then orders a clerk of the court to strike Norman for wasting everybody's time. Norman is duly struck.

'So, we're dancing,' says Norman, once he has recovered, 'and then suddenly everyone stops at once. Except for me, but I soon stop when I hear the shouting. Someone is up on stage bawling into the microphone. It's a bloke's voice and he's going, "Now you've heard it. Now you've heard the truth. The Great Old Ones have spoken to us, their children have sung to us, what are we going to do about it?"

'I shout, "Bring on Bob Dylan," but nobody's listening to me. They're all ripping off their clothes and shouting, "Back to the old ways" and "Tear up the pavements" and "Let the mighty mutant army of chimeras march across the lands" and stuff like that.

'I don't know what that's all about, but as clothes are coming off all around, I think I'd better get in on the act, so I whip off my shopcoat and fold it neatly on the ground. And I say to the girl with the Holman and the nice Charlies, "What *is* this all about?" and she says, "Whenever you speak, all rainbow-coloured sweeties come out of your mouth." Which is a bloody lie, because I don't eat sweeties any more, although I do know all about them. I know nearly everything there is to know about sweeties – you just try me, if you think I'm not telling you the truth.'

The magistrate asks Norman how they get all the different colours inside a gob-stopper. Norman says he does know, but he's not telling, because it's a trade secret. The magistrate makes a huffy face, but asks Norman to continue.

Norman continues. 'So,' continues Norman, 'I ask her again, "What is this all about?" I ask her. And she says, "The trees, the trees. The trees have told us the truth. Mankind is destroying the planet. Raping Mother Earth. Mankind must return to the old ways. Hunting and gathering and fornicating on the grass, because the grass quite enjoys it." And I say, "Me too, let's do it right away." But she isn't keen, she says that the trees have told everyone that they must tear up the pavements and burn down all the houses and plough Brentford over and plant loads of sprouts, because sprouts are like little planets and have lots of wisdom and—'

The magistrate asks Norman whether he likes sprouts. Norman says he doesn't and the magistrate says that he doesn't either and he asks for a show of hands around the court to see how many people actually do like sprouts. There are eighty-nine people present in the court and out of these only seven are prepared to own up that they do and out of these, two say that they aren't really *that* keen.

Continue, the magistrate tells Norman and Norman continues once again.

'So,' continues Norman, 'I say to this girl, in the nicest possible way and in a manner that I hope will not offend, that she is stoned out of her face and why doesn't she come back to my place for a rubber—'

'Rubber?' asks the magistrate.

'Rubber duck,' says Norman. 'Although actually I was hoping for a shag.'

The court stenographer makes a note to edit Norman's statement down to a couple of paragraphs during the lunchtime recess.

'But then,' says Norman (continuing), 'we hear the police cars. Well, *I* hear the police cars. The crowd with the kit off start shouting that they can *see* the sounds of the police car sirens. They're shrieking, "Beware the black lightning," and crazy stuff like that. Well, I don't know who actually called the police, or why they did. Although I did notice a couple of furtive-looking fellows who kept speaking into their Y-fronts. Although of course they might have been Egyptians.'

The court stenographer rolls his eyes; the magistrate nods his head.

'So,' continues Norman, yet again. 'Police cars come screaming up and all these coppers come piling out and they've all got truncheons and they all pour in through the gates and crash, bang, wallop and thud and hit and beat and bash and—'

'Have to stop you there,' says the magistrate.

'Why?' asks Norman.

'Because it's not very nice. I don't like the idea of policemen beating up unarmed naked people with truncheons. It's horrid.'

'It *was* horrid,' says Norman. 'I was there.'

'Well, I don't like the way you're describing it. It shows our police force to be little more than thugs. Imagine if the newspapers were to get hold of this. People would be thinking that we're living in a police state, rather than never having had it so good.'

'So what would you like me to say?' Norman asks.

'I don't mind what you say. But I object to the word truncheon. Call it something else.'

'Riot stick?' says Norman. 'Baton?'

'No no no. Nothing like that. Something more friendly.'

'Tulip?'

'Perfect,' says the magistrate. 'Now kindly continue.'

'Right. So the police rush in with these tulips and there's bashing and crashing and blood everywhere.

167

And people's faces are getting smashed in and the police are ramming their tulips up—'

'No no no.'

'No?' says Norman.

'No.'

'But I'm just getting to the good part.'

'Does this good part involve tulips?'

Norman made the 'so so' gesture with his raised palms. 'Not a great many tulips.'

'Well, go ahead then and I'll stop you if I don't like the sound of it.'

'Right. So the police have, you know, with the tulips and everything, but they're really outnumbered and the naked people start grabbing the policemen and tearing off their uniforms and soon you can't tell who's who and the next thing it's all turned into this sort of mass orgy and everyone's going at it like knives.'

'Sounds amazing.'

'It was quite some party, I can tell you.'

'I went to a party like that once,' says the magistrate. 'Back in 'sixty-three. What a do that was. Someone even blew up the host's dog with dynamite.'

'Eh?'

'Well, never mind about that. Orgy, you say?'

'Gang bang, big time.'

'So, you are telling me that the policemen were raped.'

'No, I'm not.'

'They must have been raped. After all, they were completely out-numbered and they only had tulips to defend themselves with.'

'Rape's a rather unpleasant word,' says Norman.

'Perhaps you could say they were "loved against their will", or something like that. Except they weren't. They were right in there, especially old Mason, and I used to go to school with him.'

In his final summing up of the case, the magistrate did not use the words *loved against their will*. He used a lot of other words though. *Rape* was one and *tulip* was another. And he used an awful lot of adjectives: terrible, horrible, loathsome, nightmarish, vile and filthy and degrading.

He said that he had no intention of holding two thousand separate trials. He would never live to see them end. And for one thing, how could witnesses be expected to recognize defendants, as all people looked the same with their clothes off.

The festival-goers were not to blame for their actions, he said. They were innocent victims of toxic poisoning.

It wasn't their fault.

So whose fault was it, then?

Of this the magistrate was in no doubt. It was all the fault of a single individual. A criminal mastermind. A modern Moriarty. A fiend in human form who had clearly known exactly what he was doing when he emptied those drums of chemical waste into the water supply.

The Doveston did not attend the trial. He was too ill to make an appearance. It was a shame really, because had he been there, I really would have liked to ask him a few questions.

Such as how those drums of chemicals came to be in my hall.

But he wasn't there, so I couldn't ask him.

And even if he had been there, would it have made any difference?

You see I had glimpsed the future and I knew that the drums of chemicals had nothing whatsoever to do with the madness. The chemicals were not to blame.

It was the Brentstock cigarettes.

Cigarettes that had been manufactured from genetically engineered tobacco. Genetically engineered from a formula laid down in the notes of Uncle Jon Peru Joans, the man who would talk with the trees.

So, what should I have said? Should I have grassed up my bestest friend? Blamed it all on him? And on what evidence? That I had glimpsed the future?

I couldn't do that.

'It wasn't me,' I told the magistrate. 'It wasn't me.'

But did he listen?

Did he bugger!

14

Send me to Newgate and the gallows. I care not. I will laugh and jest and share a pipe or two with the hangman.

Dick Turpin (1705–1739)

I really miss the 1970s.

Which is to say that I *really* missed them.

Missed every year of them. Every single month and day. Every hour and minute.

He banged me up, the magistrate did. Sent me down. Gave me fifteen years.

Fifteen years!

I wasn't pleased, I can tell you. I was angry. I was bitter and twisted and boiling and brooding. I was not a nice man to know.

They sent me first to Parkhurst and then to Pentonville. Later I was moved to Powys, then Penroth and finally to Poonudger. That each began with the letter P gave me no cause for amusement.

The Doveston wrote to me, of course. His early letters were full of apologies and promises that he would do everything within his powers to secure me an early release. Knowing well his love for dynamite, I slept nightly with my mattress over my head, to shield myself from the blast that would bring down my cell wall and herald the arrival of the getaway car that would whirl me off to freedom.

No blast came; no car arrived.

His letters became few and far between, but with them now came press cuttings. A note was enclosed with the first of these to the effect that, as his biographer and finding myself with time on my hands, I should dedicate my days to compiling an archive of his achievements as they were chronicled in the daily newspapers.

This, he suggested, would give me something worth while to do, with the added bonus that it would also keep me well informed as to what was going on in the world outside and just how well he was managing, even without my invaluable help.

We would get through this thing *together*, he wrote.

But he never once came to visit.

Norman called by every month, until they moved me north. Norman brought me news of Brentford. Mostly grim, as I recall.

The growing of tobacco on the St Mary's allotments had been banned. The plots had been split up again and it was now as if the plantation had never existed. The Mexican migrant workers had moved on. The Crad fields of Chiswick were now a council estate. In Hammersmith a woman had given birth to a child the shape of a hairdrier and there had been numerous signs and portents in the heavens.

'Surely,' said Norman, 'the End Times are upon us.'

Along with the reports of prodigious births, the

172

sightings of mythical animals and the life and troubled times of a Brentford confectioner, Norman also brought some tragic news.

Chico was dead.

Gunned down in a drive-by whilst dealing on the street.

'It was how he would have wanted to go,' said Norman.

And who could disagree with that?

Norman was not my only visitor. Brother Michael dropped in once or twice. He offered me counselling, with the view that I should purge myself of former wrong-doing and release the monk within. He told me that he had been inspired by a dream, a vision it was, which showed me as a monk in a low-cut leather habit, receiving the stigmata in a most unusual place.

Brother Michael displayed before me the holy paraphernalia that he had brought with him to effect my initiation. The crucifix and rosary; the golden icon of St Argent with his tiny nose; the Latin texts and phial of holy water; the sash of penitence; the tube of KY jelly.

Although tempting, as some may consider it, I did not become a monk. In fact my physical response to the brother's proposition, which manifested itself upon his person in a most vigorous and prolonged fashion, left him not only in some doubt as to the accuracy of visions, but also no longer predisposed to the riding of his bike.

It got me six months in solitary and put two more years on my sentence.

I was never the same man again.

I don't know whether you have ever read any Hugo Rune. But amongst the many Ultimate Truths revealed by this great twentieth-century philosopher and shoulder-rubber with the famous is one that relates to the human condition. Rune states, in terms which even the layman can understand, that IT IS THE NATURE OF MAN TO BEHAVE BADLY.

According to Rune (and who is there to doubt his words?) 'Any given person, at any given time, will be behaving as badly as he or she is able to get away with.'

According to Rune we are born behaving badly. We enter this world kicking and screaming and pooing ourselves. As children we are constantly punished for behaving badly. We are taught where the line is drawn and what will happen if we step over it. This continues throughout our lives, at school, in the workplace, in relationships and in marriage. We each behave as badly as we can get away with, stepping across a particular line at our peril.

Exactly how badly we are able to behave depends entirely on our circumstances. The poor oft-times behave very badly, as can be witnessed in football hooliganism, holidays abroad and the wearing of sports clothes. But if you wish to see real bad behaviour, bad behaviour taken to the extreme and exhibited (privately for the most part) as an art form, you must visit either the haunts of the very rich and privileged, or a long-term institution.

It is something of a cliché to state that wealth and bad behaviour go together. We have all heard the stories of best-selling authors who demand kumquats and chardonnay from harassed sales staff at signing sessions, of the antics of rock stars and cabinet ministers, matinée idols and members of the Royal Family. We know it goes on and we tut-tut-tut, but if our roles in life were reversed, we would do the same.

IT IS THE NATURE OF MAN TO BEHAVE BADLY.

And the more that you *can* get away with, the more you will *try* to get away with.

So what of the long-term institution? Well, here we have another set of circumstances. Here we have a place almost entirely peopled by folk who have stepped over the line. They are paying the price for their so doing.

Here we have the murderer whose bad behaviour has condemned him to life imprisonment. Society has condemned him to this punishment, even though this same society is forced into turning a blind eye upon the bad behaviour of its army or police. Society has said that this form of bad behaviour cannot be tolerated. Lock the bad man up for ever, get him out of our sight.

But is the murderer always a 'bad' man? If it is the nature of man to behave badly, was he not simply following the dictates of his nature? Doing what was natural to him? And what of the person he murdered? Was this an *innocent* victim?

I only touch upon this now, for reasons that will later be revealed. But I learned, whilst in prison, that the man without hope of release is the man who has no line left to put his foot across.

And you don't push in front of such a man when in

the queue for breakfast, or you will see some *very* bad behaviour.

They say that you meet the most interesting people in pubs. But this is only said by people who spend a lot of time in pubs. In my personal opinion, you meet the most interesting people in prisons. They're not *all* interesting, don't get me wrong. Heinlein said, famously, that ninety-five per cent of all science fiction was rubbish, adding that ninety-five per cent of *everything* was rubbish. This could be taken to the next logical stage, by stating that ninety-five per cent of *people* are rubbish too. It is not a view that I hold myself, but I know of some who do.

Now, having just suffered the preceding paragraphs, the reader might well believe that I have taken on a somewhat morbid mindset. In fact that I had become bitter and twisted and boiling and brooding and not a nice man to know.

Well, *you* try more than a decade in the nick and see if *you* come through grinning!

It wasn't *all* misery and I *did* meet some interesting people.

I did, for instance, meet an old acquaintance.

In Penroth Prison for the Criminally Disturbed I re-met Mr Blot. I didn't even know they'd banged him up and I got quite a shock when I saw his gangly frame making its loomy way along the corridor of C Block. I wondered if he would recognize me, but he just gave a bit of a sniff as he passed and continued on to therapy.

I sniffed at him in return and for the first time I realized what that smell was. The smell which had surrounded him at the Grange. That *odd* smell.

It was the smell of prison.

I learned all about Blot's crimes from one of the nurses who were giving me the electric-shock treatment. This, combined with the large doses of pharmaceuticals, were helping to keep my temper in check, and I hadn't bitten anybody's face off in more than a month.

The crimes of Blot were not without interest. He had, it seemed a penchant for corpses. Necrophilia, they call it. Apparently, as Blot had never had much success with live women, he had turned his amorous attentions upon those buried in the graveyard that backed on to the school playground. Easy access over the school wall had provided Mr Blot with a veritable harem. His QC argued that although none of the corpses offered their consent, nor could it be proved that they were unwilling participants, as none, it appeared, had put up any struggle.

Mr Blot had been visiting the graveyard for years, and would probably have continued to do so undiscovered, had he not begun taking his girlfriends home.

I got on well with Mr Blot. We talked a lot about the good old days and he took great joy in showing me his Bible. He had bound it himself and it had been one of the few items he had been allowed to bring with him to prison. 'They always let you bring your Bible,' he explained.

The cover was unusual. It bore a pattern on the front, the like of which I have only ever seen once before – as a tattoo upon my late granny's leg. The resemblance was quite uncanny.

So prison life wasn't *all* bad.

I met a few interesting people and I did build up the Doveston Archive. As the years slowly passed for me, the volume of material increased. I was able to follow his progress and it made for a fascinating read. It was as if luck was always on his side.

When I'd heard from Norman that the plantation was no more, I'd wondered just what the Doveston would do next. The answer to that had arrived in the post: a snipping from the *Brentford Mercury*, taken from Old Sandell's column.

UNHOLY SMOKE! WHATEVER NEXT?

Hard upon the heels of last year's yo-yo frenzy, we have the mini-pipe or Playground Briar. *Just like Daddy's*, says the advertising.

But once more there's trouble. Brentford vicar, Bernard Berry, has condemned the little mini-pipe and forbidden its use amongst choirboys in the vestry. Why?

Apparently because of the logo. What looks to me to be three small tadpoles chasing each other's tails, is, so the good vicar tells us, the Number of the Beast: 666.

Up your cassock, says Old Sandell, let the young 'uns have a puff in peace.

The mini-pipe did not enjoy the yo-yo's success. But whether this was down to Vicar Berry, who can say? If there was triumph in his pulpit following its removal from the shelves of Norman's shop, that triumph was short-lived. Old Sandell had this to report in his column, a scant three weeks later.

BERRY BLOWN TO BUGGERATION
Brentford vicar Bernard Berry got the final
surprise of his life this week when he lit up a stick
of dynamite in mistake for a communion candle.

Poor labelling on the box, allied to the vicar
having mislaid his specs, led to the tragedy.

But who ended up with the candles? Accidents
will happen, says Old Sandell, we'll have to let
God sort it out.

The failure of the mini-pipe did nothing to deter the
Doveston. It was a crap idea anyway and his sights were
set on far higher things. I collected the clippings as they
came in, filing them carefully, following how one business venture led to the next and noting how, with
striking regularity, those who stood in his way fell prey
to freak accidents of an explosive nature.

But accidents will happen, as Old Sandell says, and
we'll have to let God sort it out.

Accidents happen everywhere and a good many
happen in prison.

In Powys I met a young fellow by the name of
Derek. Derek had been convicted for murder. The
murder, it turned out, of Chico. Within just three days
of my meeting Derek, he was dead. He died, co-
incidentally, on the very day that I was leaving Powys
to be moved on to Penroth. Derek died in a freak
accident involving tied hands and a toilet bowl.

I expect old God knows what He's up to.

★

179

Had I been outside in the world to enjoy the Seventies, I would have given them the full fifty pages that I gave to each of the previous decades. But I wasn't, so I won't.

I was not released from prison until 1984, by which time most of those who had lived through the Seventies had forgotten about them anyway.

I regret, of course, that I missed out on the fashion. When I see old episodes of *Jason King* and *The Sweeney*, I get a glimpse of an era when style was king. Those big lapels, those kipper ties, those stack-soled shoes. They're all the fashion now, I know, but imagine what it must have been like to have worn that stuff back then and have nobody call you an utter twat!

On your very last day in prison, especially if you have served a long sentence, they make a bit of a fuss of you. Your cell-mates give you little presents: bits of string, or old lumps of soap. And if they are lifers with nothing to lose, you pay for these with whatever money you have been able to save up over the years.

It is a tradition, or an old charter, or something.

You don't *have* to pay, but then I suppose that you don't *have* to be able to walk.

I paid.

The governor invites you up to his office. He gives you a cup of tea, a biscuit and a pep talk. He tells you how you must behave in the outside world. And also how you must *not* behave. To encourage moral rectitude and discourage recalcitrance, two screws then enter the office and beat the holy bejasus out of you. You then receive a pack of five Woodbines, the price of a short-distance bus fare and a packet of cheese and onion crisps. The gift of crisps is symbolic of course, as you have to hand them back.

And if, like me, you are released from Poonudger, which is right in the middle of a bloody great moor, the price of a short-distance bus fare is also symbolic. And if you have five Woodbines, but no matches to light them with, this makes the gift of cigarettes similarly so.

The screws relieved me of money and fags and hurled me onto the moor.

When the door had slammed and the laughter died away, I rose slowly to my feet and breathed in freedom. It smelled of moorland and donkey doings. It smelled very heaven.

On the previous day a limousine had arrived at Purbeck to collect the Doveston Archive. I confess to being somewhat surprised that it had not returned for me.

I set out along the single-track road, expecting any minute to see it appear on the distant horizon.

But it didn't.

I should have been downhearted, but I wasn't. I was free. I marched along, my prison sandals scuffing up the dust. It was a shame that the prison laundry had mislaid my street clothes. I'd been quite looking forward to getting back into my kaftan. But, as the chap who ran the prison laundry told me, these things happen and it's always best to make a completely fresh start. As it happened, he was wearing a kaftan just like mine when he told me this, and I must say that he looked a bit of a twat.

I would make a fresh start. I just knew it. And, of

course, I *knew* that I would, because I had glimpsed the future. It was a great pity though that I hadn't glimpsed *all* of the future. Because if I had, I would never have stepped into quite so much donkey shit.

But to Hell with it all. I was free. I was free. I was free. I marched and I grinned and I sang and I whistled and I stepped in more shit and I didn't give a toss.

I was just *so* happy.

I don't know how I came to wander off the track. But in a way it was lucky that I did. If I hadn't wandered off the track, I would never have come across the little farmstead that nestled all but hidden in the shallow valley. And if I hadn't found the farmstead, I would never have found the scarecrow. And if I hadn't found the scarecrow—

Well, I *did* find the scarecrow and he provided me with a change of clothes. I crept down to the farmhouse and had a bit of a peep through the windows. I didn't want to bother anybody, but it did occur to me that I might ask whether I could use their telephone.

There was just one little old lady at home, no-one else, and as I was feeling in so jolly a mood, I thought I would play a harmless prank on her. I returned to the scarecrow and put on his big pumpkin head and then I went up and knocked at the door.

'Boo!' I said as the old lady opened it.

Well, I didn't know that she had a heart condition. But in a way it was lucky that she did. Because if she hadn't had the heart condition, she would never have had the heart attack.

And if she hadn't had the heart attack, I'll bet she

would never have let me borrow her car to drive off to the nearest telephone.

The nearest telephone was in a pub, some twenty-five miles distant from the farmhouse. The landlord there gave me the warmest of welcomes. I had thought that my appearance might put people off, but no, the landlord was all smiles.

'The last time I saw a hat, coat and trousers like that,' said the landlord, 'my dear old dad was wearing them. He was a farmer in these parts all his life, God rest his soul.'

I asked whether I might use the telephone and the landlord asked me why.

I explained to him that an old lady of my acquaintance had had a heart attack and I wanted to call for an ambulance.

The landlord shook his head sadly. There was no nearby hospital, he said, and no doctor who would come out at night. His dear old dad had died of a heart attack and he felt certain that his dear old mum, who lived some twenty-five miles distant, alone on a farm and suffered herself with a heart condition, would, in all probability, go the same way.

'It's God's will,' said the landlord. 'Let Him sort it out.'

I sighed and said, 'You're probably right.'

'Would you care for a pint on the house?'

I had a pint on the house and then another and when I had finished this, I told the landlord that I really should be on my way. The landlord, still chuckling about how much my coat looked like the one his father used to wear and which his mum now apparently used on her scarecrow, slipped a ten-pound note into its top pocket.

'You look like you could use that,' he said. 'Be lucky.'

As I drove away into the night, I felt certain that I would be. I just *knew* that I would be.

And I would.

15

A long-legged woman and a fine cigar. You got those
things. You're happy.

Al Capone (1899–1947)

I had no home to go to. My parents had disowned me
when sentence was passed. My mother wept the tears
that mothers weep and my father took it like the man
he was and said that he'd never cared much for me anyway. As I drove down to London, I had but one
destination in mind and that was the House of
Doveston.

The House of Doveston was no longer in Brentford,
but then the House of Doveston wasn't a house. It was
a very swish tobacconist's in Covent Garden.

I knew that the Doveston had sold his penthouse flat
in Hawtrey House. He'd sent me a press cutting, all
about how the council were selling off the flats and how
fortunes were being made. Another cutting covered the
trial and conviction of Councillor McMurdo, who had
apparently siphoned away millions from the borough
coffers. I never met up with McMurdo when I was
inside, I think he went off to one of the rather luxurious
open prisons, where people who have behaved badly but
have good connections are sent.

Now, I *was* impressed by the House of Doveston. It was right on the central plaza, next door to Brown's Restaurant. And it was *big*.

The style was Bauhaus: the German school of architecture and allied arts that was founded in 1919 by Walter Gropius (1883–1969). The experimental principles of functionalism that he applied to materials influenced the likes of Klee, Kandinsky and notably Le Corbusier. Although the Nazis closed down the Bauhaus in 1933, its influence remains amongst us to this day.

I gazed up at the building's façade, all black glass and chrome. The name was picked out in tall slim Art Deco lettering, which, along with the triple tadpole logo, was in polished chrome on polished black. It was austere, yet grandiloquent. Understated, yet overblown. Unadorned, yet ostentatious. Vernacular, yet vainglorious.

I hated it.

I'd never given a monkey's member for the Bauhaus movement. Give me the Victorians any day. And one thing I had learned in prison was that running gags which involve esoteric knowledge and the use of *Roget's Thesaurus* earn for the teller a well-deserved kick in the balls.

I pushed open the black glass door and swaggered into the shop.

And someone kicked me in the balls.

I toppled backwards, out into the street, passed by a shopper or two and sank to my knees in the road.

'Oooooh,' I went. 'That hurts.'

A large and well-knit black chap in a natty uniform

stepped out from the shop and glared down at me. 'Move on, sniffer,' he said. 'No place for your type in there.'

'Sniffer?' I went. 'Sniffer? How dare you?'

'Sniff your glue pot down the road. Go on now, or I'll kick your ass.'

I eased myself with care into the vertical plane. 'Now just you see here,' I said.

He raised his fist.

'I am a friend of the Doveston,' I said.

The knuckles of the fist made crackling noises.

'I have a letter here of introduction.'

My left hand moved towards my left coat pocket. He watched it carefully. I made rummaging motions with my fingers. His head leaned forward, just enough.

I brought him down with a right cross and put the boot in.

I mean, come on now, I'd just spent seventeen years in prison. Did you not think I'd learned how to fight?

I squared up my shoulders and marched back into the House of Doveston. I was not in the bestest of moods.

The shop interior was something to see and once inside I saw it. It was like a museum, everything displayed behind glass. A staggering selection of imported tobaccos and the largest variety of cigarettes I have ever laid my boggling eyes upon.

I have never been much of a poet, but standing there amongst the wonder of it all, I was almost moved to verse.

There were showcases glittering with pipes and
   snuffboxes,
Cabinets of match-holders, ashtrays and cigars.
There were tall glazed cupboards of rare tobacco
   pouches.
There was snuff of every blending in a thousand
   tiny jars.

I wandered and wondered and gaped and gazed. There were items here that were clearly not for sale. These were rare collectors' pieces. The pouches, for instance. And surely here was the famous calabash smoked by the magician Crowley. And there the now-legendary Slingsby snuff-pistol, fashioned to resemble a Derringer. And that was *not* Lincoln's corn-cob, was it? And *that* was not one of Churchill's half-smoked Coronas?

'It bloody is *too*,' said a familiar voice.

I turned around and saw him. He stood there, large as life, *bigger* than life. I looked at him and he looked at me and each one saw the other.

He saw an ex-convict, dressed in the garb of a scare-crow. The ex-convict's hands were crudely tattooed, as were other body parts, but these were hidden from view. The ex-convict's head was shaven, his cheeks scarred and shadowed by a two-day growth of beard. The ex-convict's frame was lean and hard and muscled. The ex-convict looked far older than his years, but had about him somehow the look of a survivor.

I saw a businessman. A successful businessman. Dressed in the garb of a successful businessman. A Paul Smith suit of linen that crumpled where it should. A gold watch by Piaget, that clenched the tanned left wrist. Brogues by Hobbs and haircut by Michael. Another two-day growth of beard, but this 'designer stubble'. The successful businessman's frame was going on podgy, but he looked far younger than his years.

And the look of a survivor?

Yes, I think so.

'Edwin,' said the Doveston.

'Bastard,' I replied.

The Doveston grinned and I saw a gold tooth winking. 'You made short work of my door supervisor,' he said.

'And I shall make short work of you too. It is payback time.'

'Pardon me?' The Doveston stepped back a pace.

'Seventeen long years I served for you.'

'I did my best to get you out.'

'I must have missed the explosions.'

'Crude stuff,' said the Doveston. 'I couldn't bust you out. You'd have had to spend the rest of your life on the run. But I set you up in prison, didn't I? Always kept you well supplied with money and snout.'

'You did *what*?'

'Five hundred cigarettes a week.'

'I never got any such thing.'

'But you must have got them. I sent them with the press cuttings and I know you got all those, I've seen the archive. Very nice work you did on that. Well put together.'

'Just hold on, hold on.' I raised a fist and saw him flinch. 'You sent me cigarettes? With the press cuttings?'

189

'Of course I did. Are you saying that you never got them?'

'Never.' I shook my head.

'And I suppose you never got the Christmas hampers?'

'No.'

'Oh,' said the Doveston. 'But you must have got the fresh salmon I sent every month.'

'No fresh salmon.'

'No fresh salmon.' The Doveston now shook his head. 'And why are you dressed like *that*, anyway? You'll be telling me next that you never received the suit of clothes and the wristwatch my chauffeur delivered to the prison when he picked up the archive. And where were you when he came to pick you up? Did nobody tell you what time he was coming?'

I shook my head once again. 'Bastards, bastards, bastards,' I shouted. 'Bastards, bastards, bastards.'

The Doveston made the face that says 'poor little sod'.

'I shall have to write a very stern note to the prison governor,' he said.

'A stern note? No.' I gave my head another shake. 'Why don't you send him a nice box of candles instead?'

'A nice box of candles.' The Doveston winked. 'I think that can be arranged.'

He led me upstairs to his flat. I will not bore the reader with a description. Let us just say that it was *bloody posh* and leave it at that.

'Drink?' asked the Doveston.

'Yes,' I replied.

'Smoke?' asked the Doveston.

'Don't mind if I do.'

'Canapé?' the Doveston asked.

'What the frig is that?'

'Just something left over from the party I'd organized for you last night. It's a pity you missed it, I'd set up a couple of really cracking women with lovely long legs. Gorgeous Herberts they had on them too.'

'Herberts? What are Herberts?'

'Bums, of course. Fifth generation Brentford rhyming slang. Herbert rhymes with sherbert. Sherbert dips, fish and chips. Chip off the block, sound as a rock. Rock'n'roll, bless my soul. Sole and turbot rhymes with Herbert. It's simple when you have the knack.'

'Have you seen much of Norman lately?' I asked.

'Once in a while. He keeps himself busy. Very into inventing he is, nowadays. Last year he invented a machine based on Einstein's Unified Field Theory. He teleported the Great Pyramid of Cheops into Brentford Football Ground.'

'How very interesting.'

The Doveston handed me a drink, a fag and a canapé. 'Tell me this,' he said. 'If you thought I'd stitched you up, why did you continue to work on the Doveston Archive?'

I shrugged. 'Hobby?' I suggested.

'Then tell me this also. Is there any chance of you taking a bath? You really pong.'

I took a bath. I shaved and I dressed in one of the Doveston's suits. I had to clench the belt in a bit around the waist. But the Doveston said it looked trendy. His shoes also fitted and by the time I was all togged up, I looked the business.

Emerging from the bathroom I found myself gawping at one of the most beautiful women I'd ever seen.

She was tall and slim and svelte. Her skin was clear and tanned; her legs were long and lovely. She wore one of those 'power-dressing' suits that were so popular in the Eighties. Short black skirt and jacket with the Dan Dare[1] shoulders. She balanced herself upon five-inch stilettos and her mouth was so wide that you could easily have got your whole hand in there, even if you were wearing a boxing glove.

'Hello,' she said, exposing more ivory than a big-game hunter's holdall.

'Hello to you,' I said and my voice echoed from the back of her throat.

'Are you a friend of Mr Doveston?'

'The bestest friend he ever had.'

'You're not Edwin, are you?'

'That is the name he likes to call me.'

'Well well well.' She looked me up and down. Then up and down again. And then she looked me halfway up. 'You've got a hard-on there,' she said.

I grinned painfully. 'I have no wish to offend you,' I said, 'but I don't suppose you're a prostitute?'

She smiled and shook her head, showering me with pheromones. 'No,' she said, 'but I'm shamelessly immoral. There's not much I won't do for a man in a Paul Smith suit.'

1Flash Gordon, actually. But then I *had* been in prison.

I made small gagging sounds.

'Aha,' said the Doveston, striding up. 'I see you've met Jackie.'

'Ggggmph. Mmmmph,' said I.

'Jackie's my PA.'

I nodded in a manner suggestive of comprehension.

'You don't know what a PA is, do you?'

I shook my head in a manner suggestive of the fact that I did not.

'Pert arse,' said the Doveston. 'Let's have some drink and fags and all get acquainted.'

I grinned a bit more. 'I'll just pop back into the bathroom and change my underpants,' I said.

Suavely.

I got on very well with Jackie. She showed me some tricks that she could do with canapés and I showed her a trick I'd learned in prison.

'Don't ever do that in front of a woman again,' said the Doveston when he'd brought Jackie out of her faint.

Jackie took me all around London. The Doveston gave her something called a credit card and with this magical piece of plastic she bought me many things. Suits of clothes and shirts and ties and underpants and shoes. She also bought me a Filofax.

I stared helplessly at this. 'It's an address book,' I said.

'And a diary. It's a *personal organizer*.'

'Yes. And?'

'It's fashionable. You carry it everywhere with you and always put it on the table when you're having lunch.'

I shook my head. 'But it's an address book. Only woosies have address books.'

'There are pouches in the back for putting your credit cards in and a totally useless map of the world.'

'Yes, but—'

'These are the 1980s,' said Jackie. 'And in the 1980s there are only two types of people. Those who *have* Filofaxes and those who *don't*. Believe me, it is far better to be a *have* than a *have-not*.'

'But look at the size of the bloody thing.'

'I'm sure you'll find somewhere to put it.'

'Where do you keep yours?'

Jackie pointed.

'Oh yeah,' I said. 'Of course. Silly question. I'm sorry.'

And I did get a watch. Watches were a big number in the Eighties. And none of that digital nonsense. Real watches with two hands and Roman numerals and clockwork motors. I still have the watch Jackie bought for me. And it still keeps perfect time. And *it* didn't explode at midnight before the dawn of the year two thousand. Curiously, I have no idea whatever became of my Filofax.

'You'll need a car,' said Jackie. 'What kind would you like?'

'A Morris Minor.'

'A what?'

'One like that.' I pointed to a car across the road.

'A Porsche.'

'That would be the kiddie.'

And it was.

The Doveston set me up in a little flat just off the Portobello Road. 'This area is coming up,' he told me.

I viewed the greasy lino and the broken window panes. 'It would perhaps do better for pulling down,' I suggested. 'I don't like it here.'

'You will not be here for long. Only until you have decorated the place.'

'What?'

'Once it has been decorated, we will sell it for double the price.'

'And then what?'

'I will move you into a larger flat in another area that is coming up. You will decorate that one and we will sell it once again for double the price.'

'Is this strictly legal?'

'Mark well my words, my friend,' said the Doveston. 'There is a boom going on in this country at the moment. It will not last for ever and many will go down when the plug is pulled. In the meantime, it is up to us, and those like us' – he raised his Filofax, as if it were a sword – 'to grab whatever can be grabbed. These are the 1980s, after all.'

'And tomorrow belongs to those who can see it coming.'

'Exactly. I'm not into property. Buying and selling houses holds no excitement for me. I want to make my mark on the world and I shall do that through my expertise in my chosen field of endeavour.'

'Tobacco,' I said.

'God's favourite weed.'

'I have no wish to share another Brentstock moment.'

'Ah, Brentstock,' said the Doveston. 'Those were the days, my friend.'

'They bloody weren't. Well, some of them were. But do you know what happened to me when I smoked that stuff of yours?'

'You talked to the trees.'

'More than that. I saw the future.'

'All of the future?'

'Not all. Although it seemed like all at the time. I saw glimpses. It's like *déjà vu* now. I get that all the time and sometimes I know when something bad is going to happen. But I can't do anything about it. It's pretty horrible. You did that to me.'

The Doveston went over to the tiny window and peered out through the broken pane. Turning back towards me he said, 'I am truly sorry for what happened to you at Brentstock. It was all a terrible mistake on my part. I worked from Uncle Jon Peru's notes and I thought that the genetic modifications I'd made to the tobacco would only help it to grow in the English climate. I had no idea the cigarettes would have the effect they did. I've learned a great deal more about that drug since then and I will tell you all about it when the time is right. But for now I can only ask that you accept my apologies for the awful wrong that I've done you and ask that you don't ever speak of these things to other people. You can never be certain just who is who.'

'Who is who?'

'I am followed,' said the Doveston. 'They follow me everywhere. They watch my every move and they make their reports. They know I'm on to them and that makes them all the more dangerous.'

'This wouldn't be the secret police again, would it?'

'Oh yes,' said the Doveston, grave in the face. 'Uncle Jon Peru Joans knew exactly what he was talking about. You experienced the effects of the drug. You know it's true.'

'Yes, but all that secret police stuff. I remember you saying that they would be in the crowd at Brentstock. But I thought you were only winding me up.'

'They were there and they're out there now. At some time in the future, when I consider it safe, I will show you my laboratory. You will see then how the Great Work is progressing.'

'The Great Work? Uncle Jon Peru's Great Work?'

'The very same. But we shall speak of these things at some other time. I don't want to keep you talking now.'

'You don't?'

'I don't. You've got decorating to do. You'll find all the stuff in the kitchen along with the plans for which walls you have to knock down and how to plumb in the dishwasher. Try and get it all done by next week, because I think I've got a buyer lined up.'

'You *what*?'

But the Doveston said no more.

He turned on his designer heel and, like Elvis, left the building.

He did pause briefly at the door to offer me a smile and a wave, before he went.

And it was then I saw it.

That look in his eyes.

The look that Uncle Jon Peru had had in his.

That look that the monkey in the *Mondo* movie had.

And I suppose it was at that very moment that I

realized, for the first time ever, just how absolutely mad the Doveston was.

But I wouldn't let it spoil our friendship. After all, I was on a roll here. I was in the money. I had a Paul Smith suit, a Piaget watch, a Porsche *and* a personal organizer.

All of these began with a P.

I really should have noticed that . . .

16

Beatle bones and smokin' Stones.
Don Van Vliet

For a man who was not into property, the Doveston sure bought a lot of it. During my first six months of freedom, I moved house eight times. Each to somewhere grander in a more up-market neighbourhood. By Christmas of 1984, I had made it to Brentford.

Yes, Brentford!

The Butts Estate.

And which house was I living in? Why, none other than that once owned by Uncle Jon Peru Joans. It would have been a childhood dream come true – had I ever dreamed of such a thing in childhood. The dreams I'd had in childhood, however, were formed of far humbler stuff. Never once had I thought that one day I might live on the Butts Estate.

The conservatory had been rebuilt, but not in its original style. Two local jobbing builders, Hairy Dave and Jungle John, had hobbled a nasty double-glazed atrocity of the monstrous carbuncle persuasion across the back of the house and my first job was to pull it down.

I did have a bit of a party when I moved in. But all very low key and sophisticated. I'd been hoping to get my leg over Jackie, but she wasn't having any. She told me that even though there wasn't much that she wouldn't do for a man in a Paul Smith suit, there was no way she was going to shag a bloke who was a painter and decorator. What did I think she was, a slapper?

I took that one on the chin and determined that one day . . .

One day . . .

Norman spoiled the party for me somewhat. He'd brought with him several bottles of home-brewed sprout brandy, of which he imbibed too freely. In a moment of drunken bonhomie, he called me his bestest friend and said that this was the bestest party he'd ever been to.

Except for one he'd been to back in 'sixty-three, where somebody had blown up the host's dog with dynamite.

Oh how we laughed.

I was really up for rebuilding that conservatory. I'd managed to get copies of the original plans from the Memorial Library and a nearby foundry had agreed to take on the job of casting the columns and decorative ironwork.

When, in the January of the following year, the Doveston told me that it was time to move again, I said no. I wanted to stay where I was, complete the conservatory and once again be a Brentonian.

To my great surprise the Doveston said that he didn't

mind. I could keep the house, but on one condition. He himself had recently acquired a property in Sussex. If I would decorate that for him at no charge, the house in the Butts was mine.

I readily agreed.

I was pretty nifty now, when it came to the old renovating. I had a small team of lads who worked for me and we breezed through it at the hurry-up. I figured that a month or two's work on the Doveston's property, in exchange for Uncle Jon Peru's house, was an offer I couldn't refuse.

There was just the one question that I should have asked.

And this was: 'How big is this property?'

The winter of 'eighty-five was the coldest ever on record. The River Thames froze over and thousands died from hypothermia. Few of these thousands, I suspect, left Filofaxes to their next of kin. The nation had divided itself into two separate classes. The we-have-lots and the we-have-bugger-alls. The we-have-lots were topping off their walls with razor-wire. The we-have-bugger-alls were planning revolution.

The Doveston's limo, an armoured affair with bullet-proof glass and gun-ports on the roof, picked me up on a February morning to ferry me down to Sussex. The snow had been falling non-stop for almost a month and if it hadn't been for the chains on the tyres and the snow-plough on the front, I doubt whether we could ever have completed the journey.

I'd never been to Sussex before and all I knew of the

countryside was what all Londoners knew: the folk there lived in thatched cottages, hunted foxes and shagged the sheep. When not shagging sheep, they shagged their daughters, and if their daughters weren't keen, they set to work on the chickens.

I am prepared to agree now that this commonly held view of country folk is not altogether accurate. Most country folk do *not* shag their sheep, their daughters or their chickens.

They do, however, practise human sacrifice in their worship of Satan. But who doesn't nowadays?

And they *do* make nice jam.

The Doveston's property was situated on the edge of a picture-postcard village called Bramfield, some ten miles north of Brighton.

Bramfield skulked in the South Downs. Most villages nestle, but not Bramfield. Bramfield was a definite skulker. It had its head down. It was cowering. And, as we reached the end of the High Street, it was plain to see from what.

Ahead, across the snow-covered fields, arose a terrible building. It looked as I imagine Gormenghast must look. A great black hulking Gothic nightmare of a place, all twisted towers and high cupolas, gabled roofs and flying buttresses.

'Look at that bloody horrible thing,' I said as we approached it.

The Doveston raised an eyebrow to me.

'It's *not*?' I said.

'It *is*,' was his reply.

And the nearer we got, the bigger it grew, for such is the nature of things. When we stepped from the car into three feet of snow, it was heads back all and gape up.

Jackie huddled in her mink and her mouth was so wide that I'm sure I could have climbed in there to shelter from the cold. The Doveston's chauffeur, Rapscallion, took off his cap and mopped at his African brow with an oversized red gingham handkerchief. 'Lordy, lordy, lordy,' was all he had to say.

I, however, had quite a bit more. 'Now just you see here,' I began. 'If you think I'm going to decorate this monstrosity for you, you've got another think coming. Who owned this dump before you bought it, Count Dracula?'

'Most amusing.' The Doveston grinned a bit of gold in my direction. 'I have my laboratory here. I only wish you to decorate some of the apartments.'

'Laboratory?' I shook my head, dislodging the ice that was forming on my hooter. 'I assume that you have an assistant called Igor, who procures the dead bodies.'

'He's called Blot, actually.'

'*What?*'

'Let's go inside before we freeze to death.'

'We belong dead,' I muttered, in my finest Karloff.

Inside it was all as you might have expected. Pure Hammer Films. A vast baronial hall, flagstones under-foot and vaulted ceiling high above. Sweeping staircase, heavy on the carved oak. Minstrels' gallery, heavy on the fiddly bits. Stained-glass windows, heavy on the brutal martyrdoms. Wall-hanging tapestries, heavy on the moth. Suits of armour, heavy on the rust. Authentic-looking instruments of torture.

Heavy.

It was grim and lit by candles and the fire that blazed within a monstrous inglenook. Everything about it said, 'Go back to London, young master.'

'Let's go back to London,' I suggested.

'Too late now,' the Doveston said. 'It's getting dark out. We had best stay for the night.'

I sighed a deep and dismal. 'This is undoubtedly the most sinister place I've ever been in,' I said. 'It literally reeks of evil. I'll bet you that all the previous owners came to meet terrible ends. That half of them are walled up in alcoves and that at midnight you can't move for spectres with their heads clutched underneath their arms.'

'It does have a certain ambience, doesn't it?'

'Sell the bugger,' said I. 'Or burn it down and claim the insurance money. I'll lend you my lighter if you want.'

'I have plenty of lighters of my own.' The Doveston took off his designer overcoat and warmed his hands beside the fire. 'But I have no intention of burning it down. This is more than just a place to live. A title goes with it as well.'

'The House of Doom,' I suggested.

'A title for me, you buffoon. I am now the Laird of Bramfield.'

'Well pardon me, your lordship. Does this mean that you will soon be riding to hounds?'

'It does.'

'And shagging the sheep?'

'Watch it.'

'Oh yes, excuse me. If I recall correctly, it will be the

chickens that have to keep their backs to the henhouse wall.'

A look of anger flashed in his eyes, but I knew he wouldn't dare to strike me. Those days were gone, but it wasn't too smart to upset him.

'So that's why you bought it,' I said. 'So you could be Lord of the Manor.'

'Partly. But also because it can be easily fortified. I'm having the moat redug and a high perimeter fence put up.'

'That should please the locals.'

'Stuff the locals.'

'Quite so.'

'But don't you see it? The kudos of owning a place like this? I shall be able to entertain wealthy clients here. Hold stupendous parties.'

'Hm,' I went. 'You'll have to do something about the *ambience* then.'

'Oh yes, I'll switch that off.'

'What?'

The Doveston strode back to the big front doors and flicked a tiny hidden switch. I experienced a slight popping of the ears and then a feeling of well-being began to spread through me, as if I were being warmed by a tropical sun. But not too much. Just enough.

'Mmmmmmm,' went Jackie, flinging off her mink.

'Right on,' said Rapscallion.

The Doveston grinned. 'It's clever, isn't it?'

I went, 'What?' and 'Eh?' and 'How?'

'It's an invention of Norman's. He calls it the Hartnell Home Happyfier. There's one installed in every room.'

205

I went, 'What?' and 'Eh?' and 'How?' some more.

'You see,' said the Doveston, 'Norman saw an advert in the *Brentford Mercury* for ionizers. They're all the fashion nowadays, supposed to pep up the atmosphere in offices and suchlike. Norman thought that one would be good for his shop. But when it arrived and he tried it out, he found the results to be negligible. He thought that perhaps it was broken, so he took it to pieces to see how it worked and he discovered that there was damn all inside it and what there was didn't do much anyway. So Norman got to work with his Meccano set and designed a better one. One that really did the business.

'Norman's one has three settings. *Grim*, which is what I had mine set to. That really discourages burglars, I can tell you. *Normal*, which is what you are experiencing now. And *Yaa-hoo-it's-Party-Time*, which really gets the joint a-jumping.'

'But that's incredible,' I said. 'How does it work?'

'Something to do with the trans-perambulation of pseudo-cosmic anti-matter, I believe.'

I shook my head in amazement. 'But an invention like that must be worth millions.'

'You'd think so, wouldn't you? And yet I was able to buy the patent from Norman for less than one hundred pounds.'

'Why you crooked, double-dealing—'

'Not a bit of it. I have no wish to profit financially from Norman's invention. I just wanted to make sure that it remains only in the right hands.'

'And these right hands would be the ones that often hold a Filofax?'

'I generally hold mine in my left hand. But essentially you are correct. Shall we dine?'

We dined.

And as we dined, the Doveston spoke. And as had the walrus of old, he spoke of many things. Of pipes and snuff and smoking stuff and Brentstock Super Kings.

He spoke of his plans for the house. It was currently called Bramfield Manor, but he intended to change the name to Castle Doveston. It was to be made a secure area. I assumed that this meant secure against any possible attacks from villagers with flaming torches. But I later came to understand that this meant secure against the surveillance of the so-called secret police.

He also spoke of his plans for the future. That it was his intention to open shops all over the world. I enquired as to whether each of these shops would be kitted out with a Hartnell Home Happyfier, turned up to full blast.

I did not receive an answer to this question.

Before the meal began, the Doveston had asked me to get out my Filofax and Mont Blanc pen so that I could take down all he said for the biography. I explained to him that it really wasn't necessary, what with me having total recall and everything. But he still made me get it out and stick it on the table.

I did make a few jottings and I did draw a really good picture of a big-bosomed lady riding a bike. But sadly, as this is not an illustrated book, it can't be printed here. But then neither can anything the Doveston said.

I suppose it could have been. If I'd taken the trouble to write it all up.

But frankly, I couldn't be arsed.

The meal was splendid though. A five-course Crad supper with afters. Served by the cook who had come with the house.

Afterwards, over brandy and cigars, the Doveston spoke a lot more. We were all rather drunk now and feeling very mellow. Rapscallion snoozed in an arm-chair by the fire. Jackie hiccuped and blew out the candelabrum at the far end of the room. And I wondered just how I might persuade her to come up to my room and enjoy the *Yaa-hoo-it's-Party-Time* setting of the Hartnell Home Happyfier.

As I watched the Doveston standing there beside the great fireplace, holding forth about his plans for this thing, that thing and the other, my thoughts travelled back, as thoughts will do, to times long gone and done with.

I wrote in the very first chapter about how this was to be no ordinary biography, but rather a series of personal recollections. And I have stayed true to this. Our childhood days were happy ones and I knew that there would be good times ahead.

But I also knew, for I had glimpsed the future, that there would be evil times and that the Doveston would meet a terrible end. But seeing him there, in his very prime, full of plans and full of life, it all seemed so unlikely. This was the grubby boy who had become the rich successful man. This was my bestest friend.

Whenever I am asked about the times I spent with

the Doveston, it is always the period between 1985 and the year two thousand that people want to know about. The Castle Doveston years and the Great Millennial Ball.

Did all that incredible stuff *really* happen? Was what we read in the tabloids true? Well, yes and yes. It *did* happen and it was all true.

But there was so much more.

And I will tell it here.

17

The King's condition worsened, there were terrible seizures which caused him to roll his eyes in a hideous fashion and beat upon his breast.

When the madness came upon him, he would cry out in a vulgar tongue, using phrases unchristian. Only his pipe brought comfort to him then.

Silas Camp (1742–1828)

'He's Richard, you know,' said Norman.

I looked up from my pint of Death-by-Cider. We sat together in the Jolly Gardeners, Bramfield's only decent drinking house. It was the summer of 'eighty-five, the hottest ever on record. Outside tarmac bubbled on the road and the death toll from heatstroke in London was topping off at a thousand a week. There was talk of revolution in the air. But only inside in the shade.

'Richard?' I asked.

'Richard,' said Norman. 'As in barking mad.'

'Ah,' said I. 'This would be that fifth generation Brentford rhyming slang that I find neither clever nor amusing.'

'No, it's straightforward one on one. Richard Dadd, mad. Richard Dadd (born sometime, died later) painted pictures of fairies, butchered his old man and ended his days in the nuthouse.'

'*Touché.*' I smiled a bit at Norman. The shopkeeper had grown somewhat plump with middle years. He had a good face though, an honest face, which he had hedged to the east and west with a pair of ludicrous mutton-chop side-whiskers. As to his hair, this was all but gone and the little that remained had been tortured into one of those greased-down Arthur Scargill comb-over jobs that put most women to flight.

For the most part, he had grown older with grace and with little recourse to artifice. His belly spilled over the front of his trews and his bum stuck out at the back. His shopcoat was spotless, his shoes brightly buffed and his manner was merry, if measured.

He had married, but divorced, his wife having run off with the editor of the *Brentford Mercury*. But he had taken this philosophically. 'If you marry a good-looking woman,' he said to me, 'she'll probably run off with another man and break your heart. But if, like me, you marry an ugly woman, and she runs off with another bloke, who gives a toss?'

Norman had been brought down to Castle Doveston to do some work on 'security'. He was as anxious to get back to his shop as I was to get back to my conservatory. But the Doveston kept finding us more things to do.

'So,' I said, 'he's Richard. And who are you talking about?'

'The Doveston, of course. Don't tell me it's slipped by you that the man's a raving loon.'

'He does have some eccentricities.'

'So did Richard Dadd. Here, let me show you this.'

Norman rummaged about in his shopcoat pockets and drew out a crumpled set of plans. 'Move your woosie address book off the table and let me spread this out.'

I elbowed my Filofax onto the floor. 'What have you got there?' I asked.

'Plans for the gardens of Castle Doveston.' Norman smoothed out creases and flicked away cake crumbs. 'Highly top secret and confidential, of course.'

'Of course.'

'Now, you see all this?' Norman pointed. 'That is the estate surrounding the house. About a mile square. A lot of land. All these are the existing gardens, the Victorian maze, the ornamental ponds, the tree-lined walks.'

'It's all very nice,' I said. 'I've walked around most of it.'

'Well, it's all coming up, the lot of it. The diggers are moving in next week.'

'But that's criminal.'

'They're his gardens. He can do what he likes with them.'

'You mean he can *behave* as *badly* as he likes with them.'

'Whatever. Now see this.' Norman fished a crumpled sheet of transparent acetate from another pocket and held it up. 'Recognize this?'

Printed in black upon the acetate was the distinctive Doveston logo, the logo that had so upset the late Vicar Berry. The three tadpoles chasing each other's tails.

'The Mark of the Beast,' I said with a grin.

'Don't be a prat,' said Norman. 'It's the alchemical symbol for Gaia.'

'Who?'

'Gaia, Goddess of the Earth. She bore Uranus and by him Cronus and Oceanus and the Titans. In alchemy she is often represented by the three serpents. These symbolize sulphur, salt and mercury. The union of these three elements within the cosmic furnace symbolize the conjunction of the male and female principles, which create the philosopher's stone.'

'There's no need to take the piss,' I said.

'I'm not. The symbol ultimately represents the union between the animal kingdom and the plant kingdom. Man and nature, that kind of thing. I should bloody know, I designed the logo for him.'

'Oh,' said I. 'Then pardon me.'

Norman placed the sheet of acetate over the map. 'Now what do you see?' he asked.

'A bloody big logo superimposed over the gardens of the estate.'

'And that's what you'll see from an aeroplane, once the ground has been levelled and the trees planted. The logo picked out in green trees upon brown earth.'

'He's Richard, you know,' said I.

'He worries me,' said Norman. 'And he keeps on about this invisible ink thing. I wish I'd never mentioned it to him.'

'I don't think you've mentioned it to me.'

'Top secret,' said Norman, tapping his nose.

'So?'

'So it's like this. He was talking to me about the colour he wanted for the package of his new brand of cigarettes. Said he wanted something really eye-catching, that would stand out from all the rest. And I said that you can't go wrong with red. All the most successful products have red packaging. It's something to do with blood and sex, I believe. But then I made the mistake of telling him about this new paint I was working on. It's ultraviolet.'

'But you can't see ultraviolet.' I sipped at my pint. 'It's invisible to the human eye.'

'That's the whole point. If you could create an opaque ultraviolet paint, then whatever you painted with it would become invisible.'

'That's bollocks,' I said. 'That can't be true.'

'Why not? If you paint anything with opaque paint, you can't see the thing itself, only the layer of paint.'

'Yes, but you can't see ultraviolet.'

'Exactly. So if you can't see *through* the paint, you can't see the thing underneath it, can you?'

'There has to be a flaw in this logic,' I said. 'If the paint is invisible to the human eye, then you must be able to see the object you've painted with it.'

'Not if you can't see through the paint.'

'So, have you actually made any of this paint?'

Norman shrugged. 'I might have.'

'Well, have you?'

'Dunno. I thought I had, but now I can't seem to find the jam jar I poured it into.'

I made the face that says 'you're winding me up'. 'And the Doveston would like to buy a pot or two of your miracle paint, I suppose?'

'As much as I can produce. For aesthetic reasons, he says. He wants to paint all the razor wire on the perimeter fences with it.'

I got up to get in the pints. At the bar the landlord

kindly drew my attention to the fact that I had dropped my woosie address book. 'You still working up at the big house?' he asked.

'Would I still be drinking in this dump if I wasn't?'

He topped up my newly drawn pint from the drips tray. 'I suppose not. Is it true what they say about the new laird?'

'Probably.'

The landlord whistled. 'I tried that once. Had to soak my pecker in iodine for a week to wash the smell off.'

I paid for my pints and returned to my table.

'And another thing,' said Norman. 'He has become utterly convinced that the world as we know it will come to an end at the stroke of midnight on the final day of this century. Says he's known it for years and years and that he's going to be prepared.'

'Tomorrow belongs to those who can see it coming.'

'I thought up that phrase,' said Norman. 'He nicked it off me.'

'Don't you ever get fed up with him nicking your ideas?'

'Not really. After all, he is my bestest friend.'

'But he's Richard.'

'Oh yeah, he's Richard all right. But I don't let that interfere with our friendship.'

We drank down our pints and then Norman got a couple in. 'The landlord said to tell you not to forget your woosie address book, it's still on the floor.' Norman placed the pints upon the table.

'We'd better drink these up quickly,' I said, 'and get back to work.'

'Not today. The Doveston said we are to take the afternoon off. Another of his secret meetings.'

'Bugger. I want to get finished.'

'Me too, but we're not allowed back this afternoon.'

I swallowed Death-by-Cider. 'I'd love to know what he gets up to at those secret meetings, wouldn't you?'

Norman shrugged. 'We could always sneak back and watch him on the closed-circuit TV.'

'What closed-circuit TV?'

'The one I fitted last month. There're secret cameras in every room.'

'What? Even in my bedroom?'

'Of course.'

'Then he's been watching me having sex.'

'Well, if he has, then he hasn't shown me the tapes. The only footage I've seen of you involved a mucky mag and a box of Kleenex.'

I made gagging croaking sounds.

'Oh yeah, those were the noises you were making too.'

'The bastard,' I said. '*The bastard!*'

'You think that's bad. You should see the tapes of me.'

'Of you?'

'Oh yeah. In *my* bedroom. The landlord has recommended iodine.'

'You mean there's a hidden camera in your bedroom too?'

'Of course there is. I installed it there myself.'

'But . . .' I said. 'If you . . . I mean . . . Why . . . I mean . . .'

'Precisely,' said Norman. 'It's a right liberty, isn't it?'

We finished our pints and sneaked back to Castle Doveston.

Norman let us into the grounds through a hole he'd made in the perimeter fence. 'I can't be having with all that fuss at the main gates,' he said. 'So I always come in this way.'

We skirted the great big horrible house and Norman unlocked a cellar door. 'I got this key cut for myself,' he said. 'Just for convenience.'

Once inside, Norman led me along numerous corridors, opening numerous locked doors with numerous keys he'd had cut for convenience. At last we found ourselves in an underground room, low-ceilinged and whitely painted, one wall lined with TV screens, before which stood a pair of comfy chairs. We settled into them and Norman took up a remote controller.

'Here we go,' he said, pushing buttons. 'Look, there's your bedroom and that's mine. And there's the great kitchen – and what's Rapscallion doing with that chicken?'

'It beggars belief. But there's a hidden camera in the boardroom, is there?'

'There is. Mind you, the Doveston doesn't know it's there. I just put one in for—'

'Convenience?'

'Bloody-mindedness, actually. Wanna see what's going on?'

'Damn right.'

Norman pushed a sequence of buttons and a

bird's-eye view of the boardroom table appeared on the screens. I recognized the top of the Doveston's head; the other five heads were a mystery to me. 'I wonder who those fellows are,' I wondered.

'They're not all fellows. The bald one's a woman. I know who they all are.'

'How come?'

'I can recognize them from their photographs in the Doveston's files.'

'Those would be the ones he keeps in his locked filing cabinet?'

'And a very secure filing cabinet it is too. I built it myself. It opens at the back, in case you forget where you've put your key.'

I shook my head. 'Can you turn the sound up, so we can hear what they're saying?'

'Of course and I'll explain to you who's who.'

Now history can boast to many a notable meeting. In fact, if it hadn't been for notable meetings, there probably wouldn't have been much in the way of history at all. In fact, perhaps history consists of nothing *but* notable meetings, when you get right down to it. In fact, perhaps that's all that history is.

Well, perhaps.

And perhaps it was sheer chance that Norman and I happened to be looking in on this particular notable meeting on this particular day.

Well.

Perhaps.

'That's what's-his-face, the Foreign Secretary,' said

Norman, pointing. 'And that's old silly-bollocks the Deputy Prime Minister. Those two on the end are the leaders of the Colombian drugs cartel, I forget their names, but you know the ones I'm on about. That bloke there, he's the fellow runs that big company, you know the one, the adverts are always on the telly, that actor's in them. He was in that series with the woman who does that thing with her hair. The tall woman, not the other one. The other one used to be on *Blue Peter.* The bald woman, well, you know who she is, don't you? Although she usually wears a wig in public. In fact most people don't even know it's a wig. I never did. And that bloke, the one there, where I'm pointing, that's only you-know-who, isn't it?'

'It never is!' I said.

'It is and do you know who that is, sitting beside him?'

'Not . . .?'

'It certainly is.'

'Incredible.'

'He's having an affair with the woman who used to be on that programme. You know the one.'

'The other one?'

'Not the other one, the tall woman.'

'The one on the adverts?'

'No, she was in the series. The bloke in the adverts was with her in the series.'

'But she's not the same woman that the bloke sitting next to you-know-who is having the affair with?'

'No, *that's* the other one.'

'Oh yeah, that's the other one. And who's *that*?'

'The bloke sitting opposite you-know-who?'

'No, sitting to the right of the fellow who runs that big company.'

'His right, or our right?'

'Does it matter?'

'Of course it matters. You have to be exact about these things.'

'So who is it?'

'Search me.'

'I'll tell you what,' I said to Norman.

'What?'

'That thing the tall woman used to do with her hair. I never thought that was very funny.'

'I don't think it was supposed to be funny. Are you sure you're talking about the same woman?'

But whether I was, or whether I wasn't, I never got to find out. Because just then the Doveston began to talk and we began to listen.

'Thank you,' said the Doveston. 'Thank you all for coming. Now you all know why this meeting has been called. The harsh winter, followed by the sweltering summer has led to an economic crisis. Everywhere there is talk of revolution and there have recently been several more bombings of cabinet ministers' homes by the terrorist organization known only as the Black Crad Movement. We all want these senseless dynamitings to stop and none of us want the government overthrown, do we?'

Heads shook around the table. I looked at Norman and he looked at me.

'And so,' continued the Doveston, 'I have drawn up a couple of radical proposals which I feel will sort everything out. Firstly I propose that income tax be abolished.'

A gasp went up around the table.

'I'll give that the thumbs up,' said Norman.

'Please calm down,' said the Doveston, 'and allow me to explain.'

'I am calm,' said Norman.

'He wasn't talking to you.'

'As we all know,' the Doveston said, 'no matter how much money you earn, the inland revenue will eventually get all of it. It is damn near impossible to buy anything that does not have a tax on it somewhere. Allow me to advance this argument. Say I have one hundred pounds. I go into an off-licence and buy ten bottles of whisky at ten pounds a bottle. The actual whisky only costs two pounds a bottle, all the rest is tax. So the man in the off-licence now has the difference, twenty pounds. He uses that to fill his car up with petrol. Tax on petrol represents seventy-five per cent of its market price. So now there's only five pounds left out of my one hundred pounds. The chap at the petrol station spends this on five packets of cigarettes. And we all know how much tax there is on fags. Out of my original one hundred pounds, the government now have all but one. And whatever the man in the fag shop spends that one pound on will have a tax on it somewhere.'

'Yes yes yes,' said old silly-bollocks. '*We* all know this, although we wouldn't want the man in the street to know it.'

'Precisely,' said the Doveston. 'And we're not going to tell him. Now this same man in the street is taxed roughly one-third of his weekly earnings in direct taxation. What would happen if he wasn't?'

'He'd have a third more of his money to spend every week,' said old silly-bollocks.

'And what would he spend it on?'

'Things, I suppose.'

'Precisely. Things with tax on.'

'Er, excuse me,' said what's-his-face, the Foreign Secretary. 'But if everybody in the country had a third more of their money in their pockets to spend and they *did* spend it, surely the shops would run out of things to sell?'

'Precisely. And so factories would have to manufacture more things and to do so they would have to take on more staff and so you would cut unemployment at a stroke. And you wouldn't have to increase anybody's wages, because they'd all be getting a third more in their pay packets anyway. You'd have full employment and a happy workforce. Hardly the recipe for revolution, is it?'

'There has to be a flaw in this logic,' I said to Norman.

'There has to be a flaw in this logic,' said old silly-bollocks. 'But for the life of me, I can't see what it is.'

'There is no flaw,' said the Doveston. 'And if you increase the purchase tax on all goods by a penny in the pound – which no one will complain about, because they'll have so much more money to spend – you'll be able to grab that final pound out of my original one hundred. You'll get the lot.'

All around the boardroom table chaps were rising to applaud. Even the woman with the bald head, who usually wears the wig, got up and clapped.

'Bravo,' cheered Norman.

'Sit down, you stupid sod,' I told him.

'Yeah, but he's clever. You have to admit.'

'He said he had a *couple* of radical proposals. What do you think the second one might be?'

'Now, my second radical proposal is this,' said the Doveston, once all the clappers had sat themselves down. 'I propose that the government legalize all drugs.'

'Oh well,' said Norman. 'One out of two wasn't bad. Not for a bloke who's Richard, anyway.'

Chaos reigned in the boardroom. The Doveston bashed his fists upon the table. Chaos waned and calm returned. The Doveston continued. 'Please hear me out,' he said. 'Now, as we all know, the government spends a fortune each year in the war against drugs. It is a war that the government can never win. You can't stop people enjoying themselves and there are just too many ways of bringing drugs into this country. So why does the government get so up in arms about drugs?'

'Because they're bad for you,' said what's-his-face.

'You are amongst friends here,' said the Doveston. 'You can tell the truth.'

'I'll bet he can't,' said old silly-bollocks.

'Can too.'

'Can't.'

'Can too.'

'Go on then,' said the Doveston. 'Why does the government get so up in arms about drugs?'

'Because we can't tax them, of course.'

'Precisely. But you could tax them if they were legal.'

223

'Don't think we haven't thought about it,' said old silly-bollocks. 'But no government dare legalize drugs. Even though half the population regularly use them, the other half would vote us out of office.'

'But what if they were legalized, but the man in the street didn't know they were legalized?'

'I don't quite see how you could do that.'

'What if you were to take all the money that is wasted each year in the war on drugs, go over to the areas where the drugs are originally grown, the Golden Triangle and so on, and use the money to buy *all* the crops. Ship them back to England, then market them through the existing network of pushers. You wouldn't half make a big profit.'

'That's hardly the same as legalizing them, or taxing them.'

'Well, firstly, the people who take drugs don't really want them legalized. Half the fun of taking drugs is the "forbidden fruit" aspect. They're much more exciting to take if they're illegal. Only the government will know that they're legal, which is to say that the Royal Navy will import them. You can't imagine any drug-traffickers wanting to take on the Royal Navy, can you? On arrival here, the drugs will be tested and graded, they could even be trademarked. They will be top quality, at affordable and competitive prices. Any opposition in the shape of rival drug-importers will soon be put out of business. The profits you make can be called "tax". I can't think of a better word, can you?'

'But if the rest of the world found out . . . ?' Old silly-bollocks wrung his hands.

'You mean if other governments found out? Well, tell

them. Tell them all. Get them to do the same. It will put the Mafia out of business and increase government revenues by billions all over the world.'

'But the whole world will get stoned out of its brains.'

'No it won't. No more people will be taking drugs than there are now. And fewer people in this country will be taking them.'

'How do you work that out?' old silly-bollocks asked.

'Because a great deal of drug-taking is done out of desperation. By poor unemployed people who have given up hope. In the new income-tax-free society, they'll all have jobs and money to spend. They won't be so desperate then, will they?'

'The man's a genius,' said Norman.

'The man is a master criminal,' I said. 'No wonder he's so into security. He's probably expecting the arrival of James Bond at any minute.'

So, what of the Doveston's radical proposals? What of them indeed. You will of course know that direct taxation ceased at midnight on the final day of the twentieth century, when most of the government's computer systems self-destructed. But you probably didn't know that since the summer of 1985 virtually any 'illegal' drug that you might have taken in this country was imported, graded and marketed with the approval of HM Government herself.

And that a penny in the pound on all profit made has gone directly to the man who brokered the original deal with the chaps from the Colombian drugs cartel.

And this man's name?
Well, I don't really have to spell it out.
Do I?
But I'll tell you what. It's not Richard.

18

Fame is a process of isolation.
Alice Wheeler (friend of Kurt Cobain)

I worked for a full ten years at Castle Doveston.

Ten bloody years it took me doing it up. And when I had finally finished my labours, the Doveston drew my attention to some of the first rooms I'd decorated and remarked that they were now looking somewhat shabby and would I mind just giving them another lick of paint.

I did mind and I told him so. I had my conservatory to get started on and I felt I could use a holiday.

Mind you, I'm not saying that my years at Castle Doveston weren't fun. In fact I'm prepared to say that they were some of the happiest years of my life. During those years I must have taken every conceivable drug and indulged in every conceivable form of sexual deviation known to man and beast. There was even some talk of naming a brand of iodine after me.

And I did get to meet the rich and famous. I got to watch them engaging in the bad behaviour that their status afforded them. And if I wasn't there to witness it in person, I could always watch it on video the following day.

My video library became a bit of a legend in Brentford and I derived a great deal of pleasure from standing in the saloon bar of the Flying Swan, listening to conversations about the rumoured sexual peccadillos of film stars, before chipping in that I had them captured on tape doing worse. I never charged for private screenings, although I made a fair bit of money from marketing bootleg copies.

I should never have sent that compilation tape off to *You've Been Framed* though.

The vice squad did me for Possession of Pornographic material. Another two Ps there, you notice. But the case never came to court. The Doveston's influence saw to that. His video library was far bigger than mine, with its own special magistrates' section. And anyway, he was by now so hand in glove with the government that all his employees carried diplomatic immunity. Which meant that we could behave very badly and park on double yellow lines.

It was during this period, of course, that the Doveston became world famous. He had been rich and powerful for years, but he really got off on the fame.

It was the snuff that did it. The Doveston designer snuff.

The Nineties, you see, were no laughing matter. These were the years of PC. Political Correctness. For which you can read TYRANNY. People were urged into giving things up. They gave up having casual sex. They gave up eating meat.

They gave up smoking!

They didn't want to, but they did. The Secret Government of the World decreed it and it was so.

228

And where people had to be urged that little bit harder, they were. We all know now that AIDS and BSE were not the products of nature. They were engineered. But when it came to smoking, the approach was far more subtle.

The scare stories that smoking was actually bad for your health were never going to work. No-one in his or her right mind would ever believe such nonsense. So the Secret Government saw to it that smoking was banned in public places. You could no longer smoke in certain restaurants, in cinemas, in art galleries, in theatres and shops and schools and swimming pools. Smoking was forbidden.

BUT NOT SO THE TAKING OF SNUFF.

It was almost as if he had seen it coming. Almost as if – perhaps – he'd had a hand in it. He had extensive tobacco plantations by now, in several Third World countries, along with his estates in Virginia. And was it really a coincidence that at a time when he was opening up trade with China, a vast and lucrative market which would surely swallow up everything he could produce, that smoking was suddenly being actively discouraged in the West?

And you see, the thing about snuff is that it can be produced cheaply from the dried end leaves of tobacco that are not of sufficient quality to use in cigarettes. Every plantation finds itself each year with a surplus of this stuff. It's usually just mulched up for fertilizer.

Aha! I hear you cry, the rat is smelled. But what about Political Correctness as a whole? Surely *it* wasn't just a callous hoax, played upon a gullible public for motives of profit alone?

Well sorry, my friends, I'm afraid it was. The fear of AIDS led to the abandoning of casual *unprotected* sex. Shares in condom companies boomed. The fear of BSE led people to give up eating meat and eat more vegetables. Shares in agri-chemical companies boomed. And so on and so forth and suchlike.

No matter what you gave up in the cause of PC, it benefited some rich bugger somewhere.

So what about that snuff?

The first TV commercial was a masterpiece. It featured an actress from one of the popular 'soaps'. Normally it is written into the contracts of such actresses that they cannot appear in commercials. Except, of course, if the soap itself is sponsored by the makers of the very product that is being advertised. And when the product is 'the healthy PC alternative to smoking', where could be the harm in it?

It was the very first TV commercial for a branded product ever shown on the BBC.

And the range of fashion accessories that went with the product! The snuffbox jewellery, the pendants and necklaces, bracelets and brooches. The cufflinks, the hipflasks, the snuff-dispensing pens. All, of course, with their distinctive Gaia logo. What could possibly be more PC?

But for all the design and the promo and bullshit, what of the product itself? Was the snuff any good? Did it smell nice? Did it give you a buzz? Remember, you had to stick this stuff up your hooter and the taking of snuff had formerly been regarded as solely within the province of dirty old men.

Well, come on now, what do *you* think?

It was bloody marvellous. It smelled like Heaven and set you right up for the day.

It came in fifty different blends, each the product of years of research and development. And he'd left nothing to chance. He had trademarked the name Doveston's Snuff. Which is to say that he had not only trademarked his own name, but the word 'snuff' too. How he did it is anyone's guess, although I have a few of my own. And what it meant was that no rival could use the word 'snuff' on their product. And there were to be many rivals. Any good idea spawns imitators and I still own in my private collection a packet of Virgin Sniffing Mixture.

It never caught on.

The Doveston began to make his first public appearances: on talk shows, at world premières, society functions and fight nights. He was a natural raconteur and the camera loved him. He would turn up on *Newsnight*, discussing 'Green Issues', and on *Blue Peter*, demonstrating how you could make a snuffbox for Mummy out of sticky-backed plastic and Fairy Liquid bottles with their names blacked out.

He appeared on the covers of trendy magazines and it wasn't long before photographers from *Hello!* were given the secret password to get them through the gates of Castle Doveston.

And it wasn't too long after that that the first piece of shit hit the wildly whirling fan. Some stills from a video recording found their way into the hands of a Sunday tabloid journalist. The joyful journalist passed these on to his editor. The elated editor passed on the news that he intended publication to the Doveston. The Doveston apparently then told him to publish and be damned.

Or so the story goes. Some, who are better informed, tell it that the words used were actually: *you'll be damned before you publish*. If these *were* the very words used, then they were uncannily prophetic, for the editor died the following day, in a freak accident involving his car-exhaust pipe and a stick of dynamite.

The incriminating photographs went up with him. Or should that be *down*, in the case of the damned?

But the brown stuff always sticks and even as the Doveston was making his way to Buck House to receive his OBE 'For Services to the British People' from his grateful monarch, queues of young women were forming outside the offices of the nation's press, each of these young women being eager to offer details, in exchange for nothing more than large sums of money, of how the man they now called the Sultan of Snuff had tried to coerce them into giving him blow-jobs, or got them to do rude things with cigars.[1]

And it seemed that every miffed ex-employee, or indeed anyone who had ever known the Doveston, had some lurid story they wanted to sell. Even Chico's now-aged aunty, who still ran the ever-popular House of Correction in Brentford, came forward with a ludicrous yarn about the young Doveston sexually molesting her pet chicken and running off with her favourite teapot.

But all publicity is good publicity and if you are very

[1] So now at least you know where Bill Clinton got the idea from.

very rich it doesn't matter what the tabloids print about you. Or even how true it might be. You sue and you win and the public loves you for it. And the damages make you even richer.

Mind you, there were moments when things got mighty dangerous. Someone – and it might very well have been the same someone who sent the video stills to the tabloid – someone tipped off a prominent investigative TV journalist that the British government was funding the importation of narcotics and that the Doveston was acting as middle man and taking one per cent of the profits.

It chills my very soul today when I recall the ghastly details of the freak accident which took that TV journalist from us. May his tortured body rest in peace.

But oh, I hear you say, enough of this. Relevant as all these details are and necessary to the telling of the tale, we really do want to get on with the guts and the gore.

Well, all right all right all right. I can beat about the beaver no longer, the story must be told and only I can tell it. The real guts and gore and the madness and mayhem occurred at the Great Millennial Ball.

Held at Castle Doveston, this was to be *the* social occasion of the century. Anyone who was anyone had been invited and anyone who wasn't wasn't getting in.

Evidently *I* wasn't anyone, because *I* hadn't received an invitation. The first I heard about the ball was when Norman told me about the costume he was working on that 'would really impress the ladies'.

Norman had just returned from the balloon trip. What balloon trip? Well, the one the Doveston had organized for his closest friends to rise above the clouds over the English Channel and view the total eclipse of the sun.

What total eclipse? The one that the rich people watched and *we* didn't. That's what!

'Good, was it?' I asked Norman.

'Bloody brilliant. You should have been there. Mind you, it fair put the wind up the Doveston. He's expecting the end of the world as we know it. He seemed quite certain that the eclipse was a sign. A portent in the heavens. He wee-wee'd himself. In front of the Prime Minister.'

'I'll bet that made you laugh.'

'Of course it didn't. Well, it did, a bit. Well, quite a lot really. I nearly wee-wee'd myself, trying not to.'

'So, he's still as Richard as ever?'

'Much more so. How long is it since you've seen him?'

'Four years. Ever since that business with the videos and the vice squad. He pays me a retainer, but I'm no longer welcome at Castle Doveston. I receive press packages, so that I can continue to work on the biography.'

'And how is that coming along?'

I made the face that says 'bollocks'.

'I'll get us another round in, shall I?'

As Norman went off to the bar, I looked around and about me. I was in the Flying Swan, that drinking house of legend. No-one here had any plans to celebrate the millennium. They'd already done it. Last year. It had all been down to a tradition, or an old charter, or something. I'd missed it, but I'd heard tell that it had been quite an occasion. Second coming of Christ and everything. Norman had put on the firework display. I wondered if he would be doing the same for the Doveston's bash.

'Tell me all about this ball, then,' I said when he returned with the drinks.

'Oh yes, I was telling you about my costume, wasn't I?'

'Something about a peacock, you said.'

'Yes, that's it, the peacock suit. It's not a peacock costume, that would be just plain silly. It's a peacock suit, as in peacock mating display. You see, the male peacock's tail feathers serve no purpose whatsoever, other than for attracting a mate. Female peacocks get off on males with big tail feathers. They always have. So those are the ones they mate with and, in consequence, natural selection has meant that the males have evolved bigger and bigger tail feathers. So big now that the blighters can't even get off the ground. Not that they're bothered; they're too busy having sex.'

'I'm sure there's some point to this,' I said. 'But so far it's lost on me.'

'Well,' said Norman. 'Imagine a human equivalent. A suit that a man could wear that would attract females.'

'There already is one. It's called a Paul Smith suit.'

'I seem to recall that yours didn't work very well.'

I took a wet from my glass. 'Whatever happened to Jackie,' I wondered.

'Died in a freak accident, I think. Tragic business. But I'm not talking about a very expensive suit that turns some women on just because it *is* very expensive. I'm talking about a suit that turns *all* women on. I have designed such a suit and when I wear it to the ball, I shall be able to have the pick of any women I choose.'

'That's bollocks,' I said. 'That can't be true.'

'I seem to recall that you said the same thing about my invisible paint. And where did that leave you?'

'In hospital,' I said. 'With fractured ribs.'

'Well, it served you right. The next time someone comes driving straight at you in an invisible car, hooting the horn and shouting out of the window, "Get out of the way, the brakes have bloody failed," you'll know better than to stand your ground, shouting back, "You don't fool me, it's a sound effects record," won't you?'

'Whatever happened to that car?'

'Dunno,' said Norman. 'I can't remember where I parked it.'

'So this peacock suit of yours will really pull the women, will it?'

'Listen,' said Norman, drawing me close and speaking in a confidential tone. 'I gave the prototype a road test in Sainsbury's. I was lucky to get out alive. I've adjusted the controls on the new one.'

'Controls? This suit has controls?'

'It works on a similar principle to the Hartnell Home Happyfier. But I've decided to hang on to the patent this time. I intend to prove to the world that a man with mutton-chop side-whiskers and an Arthur Scargill comb-over job can actually get to have sex with a supermodel.'

'Only by cheating.'

'Everybody cheats at something. The problem is that

I'm going to have to keep my suit on while I'm having sex.'

'How about a pair of split-crotch peacock underpants?'

'Brilliant idea,' said Norman. 'And to think that everybody says you're stupid.'

'Eh?'

Our conversation here was interrupted by a shout of: 'It's that bastard on the telly again.' Knowing full well that the Swan did not have a television, or a jukebox, or a digital telephone, I was somewhat surprised by this shout. But sure enough, it was some out-borough wally with a tiny TV attached to his mobile phone.

Norman and I helped Neville the part-time barman heave this malcontent into the street. But while we were so doing, I chanced to glimpse the tiny screen and on it the face of the bastard in question.

It was the Doveston.

The photograph was only a still and one taken some years before. A publicity photo, of the type he liked to sign and give out to people. The voice of a mid-day newscaster tinkled from the tiny TV. The voice was saying something about a freak accident.

The voice was saying that the Doveston was dead.

237

19

Da de da de da de da de candle in the wind.
Elton John (lyric rights refused)

'He's Leonardo,' said Norman.

I didn't ask. I knew what he meant.

Dead, is what he meant.

Mind you, I should have asked. Because this particular piece of Brentford rhyming slang was an ingenious twelfth-generation affair, leading from the now legendary fifteenth-century artist and innovator to several varieties of cheese, a number of well-known household products, two kinds of fish and three makes of motorcycle, before finally arriving at the word 'dead'.

Norman was nothing if not inventive.

I sat now in the shopkeeper's kitchen on one of a pair of Morris Minor front seats that Norman had converted into a sofa. If coincidence means anything, Norman's kitchen, which was also his workshop, looked very much the way I imagine Leonardo's workshop must have looked. Without the Meccano, of course.

'He can't be dead,' I said. 'He can't be. He just can't.'

Norman twiddled with the dials on his TV.

'Get a bloody move on,' I told him.

'Yes, yes, I'm trying.' The scientific shopkeeper bashed the top of the set with his fist. 'I've made a few modifications to this,' he said. 'I've always felt that TVs waste a lot of power. All those cathode rays and light and stuff coming out of the screen. So I invented this.' He adjusted a complicated apparatus that hung in front of the television. It was constructed from the inevitable Meccano. 'This is like a solar panel, but more efficient. It picks up the rays coming out of the screen, then converts them into electrical energy and feeds it back into the TV to power the set. Clever, eh?'

I nodded. 'Very clever.'

'Mind you, there does seem to be one major obstacle that so far I've been unable to overcome.'

'Tell me.'

'Just how you get the set to start without any initial power.'

'Plug it into the wall socket, you silly sod.'

'Brilliant.' Norman shook his head, dislodging ghastly strands of hair. 'And to think people say you're—'

'Just plug it in!'

Norman plugged it in.

The Doveston's face appeared once more on the screen. This time it was an even younger model, bearded and framed by long straight hair. This was the Doveston circa 'sixty-seven.

A newscaster's voice spoke over. This is what it said.

'The tragedy occurred today at a little after noon in the grounds of Castle Doveston. The Laird of

Bramfield was entertaining a number of house guests, among them the Sultan of Brunei, the President of the United States and Mr Saddam Hussein. The party were engaged in one of the Laird's favourite sporting pursuits: sheep-blasting. According to eye-witness accounts, given by several visiting heads of state, the Doveston had just drawn back on his catapult, preparatory to letting fly, when the elastic broke and the dynamite went off in his hand.'

'Freak accident,' said Norman. 'It's just how he would have wanted to go.'

I shook my head.

'But what a gent,' Norman said. 'What a gent.'

'What a gent?'

'Well, think about it. He died at noon on a Wednesday. Wednesday's my half-day closing. If he'd died on any other day, I'd have had to close the shop as a mark of respect. I'd have lost half a day's trade.'

Norman sat down beside me and tugged the cork from a bottle of home-made sprout brandy. This he handed to me by the neck.

I took a big swig. 'He can't be dead,' I said once more. 'This isn't how it happens.'

'You what?' Norman watched me carefully.

'I saw the future. I've told you about it. Back in 'sixty-seven, when I smoked those Brentstock cigarettes. I'm sure this isn't how he dies.'

Norman watched me some more. 'Perhaps you got it wrong. I don't think the future's fixed. And if he blew himself up, right in front of all those heads of state—'

'Yes, I suppose so. Oh Jesus!' I clutched at my throat. 'I'm on fire here. Jesus!'

Norman took the bottle from me. 'Serves you right for taking such a big greedy swig,' he said with a grin. 'I may not be able to predict the future (yet), but I could see that one coming.'

'It has to be a hoax,' I said, when I had regained my composure. 'That's what it is. He's faked his own death. Like Howard Hughes.'

'Don't be so obscene.'

'Obscene?'

'Howard Hughes. That's fourth generation Brentford rhyming slang. That means—'

'I don't care what it means. But I'll bet you that's what he's done.'

Norman took a small swig from the bottle. 'And why?' he asked. 'Why would he want to do that?'

'I don't know. To go into hiding, I suppose.'

'Oh yeah, right. The man who adores being in the public eye. The man who gets off mixing with the rich and famous. The man who was to host the greatest social occasion of the twentieth century. The man—'

'All right,' I said. 'You've made your point. But I still can't believe it.'

'He's Leonardo,' Norman said.

And Leonardo he was.

I was really keen to view the body. Not out of morbid curiosity – I just had to know. Could he truly be dead? It didn't seem possible. Not *the Doveston*. Not *dead*. The more I thought about it, the more certain I became that it couldn't be true. He had to have faked it. And if he had, what better way would there be than blowing himself up in public view? Leaving no recognizable pieces?

Norman said that he could think of at least six better ways. But I ignored Norman.

We both attended the funeral. We received invitations. We could pay our last respects to his body as it lay in state at Castle Doveston and even help carry the coffin to its resting place on a small island in the one remaining lake on the estate. He had apparently left instructions in his will that this was where he was to be interred.

A long black shiny armoured limo came to pick us up. Rapscallion was driving. 'Masser Doveston's gone to de Lord,' was all he had to say.

As we approached the grounds of Castle Doveston, what I saw amazed me. There were thousands of people there. Thousands and thousands. Many held candles and most were weeping. The perimeter fence was covered with bunches of flowers. With photographs of the Doveston. With really awful poems, scrawled on bits of paper. With football scarves (he owned several clubs). With Gaia logos made from sticky-backed plastic and Fairy Liquid bottles with their names blacked out. (There'd been a tribute on *Blue Peter*.)

And the news teams were there. News teams from all over the world. With cameras mounted on top of their vans. All trained upon the house.

They swung in our direction as we approached. The crowd parted and the gates opened wide. Rapscallion steered the limo up the long and winding drive.

Inside, the house was just as I remembered it. No further decorating had been done. The open coffin rested upon the dining table in the great hall and as I

242

stood there memories came flooding back of all the amazing times that I'd had here. Of the drunkenness and drug-taking and debauchery. Of things so gross that I should, perhaps, have included them in this book, to spice up some of the duller chapters.

'Shall we have a look at him?' said Norman.

I took a very deep breath.

'Best to do that now,' said Norman. 'He probably pongs a bit.'

He didn't pong.

Except for the expensive aftershave – his own brand, Snuff for Men. He lay there in his open coffin, all dressed up but nowhere nice to go. His face wore that peaceful, resigned expression so often favoured by the dead. One hand rested on his chest. Between the fingers somebody had placed a small cigar.

I could feel the emotions welling up inside me, like huge waves breaking on a stony beach. Like the wind, rushing into the mouth of a cave. Like thunder, crashing over an open plain. Like an orange turnip dancing on a cow's nest in a handbag factory.

'He doesn't look bad for a dead bloke,' said Norman.

'Eh? No, he doesn't. Especially for a man who was blown into little pieces.'

'It's mostly padding, you know. They only managed to salvage his head and his right hand. Here look, I'll open his collar. You can see where his severed neck is stitched on to the—'

'Don't you dare.' I pulled Norman's hand away. 'But he is dead, isn't he? I thought that it might be a dummy or something.'

'They fingerprinted the hand,' said Norman. 'And even if he was prepared to lose a hand in order to fake his own death, I think that losing his head might be going over the top a bit.'

I sighed. 'Then that's it. The Doveston is dead. The end of an era. The end of a long, if troubled, friendship.' I reached into my jacket and brought out a packet of cigarettes. This I slipped into the Doveston's breast pocket.

'Nice sentiment,' said Norman. 'Something for his spirit to smoke on the other side.'

I nodded solemnly.

'Pity they're not his own brand, though,' said Norman with a grin. 'That will really piss him off.'

The funeral was grim. They always are. At the service, numerous celebrities came forward to offer eulogies or recite really awful poems. Elton John had sent his apologies (he was having his hair done), but they had managed to employ the services of an ex-member of the Dave Clark Five, who sang their great hit 'Bits and Pieces'.

The actual laying to rest was not without its moments. Especially when, as we were trying to get the coffin into the rowing boat, the vicar fell in the water.

'You bloody pushed him,' I whispered to Norman. 'I saw you. Don't deny it.'

And then it was all back to the big house for drinks and fags and snuff and cakes and a lot of polite conversation about what an all-round good egg the Doveston had been.

Oh yes, and the reading of the will.

'I'm off home,' I whispered to Norman. 'There won't be anything in it for me.'

'You might be surprised. I witnessed his will, after all.'

'If it turns out to be a signed photograph, I will punch your lights out.'

I'd seen the Doveston's solicitor before. We weren't on speaking terms, but I had some amazing footage of him on video tape. So I knew what he was wearing under his jolly smart suit.

There were at least fifty of us there, seated in the great hall, facing the table that had so recently supported the coffin. Most of those present were strangers to me, but I imagined that they must be the Doveston's relatives. It's only weddings and funerals that bring these buggers out.

'So,' said the solicitor, seating himself behind the great table, secretly adjusting his corset as he did so. 'This is a very sad time for us all. Indeed for the entire nation. England has lost one of her most notable and best-loved sons. I do not think that his like will ever be seen here again.'

'He nicked that line,' said Norman.

'Yes, but not from you.'

'There are a number of bequests to charities and trusts,' the solicitor continued. 'But these need not concern us here. You'll no doubt read all about them in the newspapers, as soon as the details have been officially leaked. What concerns us here is the major part of the estate, the house and grounds, the business interests, the capital.'

'Now, first things first. The Great Millennial Ball. The Doveston has left specific instructions that the ball *must* go ahead. It will be held in his honour and hosted by his inheritor. I say inheri*tor*, rather than -*tors*, because there is only one. This one person must host the Great Millennial Ball in the *exact* manner the Doveston planned it, or forfeit the inheritance. Is this understood?'

People nodded. I didn't bother. 'Your lights are about to be punched,' I told Norman.

'The sole inheritor of the Doveston's fortune is . . .' The solicitor paused for effect. Necks craned forward, breaths were held.

'Is . . .' He produced a small golden envelope from his top pocket and opened it carefully.

Norman nudged me in the ribs. 'Exciting, isn't it? This was written into the will.'

I rolled my eyes.

'Is . . .' The solicitor glanced at the card. '*My bestest friend*—'

Norman jumped up. 'Well what a surprise. I wasn't expecting this.'

'*Edwin*,' said the solicitor.

Norman sat down. 'Only kidding,' he said. 'I told you you might be surprised.'

They brought me round with the contents of a soda siphon.

I was sorry that I'd fainted, because I missed the punch-up. Some people can be very sour losers. Apparently Norman started it.

'I can't believe it.' I gasped, spitting soda. 'He's left everything to me.'

246

'You're the new Laird of Bramfield,' said Norman. 'How does it feel?'

'I'm rich,' I replied. 'I'm a multi-multi-multi-millionaire.'

'Lend us a quid then,' said Norman.

I was really shaking as I signed all the forms the solicitor gave me. Norman kept a close eye over my shoulder, just to make sure that I didn't sign anything dodgy. The solicitor gave Norman a very bitter look and tucked several sheets of paper back into his briefcase.

'There,' I said, when I'd done. 'I'm done.'

The solicitor smiled an ingratiating smile. 'I trust, sir,' said he, 'that you will retain the services of our company.'

'Bollocks!' I said. 'On your bike.'

Norman shooed the solicitor out and then returned to me. 'So,' said Norman, 'your lairdship, would you like me to show you around your new home?'

I took snuff from a silver bowl and pinched it to my nose. 'I've seen all the house,' I said. 'I decorated most of it myself.'

'There must be something you'd like to see.'

'Ah, yes, there is.' I sneezed.

'Bless you,' said Norman.

'I would like to see the secret laboratories. See what he's really been getting up to all these years. All that stuff about the Great Work. All the genetic engineering. All the concocting of strange mind-altering drugs.'

'Oh yes,' said Norman, rubbing his hands together. 'I'd like to see all that too.'

'Then lead me to them.'

'Certainly,' said Norman. 'Which way are they?'

I made the face that says 'come on now'. 'Come on now,' I said. 'You've got your set of keys. You know everything there is to know about this house.'

'You're right there,' said Norman. 'So which way are they then?'

'Norman,' I said. 'Don't jerk me about. You know I'll see you all right. You can consider that from this minute you are a millionaire too.'

'Oh, no thanks,' said Norman. 'I don't need any money.'

'You don't?'

'No, I've got all I need to keep going. Although . . .'

'Although?'

'I could do with another box of Meccano.'

'It's yours. A van load. Now where are the secret laboratories?'

'I give up,' said Norman. 'Where are they?'

'All right then.' I took a pinch of snuff from another bowl and poked it up my hooter. 'We'll just have to search for them. Where do you think we should start?'

Norman shrugged. 'How about his office? There might be secret plans hidden away.'

'What a very good idea.'

The Doveston's office (my office now!) was on the first floor. A magnificent room, all done out in the style of Grinling Gibbons (1648–1721), the English sculptor and woodcarver, so well known for his ecclesiastical woodwork. As well as the bigness of his willy.

Well, probably more so for his ecclesiastical wood-work. But as I *am* rich now, I can say what I like.

248

'The wallpaper really spoils this room,' said Norman. 'Stars and stripes. I ask you.'

'Oh,' I said. 'I chose the wallpaper.'

'Nice,' said Norman. 'Very nice too.'

'You're just saying that to please me.'

'Of course I am. It's something you'll have to get used to, now you're rich. Everyone will want to suck up to you. And no-one will ever say anything to you that you don't want to hear.'

'Don't say that!'

'What?' said Norman. 'I never said anything.'

We searched the office. We had the back off the filing cabinet. But the filing cabinet was empty. All the desk drawers were empty too. As were all the shelves that normally held all the paperwork.

'Somebody's cleaned out this office,' I said. 'Taken everything.'

'He probably left instructions in his will. That all incriminating evidence was to be destroyed. He wouldn't have wanted anything to come out after his death and sully his memory with the general public.'

'You think that's it?'

'I do. But you're welcome to say that you thought of it first, if you want.'

'Norman,' I said, 'is the fact that I am now unthinkably rich going to mess around with our friendship?'

'Certainly not,' said Norman. 'I still don't like you very much.'

I sat down in the Doveston's chair. (My chair now!) 'So you are telling me that you have absolutely no idea whatsoever as to where the secret laboratories might be?'

'None whatsoever.' Norman sat down on the desk.

'Get your arse off my desk,' I said.

Norman stood up again. 'Sorry,' he said. 'First one up against the wall, come the revolution,' he whispered.

'What was that?'

'Nothing.'

'But the secret laboratories must be here somewhere. I'm certain that if we could find them, we would find the answer to everything. I think that the Great Work was what he lived for. It was the whole point of his life.'

Norman shrugged. 'Well, believe me, I've searched for them. Searched for them for years. But if they're here, I don't know where they are. The only secret room I ever found was the secret trophy room.'

'And where's that?'

'At the end of the secret passage.'

'Lead the way.'

Norman led the way.

It was a really good secret passage. You had to swing this suit of armour aside and crawl in on your hands and knees. Norman led the way once more. 'Don't you dare fart,' I told him.

At length we reached a secret door and Norman opened it with the secret key he'd copied for the sake of convenience.

He flicked on the light and I went, 'Blimey!'

'It's good, isn't it? Just like a little museum.'

And that was just what it was. A little museum. A little *black* museum. I wandered amongst the exhibits. Each one told its little tale of infamy.

'Hm,' I said, picking up a pair of specs. 'These would be the glasses that Vicar Berry "mislaid" before he lit the dynamite instead of the communion candle. And here's Chico's aunty's leather bondage teapot. And the box bound in human skin that Professor Merlin showed us and you—'

'I don't want to think of that, thank you.'

'And what do we have here? A badge-making machine and some badges. Let's see. The Black Crad Movement.'

'Wasn't that the terrorist movement that blew up all those cabinet ministers' houses?'

'With dynamite, yes. And look at this. Some charred photographs. They look like stills from a video tape.'

'The ones that the journalist passed on to his editor, who—'

'Aaah-Choo,' I said. 'As in dynamite.'

'Urgh,' said Norman. 'And look at this blood-stained bow tie. Didn't that bloke on the TV, who used to expose government corruption, wear one just like this? They never found all of him, did they?'

I shook my head. 'But – oh, look, Norman,' I said. 'Here's something of yours.' I passed him the item and he peered down at it.

'My yo-yo,' he said. 'My prototype yo-yo. That takes me back. Who was it, now, who ended up with the patent?'

'A certain Mr Crad, I believe. No doubt the same Mr Crad who founded The Black Crad Movement.'

'Oh,' said Norman. He looped the end of the yo-yo's string over his finger and sent the little bright wooden toy skimming down. It jammed at the bottom and didn't come up.

'Typical,' said Norman, worrying at the string. 'Oh no, hang about. There's something jammed in here. A piece of paper, look.'

'Perhaps it's a map showing the location of the secret laboratories.'

'Do you really think so?'

'No.' I snatched the tiny crumpled piece of paper from his hand and did my best to straighten it out. And then I looked at what was written on it and then I said, 'Blimey!' once again.

'What is it?' Norman asked.

'A list of six names. But I don't recognize them. Here, do they mean anything to you?'

Norman screwed up his eyes and perused the list. 'Yes, of course they do,' he said.

'So who are they?'

'Well, remember when we watched that secret meeting, when the Doveston came out with his idea for the government to take over the importation of drugs?'

'Of course I do.'

'Well, these were the six people present. That's old silly-bollocks. And that one's what's-his-face. And that's the bald-headed woman who usually wears the wig and—'

'Norman,' I said. 'Do you know what this means?'

'That one of them might know where the secret laboratories are?'

'No! Don't you understand? This list wasn't put into the yo-yo by accident. It was put there for us to find.

252

You and me, the people who watched that meeting taking place. His bestest friends. The stuff in his office wasn't taken away to be destroyed, it was nicked. By one or more of these people.'

'I don't quite see how you come to draw these conclusions.'

'Norman,' I said. 'Read what it says at the top of the list.'

Norman read the words aloud. There were just two of them.

The words were 'POTENTIAL ASSASSINS'.

'Norman,' I said. 'The Doveston did not die in any freak accident. The Doveston was murdered.'

20

Metabolically challenged: Dead.
The Politically Correct Phrasebook

'Murdered!' cried Norman and he whistled.

It was a nice enough tune, but I soon tired of it. 'Stop that bloody whistling,' I told him. 'We have to think.'

'About what?'

'About what we're going to do! Our bestest friend has been murdered.'

Norman opened his mouth to speak, but didn't.

'Go on,' I said.

'Oh, nothing. I was just going to say that it was how he would have wanted to go. But I don't suppose it was. Yet if you think about it, it was probably how he was bound to go. He must have made hundreds of enemies.'

'Yes, but we've got the list.'

'So what? If he was murdered, it could have been anybody.'

'Then we have to narrow it down to the most likely suspect.'

'That's easy,' said Norman.

'It is?'

'Of course it is. You just have to figure out which one single person had the most to gain from the Doveston's death. That will be your man for sure.'

'But how do we do that?'

'That's easy too.'

I sighed.

'Would you like me to give you a clue?'

I nodded.

'All right. The one single person who had the most to gain from the Doveston's death is standing in this room – and it isn't me.'

'You twat,' I said to Norman. 'I do have an alibi, you know. I was with you in the Flying Swan when it happened.'

'Well, you would say that, wouldn't you?'

'Turn it in. I think we have a duty to bring the Doveston's murderer to justice.'

'Why? Just look at this room. It's like Ed Gein's kitchen. Or Jonathan Doe's apartment in that movie *Seven*. All the evidence is here for the crimes he committed. He got his just desserts, why not leave it at that?'

It was a reasonable argument, but I wasn't happy with it. All the evidence *was* here. The Doveston had left us the clue in the yo-yo, but he had also left all the evidence for us to find. He had also left *me* all his money, which *did* make *me* the prime suspect, if there was ever a murder investigation. And it also made me something else.

'Oh shit!' I said.

'Excuse me?' said Norman.

'I've just had a terrible thought.'

'No change there then.'

'No, shut up and think about this. If the Doveston was murdered for the money, whoever murdered him didn't get it, did they? Because *I* got it. Which means—'

'Oh dear oh dear,' said Norman. 'Which means that they'll probably kill you next.'

'Bastard! Bastard! Bastard!'

'It's not my fault.'

'No, not you. The Doveston. He's stitched me up again. Stitched me up from beyond the grave. I get all the money, but if I don't get his murderer, his murderer gets me.'

'Still,' said Norman. 'He gave you a sporting chance. He did leave you the list of POTENTIAL ASSASSINS. That was very thoughtful of him.'

We returned to *my* office. I sat down in *my* chair and allowed Norman to park his bottom upon *my* desk. 'The six names on the list,' I said. 'Have those six people been invited to the ball, do you think?'

'Definitely.'

'And how can you be so sure?'

'Because it was my job to vet the list. I decided who got sent an invitation and who didn't.'

I gave Norman a somewhat withering look.

'Ah,' he said. 'Perhaps yours got lost in the post.'

'Get your arse off my desk,' I said.

Money being no object, I employed the services of a private detective. There was only one listed in the Brentford Yellow Pages. He went by the name of Lazlo

Woodbine. I figured that anyone who had the gall to name himself after the world's most famous fictional detective must be good for something.

Lazlo turned out to be a handsome-looking fellow. In fact he bore an uncanny resemblance to myself. He had just completed a case involving Billy Barnes. I remembered Billy from my school days at the Grange. Billy had been the boy who always knew more than was healthy for one of his age. Small world!

I explained to Lazlo that I needed all the information he could get me about the six POTENTIAL ASSASSINS. And I wanted it fast. The Great Millennial Ball was but two months away and I meant to be ready.

The final months of the twentieth century didn't amount to much. I had expected some kind of buzz. Lots of razzmatazz. But it was all rather downbeat. It seemed to rain most of the time and the newspapers became obsessed with the Millennium Bug. We'd all known about it for years. How many computer clocks would not be able to cope with the year two thousand and how computers all over the world would shut themselves down, or go berserk, or whatever. But only a very few people had actually taken it seriously and the newspapers hadn't been interested in it at all. Until now. Until it was too late to do anything about it.

Now it *was* news. Now it had the potential to spread panic.

But it didn't spread panic. The man in the street didn't seem to care. The man in the street just shrugged his shoulders. The man in the street said, 'It will be all right.'

And why did the man in the street behave in this fashion? Why the complacency? Why the couldn't care less and the glazed look in the eyes?

And why almost every man on almost every street? Why?

Well, I'll tell you for why.

The man in the street was on something.

The man in the street was drugged up to his glazed eyeballs.

The man in the street took Doveston's Snuff.

Yes, that's right, Doveston's Snuff. 'A pinch a day and the world's no longer grey.' It was all people talked about in those final months. All people did. Tried this blend, that blend and the other. This one brought you up, this one took you down and if you mixed these two together, you were off somewhere else. It was a national obsession. It was the latest craze.

Everyone was doing it. Every man on almost every street. And every woman too and every child. So what if the end of civilization was coming? Everyone seemed to agree that they could handle that − if not with a smile upon the face, then at least with a finger up the nose.

And so they wandered about like sleepwalkers. In and out of the tobacconist's. Norman said that trade had never been so good − Although he wasn't selling much in the way of sweeties.

Doveston's Snuff, eh? Who'd have thought it? Who'd have thought that there could have been anything dubious about Doveston's Snuff? That it might, per-haps, contain something more than just ground tobacco and flavourings? That it might, perhaps, contain some, how shall I put this . . . D R U G S ?

And if someone *had* thought it, would that someone have been able to work out the reason why? Would that someone have been able to uncover the fact that here was a conspiracy on a global scale? That this was in fact the work of the Secret Government of the World, covering its smelly bottom against the forthcoming downfall of civilization?

I very much doubt it.

I didn't figure it out.

Which was a shame, really. Because if I *had* figured it out, I would have been able to have done something about it. Because, after all, like that silly bugger with the razor blades, I *did* own the company. I could have taken the snuff off the shop shelves. I might even have been able to expose the conspiracy. Bring down the Secret Government of the World. Save mankind from the horrors to come.

But I didn't figure it out, so there you go.

I was far too busy to figure anything out. I was trying to hunt down a murderer *and* I was trying to organize a party: THE GREAT MILLENNIAL BALL.

The Doveston's solicitor had issued me with an enormous portfolio, containing all the details of the ball. Everything had to be done *exactly* as the Doveston had planned it. If not, and the solicitor rubbed his hands together as he told me, I would lose everything.

Everything.

I did not intend to lose everything and so I followed the instructions to the very letter. Norman was a tower of strength throughout this period. He'd had a big hand in the original planning of the ball and he arranged to have his uncle run his shop while he assisted me at Castle Doveston.

There were times, however, when he and I almost fell out.

'The dwarves are here,' he said one Friday evening, breezing into my office and plonking his bum on my desk.

'What dwarves?'

'The ones who've been hired for the ball. Fourteen of them have turned up for the audition, but we only need seven.'

'No-one ever needs more than seven dwarves,' I said, taking a green cigar from the humidor and running it under my nose. 'But what are these seven dwarves going to do?'

'They're going to have all their hair shaved off. Then, at the ball, they have to move around amongst the guests with lines of cocaine on their heads.'

The green cigar went up my left nostril. 'What?' I went. 'What? What? What?'

'You really should read all the small print.'

'It's gross,' I said. 'That's what it is.'

Norman helped himself to a cigar. 'If you think that's gross,' he said 'wait 'til you meet the human ashtrays.'

I auditioned the dwarves. It was a painful experience. Even though they were all prepared to submit to the humiliation of having their heads shaved, it didn't make me feel any better about it. In the end, I let their sex decide the matter for me.

There were seven men and seven women.

In the spirit of the Nineties, PC and positive discrimination, I dismissed all the men and chose the women.

An interior decorator called Lawrence had been engaged to spruce up the great hall for the party. Lawrence was famous. He starred in a very popular BBC television series, where neighbours were invited to redecorate each other's rooms in a manner calculated to create the maximum amount of annoyance and distress.

I loved the show and I really liked Lawrence. He was all long hair and leather trousers and he would strut about in cowboy boots, getting bad-tempered and shouting that this wasn't right and that had to be moved and that thing over there must be torn down and thrown away.

Lawrence didn't take to the Doveston's fine art collection. He hated it. He said that the Canalettos were far too old-fashioned and so he drew in some speedboats with a felt-tipped pen. I don't know much about art, but I know I liked his speedboats.

I didn't like it, though, when he told me that the two pillars supporting the minstrels' gallery would have to be demolished.

'We can't do that,' I told him. 'The minstrels' gallery will collapse.'

Lawrence stamped his cowboy boots and grew quite red in the face. 'They ruin the lines,' he shouted. 'I want to hang cascades of plastic fruit over the gallery. Either those pillars go, or I will.'

I knew that I couldn't lose Lawrence, but I knew the pillars had to stay. Luckily Norman stepped in and saved the situation. He suggested to Lawrence that he give the pillars a coat of invisible paint.

Norman's invisible paint really impressed the volatile Lawrence and he soon had the shopkeeper trailing after him, painting over Rembrandts and Caravaggios and suits of armour that couldn't be moved. And making doorways look wider and steps look lower and generally improving the look of the place.

I have no idea where the Doveston found the chef.

He was famous too, apparently, but I'd never heard of him. The chef was short and stout and swarthy and sweaty and swore a great deal of the time. Like all chefs, he was barking mad and he hated everybody. He hated Lawrence and he hated me. I introduced him to Norman. He hated Norman too.

'And this is my chauffeur, Rapscallion.'

'I hate him,' said the chef.

The chef, however, *loved* cooking. And he loved-loved-loved to cook for the rich and famous. And when I told him that he would be doing so for nearly four hundred of the buggers, he kissed me on the mouth and promised that he would prepare dishes of such an exquisite nature as to rival and surpass any that had ever been prepared in the whole of mankind's history.

And then he turned around and walked straight into an invisible pillar.

'I hate this fucking house,' said he.

*

Lazlo Woodbine kept in touch by telephone. He said that he and his associate, someone or something called Barry, were on the brink of solving the case and felt confident that they would be able to reveal the murderer's identity on the night of the Great Millennial Ball. I really liked the sound of that.

It was just like an Agatha Christie.

Mary Clarissa Christie (1890–1976), English author of numerous detective novels. Too many featuring Hercule Poirot. And if you haven't seen *The Mousetrap*, don't bother, the detective did it.

And so the final weeks of the century ticked and tocked away. Lawrence had promised me that he'd have everything done in just two days. Which was all he ever took on the telly. But apparently these were special BBC days, each of which can last up to a month.

Norman marched about the place, taking care of business. He now wore upon his head a strange contraption built from Meccano. This, he told me, exercised his hair.

Norman had become convinced that the reason your hair falls out is because it's unhealthy. So in order to keep it fit, you should give it plenty of exercise. He had invented a system that he called Hairobics. This consisted of a small gymnasium mounted on the head.

I did not expect Hairobics to rival the yo-yo's success.

Then I awoke one morning to find it all but gone.

The twentieth century.

It was 31 December. It was eight o'clock in the morning. There were just twelve hours to go before the start of the Great Millennial Ball.

I began to panic.

21

Party on, dude.
Bill (and Ted)

'Wakey wakey, rise and shine.' Norman came bluster-
ing into my bedroom, tea on a tray and the big
portfolio under his arm.

I gaped up at Norman. My panic temporarily on
hold. 'What's happened to your hair?' I asked.

'Ah.' Norman placed the tray upon a gilded bedside
table. 'That.'

'That! I've seen thin hair before, but never *fat* hair.'

'A slight problem with the old Hairobics. I didn't
exercise the follicles for a couple of days and their new
muscles have run to fat. I think I might sport a trilby
tonight. Cocked at a rakish angle. Morning, Claudia;
morning, Naomi.'

My female companions of the night before yawned
out their good mornings. Naomi put her teeth back in
and Claudia searched for her truss.

Norman sat down upon the bed.

'Gerroff!' cried a muffled voice.

'Sorry, Kate, didn't see you there.' Norman shifted
his bum. 'I've brought you these,' he said, handing me
some tablets.

'What are they?'

'Drugs, of course. I thought you might be getting a bit panicky by now. These will help.'

'Splendid.' I bunged the tablets into my mouth and washed them down with some water. 'Nothing I like better than drugs on an empty stomach.'

'Naomi just took her teeth out of that glass,' said Norman. 'But never mind. I've brought you the guest list. It would be really nice if you'd have another go at trying to remember who's who amongst the who's whos. Oh and I've just spoken with Lazlo Woodbine on the telephone. He says that he will be unmasking the murderer tonight. And that you probably won't recognize him, because he will be in disguise.'

'Why will he be in disguise?'

'To make it more exciting. So I don't want you to worry about anything. Everything's under control. The transportation for the celebs. The food, the drink, the drugs, the music, the decorations, the floor shows, the lot. All you have to do is be there. Everything is exactly how it should be.'

I sipped at my tea. No sugar. I spat out my tea. 'But will anyone actually come? I mean, the Doveston is dead, will people still want to come to his party?'

'Of course they will. And it was written on the invitations: "In the unlikely event of the host being blown into tiny pieces in a freak accident involving dynamite and catapult elastic, the party will definitely still go ahead. Bring bottle and bird. Be there or be square."'

'He certainly was a class act.'

'He was a regular Rupert.'

'Bear, or Brooke?'

266

'Bear,' said Norman. 'Definitely bear.'

Oh how we laughed. Well, it *was* a good 'un.

'Right then,' said Norman. 'That's enough of that. I have to go and make a few final adjustments to my peacock suit. You have another run through the guest list. Ta ta for now.' And with that said, he upped and left, slamming the door behind him.

I flung the portfolio onto the floor and myself on top of Naomi. I shagged and showered and shaved and shagged some more. And then I went down for my breakfast.

After breakfast, I inspected the great hall. Lawrence had finally completed his work and the vast Gothic room had been transformed into his personal vision of an oriental palace.

The ancient stone walls had been daubed a violent red, with Chinese characters crudely stencilled in yellow. Strings of plastic fruit – mandarin oranges and lychees – hung over the minstrels' gallery. A few balloons lay scattered about and a sign saying 'HAPPY NEW YEAR' had fallen down from above the doorway. Dangling from the central chandelier was something that I at first took to be a dead dog. On closer inspection this proved to be a Chinese dragon, imaginatively formed from sticky-backed plastic and Fairy Liquid bottles with their names blacked out.

Lawrence had gone a little over the five-hundred-pound budget. About one hundred and seventy-five thousand pounds over, according to his invoice.

I took up my mobile phone and tapped out a sequence of numbers. 'Hello,' I said. 'Rapscallion.

Masser Edwin here. Find Lawrence and kill him. Goodbye.'

The sun came out from behind a cloud and up on high the angels sang.

I won't bore the reader with the details of my day. You know what it's like when you're trying to organize a big party and you want everything to be 'just so'. You fuss over the silliest things. Should the Château-Lafite 1822 be served in champagne flutes or half-pint mugs? Big spoons or small spoons for *pâté de foie gras*, or just dig in with the fingers? What if the donkey you've hired for the floor show can't get a stiffy on? Will the monkeys' heads fit through the little holes you've had cut in the dining table? Does everybody's party bag have the same number of Smarties in it?

Throughout the afternoon, Norman maintained a vigilant position at the gates. I'd had him up the security at Castle Doveston. Inner fortifications had been built; pits dug and lined with bamboo spikes (painted over with invisible paint, so as not to spoil the look of the grounds). But I was still very worried. The Doveston's obsession with security had not been ill-founded, but they'd got to him and they might well get to me.

Norman was seeing to it that absolutely nothing that wasn't listed in the big portfolio got through the gates.

The Great Millennial Ball was no secret. News crews and crowds had once more formed about the perimeter fence, eager to view the arriving who's whos. Norman kept a careful eye on them.

Whenever I wasn't bothering the chef, the catering staff, the performers, the dwarves, my long-legged lady friends, the human ashtrays or the donkey, I found time to bother Norman.

'Watcha doing now?' I asked him.

'Bugger off,' said Norman. 'I'm busy.'

'What are those?' I pointed towards a convoy of long black lorries that was heading our way. Impressive-looking lorries they were, with blacked-out windscreens and the Gaia logo on their fronts.

Norman scratched at his head and then disentangled his fingers from his fat hair. 'Dunno,' he said. 'They're a bit of a mystery, actually. They're listed in the big portfolio and there are special parking places marked out for them in the grounds. But I've absolutely no idea what's inside them.'

'Perhaps it's the bouncy castles,' I suggested.

Norman made the face that says 'you twat'. 'I'm sure you're right,' he said. 'But now please bugger off.'

I buggered off.

'And bugger off from here too,' said the chef.

I buggered off to my bedroom.

I sat upon my bed and worried. I wasn't panicking too much, the drugs had seen to that. But I *was* worried. I was *déjà vu*ing all the time nowadays. And getting flashes of what was to come. I knew that something awful was going to occur, for, after all, I *had* glimpsed the future. But it was all so confused and I just couldn't get a grip on how things were going to happen.

As I sat there, memories returned to me. Memories

of another time, long long ago, when I had sat upon my bed before another party. The now legendary Puberty Party of 1963. That party had ended very badly for me and even more badly for my dear old dog, Biscuit. Biscuit had been blown to buggeration by the Doveston, now blown to buggeration himself.

How would this party end? Any better? I had my doubts.

I togged up in one of the Doveston's suits. During my few brief months of being very rich I'd managed to put on considerable weight. My own suits no longer fitted. The Doveston's did.

I chose a white Armani number, Thai silk with a Gaia-logo-patterned lining. A Hawaian shirt and a pair of open-toed sandals completed the dashing ensemble. I grinned at myself in the wardrobe mirror. 'You are one handsome son of a bitch,' I said.

At half past seven of the evening clock, there came a rapping at my chamber door.

'Come,' I called, striking a dignified pose.

The chamber door opened and in came Norman.

'Holy shit!' I said.

Norman did a little twirl. 'What do you think?' he asked.

I didn't know quite what to think. Norman's suit was simply stunning. It fitted in all the right places, but it did much more than this. It made Norman seem at least six inches taller, broader at the shoulders and a good deal slimmer at the waist. The suit was of blue, or it seemed to be blue; at certain angles it wasn't. At certain angles it came and it went and sometimes parts of it weren't there at all.

But stunning as it was (and it *was*), there was something about it I just didn't like. Something about it that frankly upset me. Something about it I actively hated.

Norman must have seen the look upon my face. 'Hang on,' he said. 'I'll turn it down a bit.' He pulled something resembling a TV remote control from his pocket and pressed a button or two. 'Like it a bit better now?' he asked.

I nodded. 'I do.'

'I don't know how I'm going to get around that particular problem,' said Norman. 'The suit is designed to make me irresistible to women. But the trouble is that it has the reverse effect on men. It makes me seem utterly obnoxious.'

'But it's an incredible suit, though. It makes you look taller and slimmer and broader at the shoulders. How does it do that?'

'Taller . . .' Norman lifted a trouser bottom to expose a platform shoe. 'Broader is the shoulder pads and as to slimmer, I just painted my belly and arse out with invisible paint.'

'It's all so simple when it's explained. So how do *I* look?'

'Well . . . um . . . er . . . we'd better be going downstairs now. The guests will soon be arriving.'

'You look a prat in that trilby,' I said.

The staff were already lined up in the great hall to greet the guests. I inspected the staff, saying things like, 'You look very smart,' and 'Do up that button,'

271

and 'Stand up straight,' and things like that.

The staff responded with polite smiles and whispered words behind the hands. I've no idea what these words were, but I'm sure that they were all complimentary.

Now, one of the major problems with holding a big celebrity bash is how to get the celebrities inside. Allow me to explain. You see, no real celebrity wants to be the first to arrive. It's not fitting to their status. It isn't cool. It makes them seem over-eager. It's just not done.

For many years this problem seemed insurmountable. At some really big celebrity bashes, no-one actually came inside the party at all. The celebs just sat about in the car park in their chaffeur-driven cars, patiently waiting for someone else to go in first. And eventually, when morning came, they went home.

This led, inevitably, to some ingenious host coming up with the idea of employing specially trained actors and actresses to play the parts of first guests. They would arrive right on time, climb from their limos, wave to the crowds and go in, thus encouraging the skulking celebs to do likewise.

It was a brilliant idea.

The trouble was that some of these specially trained actors and actresses began to become so famous for always being first at parties that they started getting all stuck up and saying that other actors and actresses should be employed to go in before *them*. And this was done and then the next bunch began demanding the same thing and so on and so forth and suchlike.

The result being that at some celebrity bashes there were no real celebrities at all, just bogus celebrities employed to arrive first and others employed to arrive before them, et cetera.

And if you've ever watched any of those big awards ceremonies on the TV, you'll know exactly what I'm talking about.

To avoid any such problems arising at his bash, the Doveston had engaged the services of a certain Colin Delaney Hughes.

Colin was a famous criminal and, as everybody knows, celebrities just *love* criminals. They love to be in the company of criminals. They love to wine and dine and dance at their nightclubs. Holiday with them at their Spanish villas and island retreats. Get involved in scandals with them when they need publicity to promote their latest movie or album.

Celebrities love criminals.

And criminals love celebrities.

So it all works out rather well.

Colin was retired now, but had been a particularly violent and merciless criminal in his day. Sawing people's faces off, gunning down the innocent, running drugs and generally getting up to mischief. As such, his autobiography had been eagerly snapped up by publishers and had become an international bestseller.

It had taken a big wodge of the folding stuff and two kilos of heroin to secure Colin's services as first arriving guest. But being the professional he was, he turned up sharp on the dot of eight, an Essex babe on either arm and a great big smile on his face.

I greeted him warmly and shook him by the hand.

'I'm very pleased to meet you,' I said.

And then I introduced him to Norman.

'Who d'you think you're looking at, you bastard?' said Colin.

And after Colin, in they came. The coaches pulled up outside the door and a steady stream of top-notch celebs filtered in, smiling and waving and loveying about and generally behaving as if they owned the place.

'What a pack of wankers,' I said to Norman.

'Bollocks,' the shopkeeper replied. 'You've buddied up with enough famous folk over the years. You're just bitter because this isn't really your party and you're afraid someone's going to murder you.'

'You're not wrong there,' I said.

'I rarely am. Here, look, there's Big-horny-beaver.'

'*Who?*'

'Sigourney Weaver. Watch while I go over and chat her up.'

Norman tottered off into the crowd. I shook more hands and offered more greetings.

There was an interesting pattern to the arrivals. Each giggling gaggle of the glittering glamorous would be followed by its negative counterpart. Grim-faced evening-suited company-chairman types, with well-dressed worn-down women on their arms. Among these, I felt, were the folk I had to fear.

I had already shaken hands with old silly-bollocks and what's-his-face, the other one. And the two fellows from the Colombian drugs cartel. The bald-headed woman who usually wore the wig had yet to arrive. As had the bloke who runs all those companies.

And if I just say the word 'jumpers' to you, you'll know the one I mean.

The great hall was filling up nicely now and everyone was rabbiting away. The catering staff were taking care of business: offering around bowls of snuff, trays of those canapé things that I'll never understand, drinks and more drinks and more drinks.

It occurred to me that no-one so far had thought to bring a bottle.

'I've brought a bottle,' said someone.

I glanced up to meet the golden smile of Professor Merlin.

'Professor,' I said. 'You look wonderful.'

And he *did* look wonderful. He hadn't aged by a day.

He cut a most fantastic figure. Powdered face and purple periwig; diamond ear-studs in his lobes and pearls upon the tips of his waxed moustachios. A velvet frock-coat in a whiter shade of pale. Silken trews and buckled shoes. His slender fingers weighed heavily with wonderful rings and his turquoise eyes twinkled merrily. 'Hello, young Edwin,' he said.

I wrung his hand between my own. 'I'm so glad you've come,' I said. 'I knew you were on the guest list, but I had no idea whether you were even still—'

'Alive?'

'Well . . .'

'I am, as you can see, alive as ever I was. And sprightly with it too.' He handed me a bottle wrapped in brown paper. 'Something rather special in there for you,' he said with a wink. 'Martian sherry. Picked it up upon my travels between the planets. I'll tell you all about them later, if you want. But for now I suppose I should get down to the job in hand.'

'The drinking?' I asked.

'The MCing, dear boy. The sadly departed Doveston had engaged me as Master of Ceremonies. Did you not know?'

I shook my head. 'I'm afraid that the big portfolio had a lot of very small print. I must have missed some of it.'

'Then as to the matter of my fee?'

'Charge whatever you like, I'm easy. Oh and, Professor, I have something of yours downstairs. A certain box, bound in human skin. I'm sure you'd like it back.'

'Like it back?' Professor Merlin laughed. 'The box was never mine in the first place. I think the Doveston bought it at a jumble sale. He asked me to weave a story around it to wind up young Norman. For reasons of his own, I suppose.'

'Yes,' I said. 'That certainly makes sense.'

'And isn't that the self-same Norman there in the trilby hat? Excuse me while I go and say hello.'

And with that he was gone into the crowd, leaving me to shake new hands and offer new hellos.

Now, one of the other problems with holding a big celebrity bash is the gatecrashers. There will always be certain other celebrities whom you haven't invited who feel it is their divine right to be there. And even with all the security I had, I felt sure that there'd be one or two of the buggers doing their best to sneak in. I'd ordered the guards to fire upon anyone they caught trying to scale the perimeter fence and already they'd managed to gun down David Bowie and Patsy Kensit. I had every confidence that by the end of the evening

276

the world would be free of Michael Jackson too.

'Hi,' said a squeaky voice. 'I'm sorry I'm late. I hope you don't mind, but I've brought Bubbles too.'

I grinned through gritted teeth. 'No problem at all, Michael,' I said. 'The chef will look after Bubbles.'

'He always has his own place at the table.'

'Michael,' I said. 'Bubbles will have his own place *in* the table.'

Norman came tottering over.

'Oooooh, hello,' said Michael. 'You look nice.'

Norman cleared his throat. 'Here,' he whispered to me. 'Did you see that? Did you see how I got on with Sigourney? I'm taking her out for lunch tomorrow.'

'I'm very impressed,' I said.

'That's nothing. Hey, look over there. It's Come-here-and-poke-my-bowels.'

'Who?'

'Camilla Parker-Bowles.'

'Norman,' I said. 'Although I find this a good deal more amusing than Brentford rhyming slang, my bet is that you won't be able to keep it up for very long.'

'I will you know. I'm on Viagra.'

Oh how we laughed.

Norman tottered off once more and then a voice said, 'Psst.'

'I'm not,' I said.

'No. Psst. Come over here.'

I turned to see Michael standing in an alcove and beckoning to me with his foolish glove.

Hello, I said to myself. What's this?

'Come over here and hurry.'

I sauntered over. 'What is it you want?' I asked.

'It's me,' said Michael.

'I know it's you,' I said.

'No. It's *me*. Lazlo.' And Lazlo lifted up a corner of his face. 'Lazlo Woodbine, private eye.'

'By God,' I said. 'You certainly had me fooled. You really are a master of disguise.'

Michael's face smiled crookedly. 'It's a bit of a cheat, really,' said Lazlo. 'The guards shot the real Michael trying to shin over the fence.'

'Then there is a God,' I said.

'The guards dumped his body in the woods. I couldn't resist the opportunity, so I sort of—'

'You sort of what?'

'Sort of flayed his body and put on his skin.'

'Thank goodness for that,' I said. 'I thought you were going to say something really disgusting.'

'How dare you! But listen, we must talk. I know who the murderer is. But I also know a lot more than that. It's a global conspiracy. The end of civilization as we know it is only a few hours away. The Secret Government of the World is going to take over, the minute all the computers crash. They've been planning it for years. We have to stop them.'

'Now hold on,' I said. 'Let's just flip back a bit here. Who is the murderer?'

'It doesn't matter about that.'

'It does. It really does.'

'It does *not*. What matters is that we warn everyone.'

'No no,' I said. 'What matters most is that you tell me who the murderer is.'

'That's not important, we—'

'It bloody *is* important. I'm paying your wages, you

bastard. Tell me who the murderer is and tell me now.'

'Oh all right,' said Lazlo. 'The murderer is . . .' And then he paused.

'Go on,' I said. 'The murderer is . . .'

'The murderer is . . .' And Lazlo clutched at his throat. 'Oh shit,' he said.

'O'Shit? Is that an Irish name?'

'Urgh,' gasped Lazlo. 'I've been shot in the throat with a poisoned dart.'

'Well, don't worry about that now. Just tell me the name of the murderer.'

But did he tell me?

Did he bugger.

He just dropped down dead on the floor.

22

Da de da de da de da de da de da de . . . thriller night.
Michael Jackson (lyric rights refused)

Now, you know that panicky feeling you get when you're hosting the biggest celebrity bash of the century and the party's hardly got started yet and the private detective you've hired to track down the killer of your bestest friend gets shot in the throat by a poisoned dart and he just happens to be wearing the skin of the world's most famous pop star?

You don't?

Well, no, I suppose it doesn't happen all *that* often.

Celebs were already beginning to stare. One of their own was down in a corner and this always draws a good crowd.

'Ooh-er,' they went, 'what's happened to Michael?'

'Michael's fine,' I told them. 'Michael's fine. He's just had too much brown ale. You know what he's like.'

I tried to lift Lazlo onto his feet. I don't know why. To pretend that he hadn't been shot in the throat by a poisoned dart, I suppose. You don't always behave altogether rationally under these circumstances.

I succeeded in getting him into a kneeling position. But my attempts at doing much more were being sorely hampered by Bubbles the chimp, who had become amorously involved with my left leg.

'Get off, you stupid ape,' I told him, kicking out and struggling. At which point Lazlo's head sort of toppled forward into my crotch and Michael's hair got all entangled with my belt buckle.

At which point the staring celebs began to applaud. Drawing an even bigger crowd.

Happily with Norman amongst it.

'Blimey,' said Norman. 'This is one for the album.'

'Don't just stand there,' I shouted. 'Give me a hand.'

'No thanks,' said Norman. 'It's not really my thing. And anyway, I've just got Camilla warmed up.'

'Come here, you bloody fool.'

Norman clip-clopped over on his stack-soled shoes.

'He's dead,' I whispered to him.

'Then there is a God.' And Norman laughed. 'What's really happened?'

'He's really dead, look at him. Get off me, Bubbles!'

'Really dead?' Norman gaped and gazed. 'Well, if he's really dead, then I think what you're doing to him is in very bad taste. And in front of all these people and everything.'

If I'd had a spare hand, I'd have clouted Norman with it. 'It isn't Michael Jackson,' I whispered, teeth all clenched and left leg kicking. 'It's Lazlo Woodbine.'

'Then he really *is* a master of disguise.'

'He's wearing Michael Jackson's skin.'

'Now hang about,' said Norman. 'Let's just get this straight.'

'I don't have time for that. For God's sake, help me shift him out of here.'

'The things I do for you,' said Norman. 'Come on then, let's lift him up.'

Now, all right. I know it wasn't Norman's fault. He was only trying to help. And I'm sure that if I'd been wearing big built-up shoes like his, I'd have found it difficult to keep *my* balance. And matters weren't improved any by that damned chimp who was humping away at my leg and the fact that Michael's hair was still all tangled up in my belt buckle.

Norman sort of tugged at Lazlo's shoulders. Norman sort of tugged, then sort of toppled. And he elbowed me right in the face and I sort of fell backwards into the crowd, bringing Michael's headskin with me and this sort of ended up in my lap like a big hairy sporran. And Lazlo's body sort of slumped over, with his head all sort of gory and Bubbles sort of freaked out and went sort of berserk.

Sort of.

It was the first major embarrassment of the evening.

And it really took some explaining away, I can tell you.

I let Norman do it.

I dragged the body outside and stood about freezing my million-dollar nuts off. Finally Norman joined me. He was in a right old strop.

'You stupid bastard!' he shouted.

'What?'

'Is there something you'd like to say to me?'

'Thanks for sorting out the situation?'

'No. Not that.' Norman stamped his foot and nearly broke his ankle.

'If it's about me leaving the top off your iodine bottle—'

'No. It's not about that. I've just been on the walkie-talkie to the guards at the gate.'

'Ah,' I said.

'Yes, ah. You ordered the guards to shoot anyone who tried to climb over the fence. And they've just shot Jeffrey Archer.'

'Then there is a God.'

'It's no laughing matter. Have you gone completely mad? You can't have famous people killed. This isn't France, you know.'

'Eh?'

'I mean, it's all right with Michael.'

'It is?'

'Of course it is. I can rebuild *him*. He's mostly made out of Meccano anyway.'

'Allegedly,' I said. 'Allegedly.'

'I've ordered the guards to put away their guns. Before someone who matters gets hurt. So what have you done with the body?'

'I rolled it under that big black lorry over there.'

'We'd better have a look at it.'

'Why?'

'To search for clues, of course. If Lazlo was shot with a blow-dart, then we'll have forensic evidence. You have to put the flight of the dart in your mouth when you blow it. So there'll be traces of saliva

283

and we can get DNA from those.'

'And?'

'And then all we have to do is get DNA samples from every guest present and we can identify the killer.'

I looked at Norman.

And he looked at me.

'Right,' said Norman. 'OK. Forget that. But let's have a look at the dart anyway.'

'Here you go then,' I said. 'Careful you don't prick yourself.'

'Oh. You've already had a look at it.'

'Of course I bloody have. And see what's on the end.'

Norman held up the dart and examined it by the light that fell from one of the great hall windows. 'Lipstick,' he said. 'Pale green lipstick.'

'Sprout green,' I said. 'From the Snuff for Women allotment range. Very expensive.'

'All right then, time for action.' Norman flung the dart aside, nearly catching me one in the cobblers. 'All we have to do is find the woman who's wearing this lipstick.'

'That's all *you* have to do. I'm not going back in there without at least six bodyguards.'

'Don't be such a woosie. If she'd wanted to kill you, she could easily have done it. It was Lazlo she murdered. Did he say anything to you before he died?'

'Only some old rubbish about the end of civilization as we know it being only a few hours away and the Secret Government of the World taking over the minute all the computers crash.'

'Of course,' said Norman. 'That has to be it. The

Doveston was always going on about the secret police being out to get him. It seems he was right. An interview with this woman should prove most instructive.'

'She might not be too keen to tell us anything.'

'There are ways,' said Norman.

'Oh, right. You mean we should torture it out of her. Good idea.'

'No! That is *not* what I mean at all.'

'What then?'

Norman preened at his lapels. 'Leave this to the man in the peacock suit,' said he.

I followed the man in the peacock suit back into the ball.

'Oh look,' said Norman, 'It's You'll-lick-a-giant's-one.'

'Hold on,' I said. 'I'll get this. You'll-lick-a-giant's-one? Don't give me any clues. Yes, I've got it. You'll-lick-a-giant's-one. Ulrika Jonsson.'

'No,' said Norman. 'It's Kate Moss. I was just thinking out loud that time.'

Norman cranked up the Hartnell Home Happyfier a couple of notches, set his peacock suit on stun and swaggered off into the crowd, going, 'Whoops,' and 'S'cuse me please,' and 'Mind your backs,' and 'Sorry, did I step on your foot?'

I snorted up a couple of lines from the head of a passing dwarf and determined that I would get right into the party spirit, no matter what. If I wasn't on the immediate hit list, then at least I could enjoy myself. I was the host of this bash after all, so I should be having a bloody good time. Let Norman sort it out.

I would party.

And so, with a hooter full of Charlie and a big fat smile on my face, I squeezed myself into the happy throng.

I grinned at Caprice, leered at a couple of Spice Girls, smiled warmly on Joanna Lumley (you have to remember my age), tipped the wink to Tom and Nicole, roundly ignored Hugh and Liz and stepped over a *Blue Peter* presenter.

And then I ran into Colin.

'Having a good time?' I asked him.

'Damn right, old son,' said Colin, slapping me upon the back and loosening several vertebrae. 'How about you? Enjoying yourself?'

'I am,' I said. 'And I'm determined that nothing will spoil this party for me.'

'Good on you,' said Colin. 'The last time I was at a party as good as this was back in 'sixty-three. Someone blew up the host's dog with dynamite. Oh how we laughed.'

'Excuse me,' I said. 'I have to mingle.'

'Be happy,' said Colin.

Actually I didn't mingle. I just drifted about, listening in to other people's conversations.

Have you ever noticed how, when you do that, the snippets of conversation you hear always begin with the words 'so I said'?

'. . . so I said to Val Parnell, "If my name doesn't go above the jugglers, I will not appear."'

'. . . so I said, "I don't like the look of you, young man." And he said, "Can I smell your armpits?" And I said, "Certainly not!" And he said, "Oh, it must be your feet then."'

'. . . so I said, "I'll tell you my wife's favourite sexual position. Next door, that's what."'

'. . . so I said to the police that actually I didn't know I'd been raped until the cheque bounced.'

'. . . so I said, "I'll meet you at that new naturist restaurant. You know the one, it's called Eat Your Food Nude."'

'. . . so I said, there were these two sperms swimming along and one says to the other, "Are we at the fallopian tubes yet?" And the other one says, "No, we're hardly past the tonsils."'

'. . . so I said, that's because you don't understand how the Secret Government of the World functions. Conventional governments think that they'll be able to control the chaos caused by the Millennium Bug. But what they don't know is that their own systems have been sabotaged. Agents of the Secret Government have been infiltrating them for years, pretending to solve the problem, whilst actually making it worse.

'Revolution in any country is only three square meals away and when the infrastructure collapses and food no longer reaches the shop shelves, there will be a world crisis. And that's when the Secret Government will take over. They've been planning it for years, because they know what's going to happen. And you know what they say: "Tomorrow belongs to those who can see it coming."'

Now, I paused quite abruptly when I caught this particular snippet. 'Er, excuse me,' I said, easing my way into the little knot of chatterers. 'Do you mind if I join you?'

The chap who'd been speaking eyed me suspiciously. Which I thought was a bit of a cheek, considering that it was *my* party. He was young and pale and drawn and rather spotty. He wore a ragged T-shirt with the words 'FAST AND BULBOUS' printed on the front, grubby old trainers and baggy old jeans. I did not recall greeting him at the door.

'What do you want?' he asked, in a manner that could only be described as surly.

'I overheard what you were saying about the Secret Government.'

'But I'll bet you don't believe it.'

'On the contrary, I do. But what I'd like to know is where you got your information from.'

'Who are you?'

'I'm the host of this party.'

'Oh shit. Then I suppose you'll be throwing me out.'

'Why would I want to do that?'

'Because I just sneaked in through a hole in the fence.'

'It's OK,' I said. 'I don't mind. I just want to know about the Secret Government. Who are *you*, by the way?'

'I'm Danbury Collins.'

'Not *the* Danbury Collins?'

'The very same.'

I almost reached out to shake his hand. Almost.

For the benefit of any readers who are not acquainted with the name of Danbury Collins, allow me to explain that he is the famous psychic youth and masturbator, whose exploits, along with those of Sir John Rimmer and Dr Harney, are chronicled in the fantasy novels of P. P. Penrose.

And P. P. Penrose, as you *all will* know, was the author of the best-selling books of the twentieth century: the Lazlo Woodbine thrillers. Small world!

'But what are *you* doing here?' I asked the psychic youth.

'I got a tip-off that something big was going to happen.'

'And who tipped you off?'

'I'd rather not say.'

'Was it Lazlo Woodbine?'

'I'd rather not say.'

'Fair enough,' I said. 'But just tell me one thing. Do you think the Secret Government murdered the Doveston?'

'No I don't,' said Danbury.

'Oh.'

'Because I don't believe that the Doveston's dead.'

'Trust me,' I said. 'I've seen the body. He is dead.'

'Seeing the body doesn't mean anything. People saw Elvis's body, but Elvis isn't dead.'

'I think you'll find that Elvis *is* dead,' I said.

'Oh yeah? So who's that over there chatting up the singing nun?'

'Chatting up *who*?'

'Oh no, it's Giant Haystacks. I think my eyesight's going.'

I peered in the direction of his pointing. 'Ah,' I said.

'Precisely,' said Danbury. 'When you're really really famous, being dead doesn't have to mean that you actually *are* dead. Not if you're in cahoots with the Secret Government. They can arrange anything. Elvis entered a parallel universe in order to save mankind from the Antichrist. I thought everybody knew that.'

'Yeah, right,' I said. 'Then just tell me this. If you're wrong about the Doveston and he really is dead, who do you think could have murdered him?'

Danbury made a thoughtful face and stuck his hands into his baggy jean pockets. 'Come over here,' he said, beckoning me towards an alcove with a nifty elbow-gesture.

I followed him over and to my credit I hardly laughed at all when he smacked his head on an invisible suit of armour.

'Now listen,' he whispered. 'If the Doveston really is dead, it can mean only one thing. That he defied the Secret Government. That they approached him, tried to enlist him, and he refused them.'

'That sounds plausible. He was very much his own man.'

'Well, that wouldn't suit the Secret Government. They're into total control.'

'But who *are* these people who run this Secret Government?'

Danbury shrugged. 'You perhaps. How would I know?'

'You know they exist.'

'Everyone knows they exist. People just won't own up to the fact. Look around you, what do you see?'

I looked around. 'Lots of rich and famous people.'

'And how come they got to be rich and famous?'

'Because they're more talented than other people?'

Danbury looked at me.

And I looked back at Danbury.

'No, OK,' I said. 'Forget that.'

'It's all a conspiracy,' said Danbury. 'Everything's a conspiracy. The only people who get on in this world are the ones with the right connections. And when original thinkers come along, what happens to them? Either they vanish without trace, or they get sucked into the fame system and end up turning out pap for their masters. They take the money and sell out.'

'To the Secret Government.'

'Ultimately. Most of them don't know that. But actors can only work when they're offered scripts and rock stars soon find themselves back on the dole if they play up too much.'

'They all behave badly.'

'Perk of the job. But the products they turn out are all strictly "safe". They don't invite rebellion. They don't stir up the masses. They maintain the status quo.'

'I've heard all this stuff before,' I said. 'Mostly from people who've failed to make it big.'

'I'm not trying to convince you,' said Danbury. 'But let me tell you this: the one thing the Secret Government, or any other government, fears more than anything else is information. The free exchange of information. And with the World Wide Web and information technology, ideas can be passed around the world in seconds. And that's why it's all going down tonight. When the systems crash because of the Millennium Bug, there will be no more exchanging of information. Unless you own a carrier pigeon, of course.'

'And you really believe that this is going to happen?'

'We'll soon find out, won't we?'

'But if it is true, then we should do something about it.'

'And what would you suggest?'

'I don't know. Tell people. Get it all on the World Wide Web.'

'It's on the Web,' said Danbury. 'There are thousands of conspiracy pages on the Web. Many put there by the Secret Government to confuse the situation further. There is no way of stopping what's going to happen. Well, there's one way, but as that can't be arranged, there's really no way.'

'What would the one way be?'

'Assemble all the members of the Secret Government in one big room and then blow the lot of them to kingdom come.'

'Not very likely.'

'Although . . .'

'Although *what*?'

'Well, you'll laugh when I tell you. But something really obvious has just occurred to me.'

'Go on.'

'Well, it's . . .' Danbury's right hand was moving in his trouser pocket.

'Go on!'

'It's . . .'

Something whistled past my ear and Danbury's left hand clutched at his throat.

And was that something a poisoned dart?

Well, yes of course it was.

And did Danbury manage to blurt out the really obvious thing that had occurred to him?

Did he bugger!

23

'Tis pretty for an afternoon box, I grant you. But one
would never take it out to dine.
Beau Brummell (1778–1840), on his snuffbox collection

I didn't panic.

I could have, but I didn't.

I was far too angry this time. I'd had sufficient. I
mean to say, one cold-blooded murder at your party is
bad enough. But two! That's really taking the piss.

I glanced about in search of the assassin. But none was
to be found standing conveniently by holding a blow-
pipe in one hand whilst waving to me with the other.

Folk were gaily dancing now to the music of the
mariachi band upon the minstrels' gallery. Everyone
seemed to be having a jolly good time.

Everyone but me.

But I didn't panic. No. I was angry, but I was cool. I
was *so* cool. Do you know what I did? Well, I'll tell you
what I did. I dragged Danbury to his feet. Danced him
over to the invisible suit of armour. And then rammed his
body into the back of it. Pretty damn cool, eh?

And if you've ever tried to ram a corpse into the
back of an invisible suit of armour, you'll know that it
can be pretty tricky.

Especially if the corpse is sporting an erection.

Then I went searching for Norman.

I was angry with Norman.

The shopkeeper wasn't hard to find. He was doing the Twist. All on his own. But being cheered on by a circle of adoring females. I thrust my way through this circle, much to their annoyance.

'Norman! You twat!' I shouted at him.

Norman flapped his fingers at me. 'Go away,' he shouted back. 'I've got these women eating out of my hand. Look at Tear-apart-my-two-limbs-son.'

'Who?'

'Tara Palmer-Tomkinson.'

It wasn't bad, but I wasn't in the mood.

'Norman!' I shouted. 'It's happened again!'

'Then put some more iodine on it.'

I made fists at Norman. Much to the horror of the womenfolk.

'Stop dancing,' I shouted. 'There's been another murder.'

'Oh,' and Norman stopped dancing.

'Aaaaaaaaaaw,' went the womenfolk. 'Dance some more for us, Norman.'

'Switch your bloody suit off,' I told him.

Norman did so, grudgingly.

The womenfolk lost interest in Norman. They sort of coughed politely and drifted away and I stopped hating Norman quite so much.

'Another murder, you say?' he said.

'Danbury Collins.'

'Danbury Collins?'

'Danbury Collins.'

Norman lifted his trilby and scratched at his head. 'No,' he said. 'I don't get that one. Do you want to give me a clue?'

I shook Norman by his smart lapels. 'It's not one of your stupid name-pun things. It's the victim's real name. Danbury Collins.'

'Not *the* Danbury Collins?'

'The very same.'

'Not the one who's always . . .' Norman mimed the appropriate wrist actions.

'He was doing it when he died.'

'It's how he would have wanted to go.'

I couldn't disagree with that.

'But dip my dick in Duckham's,' said Norman. 'Lazlo Woodbine *and* Danbury Collins on the same night. If P. P. Penrose were alive today, he'd be turning in his grave.'

'Listen,' I yelled at Norman, 'we can't waste any more time. We have to find this murdering—'

And the music of the mariachis ended.

'—*bitch!*'

It was quite amazing, the way my voice carried right around the momentarily silent hall. And as for the way that all heads turned in my direction . . .

That was quite amazing too.

It was the second major embarrassment of the evening. And it was early yet.

'Nice one,' whispered Norman. 'Very 1990s. Very PC.'

And then *clash* went some cymbals, sparing Norman a walloping.

'Boom shanka,' came a voice from on high, the

voice of Professor Merlin. Heads turned and tilted. The ancient showman stood upon the balcony rail of the minstrels' gallery, arms flung wide and long fingers wiggling.

'Boom shanka boom boom boom,' cried the oldster. 'I am Professor Merlin and I welcome you to the Great Millennial Ball.'

The crowd, well-fuelled on drink and drugs and all loved-up by the Hartnell Home Happyfier, roared approval and clap–clap–clapped.

'I hate that old bugger,' said Norman.

I displayed my fist. 'As soon as he's finished, we search for the murdering you-know-what.'

'Dearly beloved,' said Professor Merlin, folding his hands as in prayer. 'We are gathered here tonight in the presence of this recherché décor . . .' He gestured towards Lawrence's dangling dog-dragon thing and the crowd guffawed aplenty. 'We are here', the professor continued, 'to celebrate the birth of a new millennium. But also to celebrate the life of a most remarkable man. You knew him as the King of the Corona. The Grandee of the golden leaf. The Caesar of the ciggie. The Rajah of the roll-up. He was the Saxe-Coburg-Gotha of the small cigar. He was the Sheik of snout. I speak to you, of course, of Mr Doveston.'

Clap, clap and whistle went the crowd.

And cheer, also.

'You' – Professor Merlin raised a forefinger and swung it about to encompass all – 'you folk are the great folk. The rulers and makers of men. The lords of high office. The grand muck-a-mucks. The captains of industry. The fair maidens of fashion.' Professor Merlin bowed gallantly. 'You are the stars of the silvery screen. You are the thespians. You are the musicians. You, my dear friends, are the business.'

More cheering and clapping and whistling too.

'And so you are deserving of an entertainment.' Professor Merlin snapped his fingers and a glittering yo-yo appeared in his hand.

'Ooooooooooooooooh,' went the crowd, most impressed.

'Easy trick,' muttered Norman. 'I could do that.'

Professor Merlin twinkle-eyed the mosaic of faces beneath him and then sent the yo-yo skimming above. It sparkled like a gemstone as he whisked it in mighty arcs out to the left and the right.

'Piece of piss,' muttered Norman.

'On this night of nights,' called the professor, 'on this final moment of our age, I shall present a special entertainment. An amusement. A frippery. A bit of fol de rol—

'To bewitch and bewilder, beguile and amuse.
To instruct and construct and perhaps to bemuse.
Will you see what you're seeing?
Or hear what you hear?
Will you say to yourself
This is all rather queer?
Does it mean what it says?
Does it say what it means?
Is he bashing the bishop
Or straining the greens?'

And he danced his yo-yo through a dazzling series of

298

tricks which naturally included the ever-popular 'stuffing the stoat'. As well as 'porking the penguin', 'furtling the flounder' and 'giving the gibbon a gobble'.

'You can't do *that*,' I said to Norman.

'I'm not altogether sure I'd want to.'

'Now be mindful, my friends,' said Professor Merlin, 'because the swiftness of the hand deceives the eye.' And he flung his yo-yo once more over the crowd. And lo and behold, it just wasn't there. 'The more you see,' the old man said, 'the more you think you know.'

And then he clapped his hands. 'Come, carpets, cushions and kilims,' he called. 'Come cosset and comfy our cool congregation.'

From all sides of the great hall came serving folk, members of the catering staff, baldy-headed lady dwarves and those littlest-said-about-them-the-better human ashtrays. They carried carpets and cushions and kilims and they walked about amongst the guests, setting these down on the flagstoned floor.

'Please be seated,' called the showman. 'Sit ye down, oh yes indeedy do.'

With general hilarity all round, and with much trouser-knee-adjustment from the men and tight-skirt-bottom-wriggling from the women, the party guests set to settling down on the out-spread rugs and comfy cushions.

'I think I'll just nip off to the bog now,' said Norman.

'No you bloody won't. Just sit down here until he's finished.'

Norman sat.

And I sat.

Sit sit sit.

'Now,' cried Professor Merlin. 'As you watch and marvel at our show, why not tuck a little tucker into your laughing gear? Dine upon delicacies, Nirvana to the nasal parts and positively paradisical to the palate. Vivacious viandes. Magical morsels. Tantalizing titbits. Knock-out nosebag. Johnny B. Goode, by golly.'

And once more he clapped his hands.

There came a fanfare from the mariachi men and beneath the minstrels' gallery, to the rear of the invisible pillars, the door that led to the kitchens opened and out strode the famous chef.

> He clapped together hands of his own,
> And swung on a polished heel.
> And he called to his waiting waiters,
> To bring on the marvellous meal.

'Get a move on, you fuckwits,' he called.

And out from the kitchen marched the waiters, looking every bit the way that waiters should. They had crisp white shirts and smart dickie-bows and sleek tail-coats and slicked-back hair with killer sideburns. And they were all gym-trained and Club-Med-tanned and they all had those 'rose-for-the-lovely-lady?' eyes.

'Fuckwits to a man,' whispered Norman.

Oh, but what they carried on their burnished silver trays. What toothsome taste-bud ticklers. What choice and chewsome chomperies. As the waiters moved amongst the party guests, bowing with their trays to offer up their bounty, the professor called down from on high and pointed to the platters as each passed beneath him.

'Lo and behold,' he called. 'A beano, a beanfeast, a banquet. A Saranapalian swallow-me-down. An Epicurean eat-'em-up. Lo and behold and look you there,' and he pointed. 'Fillet mignon of *Alytes obstreticans*, lightly fried in Ranidae miluh and served upon a bed of *Taraxacum*.'

'Sounds delicious,' I said.

Norman made a face. 'If you happen to like midwife toad, cooked in frog's milk and bunged on a bunch of dandelion leaves.'

'Some of these foreign dishes do lose a bit in the translation, don't they?'

'Hmmph,' went Norman, waving a waiter away.

The professor continued to point and proclaim, naming each dish that passed beneath him and loudly extolling its virtues.

To which Norman added his clever-Dick-I-did-languages-at-Grammar-school translations.

I passed on the lungs and the livers and lights. The bollocks of boar and the wildebeest's whangers. The monkey's brains, although fresh and piping hot (and Bubbles's looked particularly tasty in the fresh Crad sauce) didn't thrill me at all.

Not that I wasn't hungry.

Actually, I was starving.

But, well . . .

When you have so many wonderful things to choose from, you hardly know where to start. Eventually I did make up my mind. I decided to keep it simple. Nothing rich, that might be likely to 'repeat'. Good, wholesome, plain old down-home cooking.

'Beans on toast, sir?' the waiter asked.

'No thanks, mush,' I told him. 'I'll have the Rocky Mountain oysters, the belly-cut of long pig and the sheep's vagina, stewed in its own special juices. Oh and a pint of Château-Lafite 1822 and put it in my personal pewter tankard.'

Class act, or what?

I do have to say that I got quite a kick out of watching the party guests tuck in. It was a real joy to see top-notch gourmets trenchering it down. I perused them as they picked prettily at penis pasties and pork-sword pilaffs and popped portions of their preferred provender onto proffered plates.

Pretty much all Ps there again, by my reckoning.

'What are you having, Norman?' I asked.

'Just the beans on toast for me.'

'Something wrong with the other stuff?'

'Heavens no,' said Norman, 'perish the thought. It's just that I'm not very hungry. I think I ate too much elephant's dongler for tea.'

Now, whilst all the face-filling was in progress, things had been happening beneath the minstrels' gallery. A small stage had been erected, with a row of footlights and painted background scenery.

We were somewhere into the sixth or seventh course when the cymbals clashed and the voice of Professor Merlin was once more to be heard.

'Boom shanka boom boom boom,' it went. 'You dine and you sup. Let sweet champagne be danced around and let the lights be dimmed a tad and soft the music play.'

Then every damn light in the hall went out and we were left in the dark.

But not for long. The footlights glowed; the stage shone bright. Professor Merlin strode onto it. He struck up a noble splay-legged pose, his hands upon his hips. The mariachis played a sweet refrain and the professor said simply, 'Let our show begin.'

And then there was a flash, a puff of smoke and he was gone.

'I could do that too,' whispered Norman.

Now, what followed next was undoubtedly the most extraordinary piece of theatre that I have ever witnessed. It was ludicrous, though laudable. Absurd, yet absolutist. It was wacky, but wise. It was zany, but Zen. It was monstrous strange, and I fear that we will not see the like of it ever again.

'Om,' called the voice of Professor Merlin. 'Om,' it called once more. 'Om, which is the sacred syllable of the Most High. Typifying the triumvirate of Gods. Brahma, Vishnu and Siva. Birth, life and death. For our playlet comes to you in these three vital parts. The stuff of which we all are made. We're born. We live. We're cast away. Behold the Boy.'

We beheld the Boy. He rose up in the midst of us from beneath a rug, where he'd lain in wait. We applauded the Boy's appearance. We applauded loud and long.

For this boy was undoubtedly a Principal Boy. This boy was played by a girl. A beautiful girl, as it happened. Young and tender-limbed and slender. Wide of mouth and eye. Some toffs amongst the crowd wolf-whistled and did their Terry-Thomas 'well, hellloooooos'.

The Boy moved slowly through the crowd. Slowly on shuffling feet. Wearily he climbed onto the stage. Turned to face the audience, offered up a sigh, suggestive of a day's hard labours done. Then gave a long languid yawn.

Which set Norman off. I mimed a fist to the face.

The Boy settled down upon the stage. He wore rags and had nothing to cover him. He seemed pretty down upon his luck.

However, no sooner was he asleep than he began to dream and we were treated to a lavishly presented dream sequence with sparkly fairy folk flittering round and a big fat angel in a liberty bodice and wellington boots, who took a shine to the Boy and showered him with shimmering dust.

'Would this be the ludicrous yet laudable bit?' Norman asked.

The voice of Professor Merlin spoke. 'A gift is given. A gift is received,' is what I think it said.

Now, as far as I can make out, the basic story went like this. There is this little boy and he's given something special by an angel in a dream. We don't know what this special something is, but it must be really special, because everyone he meets wants to snatch it away from him.

First up is this sort of wicked uncle chap. He wears a black turban and has a painted-on beard and bad breath. The bad breath business got a lot of laughs, as did the posturing of this wicked uncle chap, who tries and tries again to bully the special something away from the Boy.

We jeer and catcall and roundly boo this uncle.

Then there is this group of good-time Charlies. They pretend to be chums of the Boy. But we all know what they're after. They get the Boy drunk, but he won't part with his special something and the good-time Charlies caper about and bump into the invisible pillars and fall down a lot. And we laugh.

Then we get to the real baddy. The Evil Prince. The Evil Prince has a stonking great palace, with hand-maidens and his own full-size indoor crazy golf course and everything.

His approach to the Boy is more subtle.

He invites the Boy into his palace. Lets him play a round of crazy golf for free. And gives the Boy presents and makes a big fuss of him and pats his head a lot.

The harem scene made the show for me. I thought I knew of every inconceivable permutation of man and beast and fowl and fish that there was to know. And, after all, I had seen all those video tapes of cabinet ministers doing what comes so naturally to them, within the walls of Castle Doveston.

I was impressed.

And just a little horny.

I won't recount the details here, because they're not really relevant to the plot of the play. But trust me on this, it was INCREDIBLE.

So, anyhow. The Boy, having given his all in the harem orgy, and got a fair bit in return, offers the special something (which he has somehow managed to hang on to even whilst doing that weird thing with the trout) to the Evil Prince. He gives it to him as a present for being so kind.

And, without a by-your-leave, or even a kiss-my-elbow, the Boy is seized by the palace guards, dragged beyond the walls, given a sound duffing up and left for dead.

We all boo a lot at this. Although we do agree that the Boy has been a trifle foolish in trusting that Evil Prince.

The Boy then falls into a bit of a coma and the fat angel comes back and puts the wellington boot in. But then the fat angel forgives the Boy and bungs him what seems to be a bag of magic dust.

In the final scene, the Boy returns to the palace. The Evil Prince is enjoying a right royal blow-out and laughing himself stupid, because he now owns the special something.

But the Boy springs up from under the table and flings the magic dust from his bag onto a candle flame. There is a bloody big bang, a good deal of smoke and when this finally clears, we see that everyone in the palace is dead. Except for the Boy, who has somehow miraculously survived.

He takes a big bow, receives a bunch of flowers and the show is over.

Apart, of course, from the rest of the bowing. We all boo the wicked uncle and the good-time Charlies and the Evil Prince and we cheer the fat angel and the flittering fairies and again the Boy.

And that's that.

Well, almost that.

Professor Merlin appears to great applause. He climbs onto the stage and he bows. He makes a very brief speech of thanks and then he takes out his snuff-box. It's the slim silver number, shaped like a coffin. He taps three times upon the lid, for Father, Son and Holy Ghost, then he takes up snuff and pinches it to his nostrils.

And then he lets fly with a very big *aaah-choo*! The cymbals clash a final time. There is a flash and a puff of smoke.

And there he is, gone.

Vanished.

24

Aaah-choo!
Bless you.
                    Trad.

The riotous applause and cheering died away. The
footlights dimmed, the hall's lights glowed again. On
cue came the waiters, bearing trays of sweetmeats.
Cheesy things and chocolates. Cognac and cheroots.
Strawberries in crack and schooners of absinthe and
mescal.

The mariachi band struck up once more and folk
jigged and wriggled, but few made the effort to climb
to their feet and dance. They were all bloated and not
a little stoned.

'Well, that was a load of old toot,' said Norman.

'Come off it,' I said. 'It was brilliant.'

'So what did it all mean, then?'

I made expansive gestures.

'You haven't the foggiest,' said Norman. 'I did like
the donkey, though.'

'Well, I'm going to say thanks a lot to Professor
Merlin. I wonder where he went.'

'Gone,' said Norman. 'Off'd it. A big aaah-choo and
goodbye to everyone.'

'What's the time?' I asked.

Norman tugged a fob watch from his pocket. It had more than the hint of Meccano about it. 'A quarter to twelve,' he said. 'Doesn't time just fly when you're enjoying yourself?'

'OK.' I stood up and squared my shoulders and then I did that breathing in deeply through the nose and out again through the mouth thing that people do before they take on something big.

A bungee jump, perhaps. Or a leap through a ring of fire on a motorbike.

Or even a daring dive from the top of a waterfall. Or a sabre charge on horseback into the mouths of the Russian guns at Sebastopol.

Or—

'What are you doing?' asked Norman.

'Preparing myself for the big one.'

'I've no wish to hear about your bowel movements.'

I showed Norman my fist again and mimed repeated violent blows. 'Biff biff biff,' I said. 'And Norman's out for the count.'

Norman rolled his eyes and got to his feet. 'OK,' he said. 'I know what we have to do. Find the woman with the green lipstick. If she has any green lipstick left. She's probably smeared it all off, pushing porcupine's peckers down her gob.'

'I never knew there were porcupine's peckers.'

'Yeah, well, there were only a few left. I had most of them at lunchtime.'

'Come on,' I said to Norman. 'Crank up your peacock suit and let's get this done. I'll feel a lot better about ringing in the New Year once we've grabbed this

309

woman, tied her up and bunged her in the cellar.'

'Fair enough.' Norman tinkered with his remote control. 'This lad's on the blink,' he said, shaking it about. 'I think some of the circuits have come unstuck.' He gave the delicate piece of equipment several hearty thumps. 'That's got it,' he said.

'Right then.' I explained to Norman the cunning strategy that I felt we should employ. It was simple, but it would prove effective. All we had to do, I told him, was to shuffle nonchalantly amongst the lolling guests in a manner that would arouse no hint of suspicion, and bid each of the womenfolk a casual how-d'you-do whilst having a furtive peer at their lipstick. Then whichever one of us found her would simply shout across to the other: 'Here's the murdering bitch,' and together we'd make the citizen's arrest.

Whatever could go wrong with a strategy like that?

Nothing.

Also, I felt that doing it this way would give me the opportunity to chat up some of the top notch totty and perhaps see myself all right for a bunk-up to bring in the New Year.

It was only fair. It was *my* party.

'Go on,' I said to Norman. 'Off you go.'

Norman went off, going how-d'you-do, and I went off, doing likewise.

'How-d'you-do,' I went, 'enjoying the party?

'Hope everything's OK.

'Please don't stub your cigar butts on the floor. Kindly use the human ashtrays provided.

'A little more Charlie with your strawberries, your Royal Highness?'

And so on and so forth and suchlike.

I thought we were doing rather well, actually. We were quartering the hall, moving in almost orchestrated shuffling zig-zag parallels not altogether unlike a combination of Rommell's now legendary pincer movement and the ever-popular 'Hokey Cokey'.

I rather hoped we'd be doing that later. Along with 'Knees Up Mother Brown' and the 'Birdy Song'. They really make the party go with a whizz in my opinion.

I suppose I must have how-d'you-do'd my way through at least fifty women before I chanced to glance across to see how Norman was doing. He appeared to be doing rather well, by all accounts. For where all my how-d'you-dos had ended with me shuffling on alone, Norman's hadn't. It seemed that all the women Norman had how-d'you-do'd to were now following him.

They trailed along behind in a giggling all-girl conga line.

I sighed and shook my head and did some more how-d'you-dos. I was getting rather fed up with how-d'you-dos, as it happened. So I thought I'd switch to hi-hello-theres, just to liven things up.

Mind you, I don't know why I even bothered with any pleasantries at all. None of the well-heeled, well-fed, well-sloshed, well-stoned women even showed the faintest interest in me.

I was well pissed off, I can tell you.

I mean to say, this was *my* party and they were scoffing *my* grub and getting pissed on *my* booze and spacing themselves out on *my* dope. The least that one of these stuck-up tarts could have done was to offer me a blow-job.

But did any of them?

Did they bugger!

I thought I'd slip into Irish mode. Women always go for Irish blokes. It's their charm and the melody of their language. Or it's the hint of danger about them. Or it's something else about them. But I reckon it's the accent.

Well, I thought it was worth a try.

'Top of the morning to you,' I said to Ma'll-yell-if-you-thrust-it-up.[1]

She looked strangely unimpressed.

But her boyfriend looked rather upset.

'Bugger off, you bog-trotting loon,' was what he had to say.

I leaned low in his direction. I recognized him immediately. He was that honourable literary chap, Old-Hairy-fat-prick.[2]

'Off about your business,' he drawled. 'Or I'll know the reason why.'

I stared the fellow eye to eye and then I head-butted him straight in the face. Well, it had been a long and trying day.

Old Hairy fell back in a crumpled heap and I smiled over to Ma'll-yell. 'Fainted,' I said. 'Too much brown ale. You know what he's like.'

I shuffled off some more.

[1] Work it out for yourself.
[2] Ernest Hemingway?

And then, do you know what, out of the blue it just hit me. I suddenly paused and thought, What am I doing here? I mean, *what* am I doing here? (Not what am I doing *here*?)

I thought, bloody Hell, I know what I'm doing here.

I'm shuffling!

Shuffling. I hadn't shuffled for years. But here I was doing it now. I was shuffling about amongst all these rich folk. These *really really famous folk*. A complete stranger. Someone who didn't belong here at all.

I was a shuffler, me. Always had been, always would be. All the wealth I'd been left by the Doveston couldn't change what was really inside. I was just a shuffler. I was shuffling in the way that long ago the Doveston had shuffled. The way that the Principal Boy in the play had shuffled. It was the very same shuffle.

The very same shuffle.

And then, of course it hit me. I realized exactly what the professor's play meant.[1]

It was the life of the Doveston. The whole bit. Birth, life and death. As in 'Om'. Brahma, Vishnu and Siva. And how had the play ended? With the downfall of the palace and the Evil Prince. And how had the professor concluded the entire performance?

With a *big aaah-choo!*

And what was it Danbury Collins had said?

Assemble all the members of the Secret Government in one big room and then blow the lot of them to kingdom come.

---

[1] Yes, OK. I'm sure you already figured it out. But then I bet you went to grammar school.

With dynamite, perhaps?

The Big Aaah-Choo!

'Oh shit!' I went. 'Oh shit! Oh shit! Oh shit!'

'You have me fair and square,' said a voice. An Irish voice as it happened. A fellow stood up, a fellow in a frock. A fellow wearing green lipstick and brandishing a blow-pipe. 'O'Shit's the name,' he said. 'Cross-dressing Secret Government hit man. How did I give myself away? Should I have shaved off me beard?'

'Forget it,' I told him. 'Don't you realize what's going to happen?'

'Well,' said O'Shit. 'My guess would be that you'll try to take me in. But I'm thinking you won't get as far as the door, before me mate O'Bastard over there takes the head right off you with his Uzi.'

'No,' I said, shaking him by the sequinned shoulders. 'We're all gonna die.'

'You before the rest of us, I'm thinking.'

'Get out of my way. Get out of my way.' I pushed O'Shit from his feet and shouted over to Norman. 'Norman,' I shouted. 'Come here quick, we're in trouble.'

'All right,' called Norman. 'I'm coming.'

Down, but not out, O'Shit was struggling. He had fallen amongst toffs. Which can prove tricky if you're a man and you happen to be wearing a dress.

'Well, helllooooo,' went the toffs.

'Get your fecking hands off me bum,' went O'Shit. 'Norman. Get over here.'

'I'm coming. I'm coming.' Norman shuffled over. Shuffled. That's what he did.

'Have you found her then?' Norman asked as he

314

shuffled. 'Oh sorry, did I tread on you?' he continued as his foolish platform shoe came down on some poor blighter's fingers.

'Norman. Hurry up.'

Behind Norman came his all-girl conga line. And behind this now came men of the mightily miffed persuasion.

I did some more of those big breaths up the nose and out of the mouth and grabbed at Norman as he stepped upon O'Shit.

'Norman,' I puffed and panted. 'Norman, I've worked it out. I've worked it out.'

'I told you I didn't want to hear about your bowel movements.'

I punched Norman right on the nose. I'm sorry, but I did. Heat of the moment.

'Ooooooooooooooooh,' went Norman's female followers. 'Leave our lovely boy alone.'

'Stay out of this,' I told them. I had Norman by the lapels; I didn't let him fall. 'The time?' I gasped. 'What is the time?'

Norman clutched at his nose. 'You hit me. You punched my hooter.'

'Tell me the time. Quickly, or—'

'OK. OK.' Norman fumbled out his watch. The women were gathering round us now, stepping on the sitters and getting in a state. Their boyfriends, lovers, husbands or whatevers were tugging at them and telling them to come away.

'It's five to twelve,' said Norman, dabbing at his conk with his sleeve. 'All this fuss just because you wanted to know the time. But hang about. Shouldn't we be organizing the "Auld Lang Syne" business?'

'Norman.' I shook him all about. 'I've worked it out. There's not going to be any "Auld Lang Syne". I know what's going to happen.'

'You always say that when you've had a few.'

'Norman, you shithead, just listen to me.'

'You leave Norman alone,' said some woman, welting me one with her handbag.

'Don't worry, love,' said Norman. 'I can handle him, he's just a bit pissed.' And then Norman became aware for the very first time of just how many women now surrounded us. 'Well, helllooooo, ladies,' said Norman.

'Listen, listen.' I flapped my hands about. 'Listen to what I'm saying. The professor's play, right? It was all about the Doveston.'

'Well, I'd worked that out,' said Norman. 'But then I did go to grammar school.'

'Yes, all right. But the bit at the end, where the boy in the play blows everybody up. And the professor. *The Big Aaah-Choo!* Don't you understand what I'm saying?'

Norman nodded thoughtfully. 'No,' he said.

'Everybody here,' I said. 'Everybody here,' and I had to speak up quite a bit, because the mob about us was pushing and stepping on people. 'Everybody here, all these people. This is them. This lot. The Secret Government. The rulers and makers of men, the grand muck-a-mucks, like the professor said. The Doveston invited all these people here, and they all came, even though he was dead. Because they knew they'd get the bash of the century. But don't you see, that's what they

316

really are going to get. The big bash. The Big Aaah-Choo!'

'What exactly are you trying to say?'

I kicked at O'Shit, who was biting my ankle. 'I'm saying, Norman, that this place is going to blow. The professor warned us. He never sneezes when he takes snuff. He warned us, you and me, so we could get out in time. Don't you see? The Doveston is going to get his revenge from beyond the grave. I'll bet this place is packed with dynamite. And I'll bet, I'll just bet, it's timed to go off at midnight. Come on, Norman, you knew the Doveston as well as I did. Isn't it exactly what he'd do?'

'There has to be a flaw in this logic,' said Norman. 'But for the life of me, I can't see what it is.'

I looked at Norman.

And Norman looked at me.

'*Fire!*' shouted Norman. 'Everybody out! Everybody out!'

'What are you doing?' I clapped my hand across his mouth.

'Just leave him alone,' said some other woman, welting me with *her* handbag.

'Keep out of this,' and I pushed her.

'How dare you push my wife, sir,' and some twat took a swing at me. I ducked out of the way, but O'Shit had a hold on my ankle and I fell forwards, bringing Norman with me. We went down amongst the toffs, who were floundering about and trying to stand up, whilst being kneed this way and that by Norman's female fan club and the men of mighty miffedness.

317

'Get off me,' cried Norman. 'We've got to warn everyone.'

'Why?' I gasped. 'Why? This lot are the Secret Government. They're the enemy. This bunch murdered the Doveston.'

'Yes,' agreed Norman. 'You're right there.' He dodged a foot that swung in his direction. 'Stuff 'em,' said Norman. 'Stuff 'em.'

Now, it does have to be said that Norman and I were up the minstrels' gallery end of the great hall. Which was not the end we wished to be at. The end we wished to be at was the other end. The end with the big entrance doors. The struggling and pushing and kicking and general bad behaviour that was going on around us was an isolated sort of chaos. The majority of the party guests weren't involved. They *were* showing considerable interest by now, but they were mostly just lolling about. And there were an awful lot of them and they were packed pretty densely and if Norman and I were to make our escape we were going to have to get through them.

'Come on.' I hauled Norman up. 'Act casual. Make for the door.'

We fought our way out of the scrum in as casual a way as we could. Which was not, perhaps, quite as casual as it might have been, but time *was* ticking away.

'I think we should forget "act casual",' said Norman. 'I think we should go for "run for our lives".'

'I think you're right.'

We ran for our lives.

But could we run?

Could we bugger!

We were reduced to doing a lot of leaping about, trying not to step on people's faces. It was a bit like that ludicrous hop, skip and jump thing they do in the Olympics.

I had hoped for a clean getaway, but Norman's fans weren't having that. They came in hot pursuit.

'Switch off your bloody suit,' I shouted at him.

Norman fumbled once more in his pocket. But this isn't easy to do when you're hop, skip and jumping.

What happened next had an elegant, almost slow-motion quality about it. The remote control slipped from Norman's fingers. It arced through the air. It fell towards the floor. It struck the floor and Norman's big left platform shoe came crunching down upon it. And then there was a sort of sparkler fizzing. It came from Norman's suit. The suit began to throb, to pulsate. It began to glow.

There was a sort of ear-splitting whine that turned every head in the place.

And what happened next wasn't elegant.

What happened next was pure chaos.

25

Tomorrow belongs to those who can see it coming.
                                        The Doveston

Allow me to set the scene, as it were.

Try to imagine that moment before the chaos kicked in.

Picture, if you will, the great hall.

Picture the duff decorations. The crudely daubed and badly stencilled walls. That vile dog-dragon thing that dangles from the chandelier. Picture the mariachi band, on high in the minstrels' gallery. It's the very band that once played Brentstock. Older now, of course, but still with lots of puff. And see their instruments. The trumpets and the flugelhorns, the cornets, the euphoniums, and indeed the ophicleides.

Now picture the people below them. All those beautiful people. Those rich and famous people. Those have-it-alls at the very top. Those people of the Secret Government. See how very well dressed they all are. How gorgeously attired. Some are on their feet, but most still loll about, languidly beckoning to waiters and shaven-headed dwarves.

And try if you can to picture Norman. He's right

down there in the very middle of the great hall. He's still got his trilby on his head. Oh no, he hasn't, no. He's torn his trilby off his head. He's beating at himself with it. He seems to be on fire. There's this big corona of light all around him. There's smoke rising up from his shoulders. And he's flashing on and off. His suit. It's going like a stroboscope. And there's this awful noise now. It's coming from the suit. It's a high-pitched whining sound. A real teeth-clencher, an ear-drum-piercer.

All eyes are upon Norman. The lollers are scrambling to their feet, covering their ears and howling.

And now the chaos kicks in.

'Ooooh!' went Norman, beating at himself. 'I'm reaching critical mass.'

Now, generally speaking, your really big punch-up starts small and works its way towards a crescendo. A bit like a military campaign. Minor skirmishes, leading to the battle proper. Usually the two opposing sides get the chance to size each other up before charging head-long. That's the way it's done. You wouldn't just jumble the two sides together, bung everyone into a big room and simply blow a whistle, would you?

That would be chaos.

Wouldn't it?

Yet here, suddenly, in the great hall, were two utterly opposing sides, all jumbled up together. What sides are these, I hear you ask. One male side and one female, is the answer.

As Norman's suit reached critical mass it discharged such a rush of power that there could be no middle

321

ground. The force was overwhelming. The women overwhelmed with love, the men with absolute hatred. Norman was no longer Norman at all. To the women he was a God-like being. To the men, the Devil Incarnate.

Now, women always know what men are thinking and a woman will fight hard to save the man she loves. So, as the men rose up as one to slay the evil demon, the womenfolk rose up as one to save the man they loved.

And if you've ever seen two hundred women take on two hundred men in a no-holds-barred grand-slam tag-team main event, then you'll know what I mean when I tell you it was brutal.

I got welted with another bloody handbag.

It was the war of the sexes. A kind of simultaneous female uprising of the kind no doubt dreamed about by Emmeline Pankhurst (1858–1928) that now legendary English suffragette leader, who in 1903 founded the militant Women's Social and Political Union.

It was war.

But then war, what is it good for? I ask you. Absolutely nothing (Good God y'all).

The women beat upon the men and the men lashed out at the women. Norman tore his jacket off and flung it into the air. As waiters' trays went sailing overhead and love-sick dwarves bit waiters in the nadgers, I did that thing that the handyman's dog did. I made a bolt for the door.

I was not alone in doing this. Norman, on his hands and knees, his trousers round his ankles, caught me up.

He had his bunch of convenient keys in his hand.

'Out,' went Norman, 'Out. Come on, I'll lock the door.'

We scuttled out and slammed the front door shut upon the chaos. Norman turned the key in the lock. 'That should keep them at bay,' he said.

'What's the time? What's the time?'

'Damn,' said Norman, kicking off his platform shoes and pulling up his smouldering trews. 'My watch is in my jacket. But there can't be much time left. A couple of minutes at most.'

'Let's head for the gates then. I'll race you.'

I was on the starting blocks and I was almost off, but Norman said, 'Hold on.'

'What?' I said. 'What is it?'

Norman peered into the darkness. 'There's something wrong out there,' he said. 'I can feel it.'

I squinted about. 'Don't be stupid,' I told him. 'This is no time to be scared of the dark.'

'It's too quiet. Too still.'

'It's not back in there.'

Sounds of battle issued from within the walls of Castle Doveston. Breakings of glass and smashings of furniture. And the occasional thud as someone blundered into an invisible pillar. Although, in all the hullaballoo, you really couldn't hear those.

'Look,' and Norman pointed. By the light that issued from the windows of the great hall, a rather dancing light with lots of moving silhouettes, we could see the big black lorries. They now had their tailgates down and ramps leading from their open rear ends to the ground. Norman limped on stockinged feet across to the nearest lorry.

'We don't have time,' I shouted to him. 'Come on, Norman, let's go.'

'No, wait.' Norman sniffed at the ramp. 'Offal,' he said, 'dead meat. The lorries are empty, but whatever was in them dines upon meat.'

'Wild animals.' I was soon at Norman's side. 'Set free in the grounds, just in case anyone was to escape the explosion.'

'He didn't miss a trick, the Doveston, did he?'

'He never left anything to chance.'

'Oh Gawd,' said Norman and he pointed again. This time out into the night. I peered in the direction of his pointing and I didn't like what I saw.

There had to be hundreds of them out there. Thousands, perhaps. Lurking where the hall's light dimmed to night. Lurking on the edge of darkness, as it were.

Chimeras.

Fully grown? Half grown? Maybe just a quarter grown. But great big sons of bitches none the less. Towering well above the eight foot mark, fanged-mouths opening and closing.

Chimeras.

Part sprout. Part basilisk. All predator.

Actually, if they ever come up with the technology again to make movies and they choose to make one out of this book, that would be great for the trailer. Imagine the bloke with the gravelly voice going, 'They came from the night. Part sprout. Part basilisk. All predator.'

Mel Gibson could play me and perhaps Danny de Vito might be persuaded to play Norman.

'What in the name of Meccano are those?' Norman asked. 'Are they triffids, or what?'

'They're *what* and we're surrounded and time is running out.'

'They'll eat us,' said Norman, shivering horribly. 'I just know they will.'

'Damn right they will. Norman, think of something.'

'*Me?* Why *me?*'

'Because you're the one with the inventive mind. Come up with something. Get us out of here.'

'Right,' said Norman. 'Right. OK. Yes. Well, all right. Let's imagine this is a movie.'

'*What?*'

'It's a movie and famous movie stars are playing us. You're being played by Danny de Vito and I'm being played by Arnold Schwarzenegger.'

'Norman, we don't have time for this.'

'No, think. In a situation like this, what would Arnie do?'

I looked at Norman.

And Norman looked at me.

'Arnie would drive the big truck,' I said.

'Into the big truck,' cried Norman and we made a dash for the cab. We dashed pretty fast, I can tell you. But you do have to hand it to the vegetable kingdom. When it gets the chance to do what it really wants to do, which, as Uncle Jon Peru Joans had told me all those years before, is, 'get about', it gets up and about at the hurry-up.

The chimeras swept towards us: a big green ugly snapping sproutish horde of horrors. We were hardly

325

inside the lorry's cab before they were all about us, evil tendrils whipping and big teeth going snap snap snap.

We locked the doors, I can tell you.

Norman was in the driving seat. 'Drive,' I told him. 'Drive.'

'Where are the keys?' Norman asked.

'I don't know. Won't one of yours fit it?'

'Now you're just being silly.'

'Oh shit! Oh shit! Oh shit!' I caught sight of the little dashboard clock. One of those digital jobbies. It read 23:59. '*OH SHIT!*'

Crack! went the window on my side. Snap snap snap went teeth.

'You drive,' yelled Norman. 'I'll reach down under the dash and hot-wire it.'

'How?'

'Do you really want me to spend time explaining to you how?'

'No. Just do it.'

I climbed over Norman and he climbed under me. The crashing and bashing was deafening and the lorry was rocking from side to side. Then the passenger window went and we were in *really* big trouble.

Norman was frantically tinkering under the dash. I was clinging to the wheel and wondering just how you drove a big lorry when suddenly everything went a bit green. Very green indeed.

'Aaaaagh! Get it off me!' Norman kicked and screamed. The cab was a thrashing maelstrom of tendrils, gnashing teeth and really horrible sprouty breath. 'Aaaaagh!' wailed Norman. 'It's got me. It's got me.'

326

And it had got him.

I tried to beat the thing off, but I couldn't do much with my fists. There was one of those big sunshield visor things above the windscreen. I figured that if I could rip that off, I could use it as some kind of weapon. I reached up and tried to tear it loose.

And guess what? There was a spare set of keys up there, stuck under the sun visor thing.

Just like there always was for Arnie.

'Hold on, Norman,' I shouted. 'We're on our way.'

I rammed the key into the ignition. Chose a gear at random and put my foot to the floor.

And we went into reverse.

Now I'm damn sure that that never happened to Arnie.

The big lorry ploughed back into Castle Doveston, demolishing stonework and stained glass. I chose another gear. It was a good'n this time. The lorry lurched forward, bringing down further stonework and stained glass. Revealing the chaos within to the monsters without. But whatever horrors followed then, I didn't see them.

I just kept my foot down hard and we took off at a gallop.

Now, big and mean and ugly the chimeras may have been, but they were no match for the lorry. We ripped through their ranks, mashing them under, me clinging onto the steering wheel and Norman clinging onto me.

'The time,' I shouted. 'The time.'

'I don't think there's any time left,' shouted Norman.

But there was.

Just a wee bit.

Just a final ten seconds.

Ten . . .

I whacked us up a gear and kept the throttle down.

Nine . . .

Inside the great hall, chimeras wreaking bloody mayhem.

Eight . . .

More chimeras up ahead.

Seven . . .

O'Shit and O'Bastard on the minstrels' gallery bravely letting fly with their Uzis.

Six . . .

Splatter and splat as the big lorry mows down further chimeras.

Five . . .

Castle Doveston silhouetted against the full moon.

Four . . .

Blood and guts and gore and ghastliness.

Three . . .

Big lorry, engine roaring, ploughs towards the gates.

Two . . .

Danbury Collins awakens to find himself inside an invisible suit of armour. 'What's all this noise?' he asks.

One . . .

Big lorry smashes through the gates of Castle Doveston.

Zero . . .

A very brief moment of absolute silence. Again Castle Doveston standing tall and proud and unsightly against that old full moon,

And then . . .
BOOOOM.

The biggest BIG AAAH-CHOO! that ever there was.

26

Are we dead then?
Norman Hartnell

I didn't see it.

Though I really wish I had.

They told me that the explosion was really quite spectacular.

Some Bramfielders conga-lining around the car park at the back of the Jolly Gardeners, singing in the New Year and the new millennium, thought at first it was a firework display that the Laird had generously laid on for them.

The charges had been so perfectly placed, you see, and the beauty of it was, as I later came to understand, they were not triggered by any pre-set timing mechanism. The Doveston had let fate set them off.

Allow me to explain.

It had been his obsession that the end of civilization as we knew it would occur at the stroke of midnight on the final night of the twentieth century. He said that he knew it. Had seen it. Had felt it. Whatever. And he was so absolutely certain of this, that this is how he triggered the bomb.

A simple cut-out switch linked to the detonator. As long as the electrical mains supply to Castle Doveston remained on, the bomb remained harmless. But should the power fail, the cut-out switch would trigger the bomb.

And so, of course, if the Secret Government of the World had not really engineered the Millennium Bug and sabotaged all those computer systems, the power would remain on. But if they had and the National Grid failed . . .

The Big Aaah-Choo!

And, at the very stroke of midnight, the computer systems went down and the National Grid failed.

From beyond the grave, he'd had his revenge.

And, love him or hate him, you had to admire him. It *was* a masterstroke.

But I was telling you about how the charges had been so perfectly placed.

Three separate charges there were. Cunningly angled. They totally atomized Castle Doveston. But through the nature of their positioning, they did something more. They sent three rolling fireballs into the sky.

Three rolling fireballs that formed for a moment the triple snake Gaia logo of the Doveston.

Pretty damn clever, eh?

But, as I said, I didn't see it. The big lorry I was trying to drive smashed through the gates, hurtled along the road towards the village and then came to that rather tricky bend just before you reach the Jolly Gardeners.

Well, it was dark, very dark now, no street lights or

anything. And I hadn't managed to figure out how to work the headlights on the big lorry and there *was* a lot of ice on the road and we *were* going very fast.

I turned the wheel and I put my foot down hard upon the brake, but that bend *was* rather tricky at the very best of times.

'Aaaaaaaaaaaaaagh!' went Norman.

'Aaaaaaaaaaaaaagh!' I agreed.

I do have some recollection of the big lorry's rear end overtaking us and all these trees appearing out of nowhere and then suddenly we were rolling over and then everything went rather dark.

We missed the Jolly Gardeners by inches, but we did hit that very picturesque-looking Tudor house opposite. The one with the carefully tended knot garden and the preservation order on it and everything.

It didn't half make a noise, I can tell you.

I awoke to find that Norman and I were all tangled up together on the ceiling of the cab, which had now become the floor.

'Are we dead then?' Norman asked.

'No,' I told him. 'We're not dead. We've survived. We're safe.'

Now, I don't know why I said that. I know I shouldn't have. I know, as we all know, that if you say that, then you leave yourself open for something really bad to happen.

You bring down upon yourself THE TRICK ENDING.

Don't ask me why this is. Perhaps it's a tradition, or an old charter, or something. But I *did* say it. And once I had said it, I couldn't very well take it back.

'What's that funny noise?' Norman asked. 'That funny scratching noise?'

That funny scratching noise. Now what could that be?

Could that perhaps be one of the chimeras that had somehow managed to get aboard the big lorry and was even now making its wicked way along inside the back, before plunging into the cab to rip us limb from limb and gulp us down?

Well, it could have been, but it wasn't.

It was just the wind in the trees.

Phew.

'Tell me we're safe,' said Norman.

'We're safe,' I said. 'No, hang about. Can you smell petrol?'

27

The show's not over 'til the fat bloke snuffs.
Winston Churchill (1874–1965)

No, of course we didn't die.

We weren't blown to buggeration.

We were out of that lorry and into the Jolly Gardeners with seconds to spare before the fuel tank exploded.

There was hardly any damage at all done to the pub. The Tudor house took most of the blast. Which was a pity, seeing as how it was so old and well kept and picturesque and everything.

But, as I've told you before, I'm very much a Victorian man myself. I could never be having with Tudor architecture.

Norman had no money on him, so I had to pay for the pints.

Not that there were any pints on offer. Not with all the electrics off. The pumps wouldn't work any more.

'All the bloody power's gone,' declared the landlord. 'It will be that centennial mouse we've been hearing so much about.'

'Millennium Bug,' said Norman.

'Who said that?' asked the landlord. 'I can see sod all in this dark.'

Actually it really wasn't all that dark. The light from the burning Tudor house opposite offered a comfortable glow.

'Just give us two doubles out of the nearest optic,' I told the landlord. 'And don't trouble yourself with the ice and a slice.'

'Coming right up.' And the landlord blundered off.

'Do you know what this reminds me of?' said some old bloke in the corner. 'This reminds me of the war. Why don't we all have a sing-song, eh? Revive some of that old Blitz spirit, that made the working classes what we were and what we are today.'

'And what are we?' I asked.

'Shufflers,' said the old bloke. 'Shufflers and proud of it.'

Well, that was good enough for me, so I sang along with the others. These were my people. I was a part of them and they were a part of me. I was home at last amongst my own. And we sang, our voices raised. A song that we all knew and loved. A song that meant so much to us.

It was a song of hope. An anthem. A song that said, in its way, everything there was to say about us.

There were tears in my eyes as we sang it.

>'Here we go, here we go, here we go.
>Here we go, here we go, here we go-oh.
>Here we go, here we go, here we go.
>Here we go-oh, here we go.'

I forget how the second verse went.

What happened as the clocks struck twelve on that final night of the twentieth century has now passed into history. Oral history, that is. Because there is no other. Oral history, fireside tales, and no two tales the same.

As with the assassination of JKF, everyone remembers where they were on the night the lights went out.

Because, for most of us, they never went on again.

A chain, it is said, is only as strong as its weakest link. We learn that in infants' school. So what of technology's chain? All those systems, linked together? All those computer networks, exchanging information, feeding off each other's data-flows?

Throughout 1999, the British government had worn its bravest face. At most, only one per cent of all systems will be affected, they said. A measly one per cent. Nothing much to worry about.

So only one link in every hundred.

But wouldn't that mean that the chain would still snap?

As it turned out, of course, they were way off the mark. The agents of the Secret Government had been very thorough.

Nearly forty per cent of all vital systems failed.

Everything went down.

Everything.

Road-traffic signal systems: Gone.

Airport flight-control systems: Gone.

Railway point systems: Gone.

Telecommunications: Gone.

Banking systems: Gone.

Health-care facilities: Gone.

And they would all stay gone. Because all power had gone. The National Grid was dead.

And what about military hardware? What about their radar systems? And missile-tracking systems? And anti-missile-missile-launch systems? Did they fail too?

Oh yes, they failed.

In England everything switched itself off. In Russia things were different. The Secret Government hadn't troubled with Russia. Russia had so many clapped-out old systems that Russia would collapse without 'help'.

Unfortunately, and evidently unforeseen, the sudden loss of power in Russia had the same effect upon some of the Russian nuclear arsenal as it had upon the Doveston's dynamite.

Only five missiles went up. Which was pretty good, considering. The other 13,055 stayed on the ground. But once those five were in the air, that was it. You couldn't bring them back. And you couldn't telephone anyone to warn them they were on their way and say that you were very sorry and it had all been an accident and not to take it personally.

The West could do nothing to stop them.

And the West didn't know they were coming, or where they were coming from.

The West was power dead. A great slice of it was in darkness: Auld Lang Syners halted in mid-flow; people searching around for candles and wondering how badly they could behave before the power came back on; pretty much everyone drunk.

And five nukes on the way.

They fell somewhat haphazardly.

The one that should have hit central London hit Penge. Which I'm told was a very nice place, although I feel disinclined to visit it nowadays.

Another hit Dublin. Which was bloody unfair. Because, come on, who have the Irish ever attacked, apart from the English? Nobody, that's who.

Paris copped one. But bugger Paris.

The one that made it to America came down in the Grand Canyon. Causing no loss of life and no damage to property. Now was *that* fair, I ask you?

The last one came down upon Brighton. Brighton! Why Brighton! Why not Switzerland, or Holland, or Belgium. Or Germany?

Two on England and one of these on Brighton. That wasn't fair. It just wasn't.

Especially as Bramfield is only ten miles north of Brighton.

But ten miles *is* ten miles. And there were the South Downs in between.

Ten miles from the blast meant only a bit of minor roasting and a few flattened buildings. Ten miles from the blast was a doddle.

I think we were into our eighth or ninth double when the shock wave hit. I recall Norman saying, 'What's that funny noise?' again. And I recall the way the south wall of the pub began to make its way towards the north wall. And I remember telling Norman that I thought we'd better run again. And I remember that Norman agreed.

We ran and once more we survived.

Few people knew exactly what had really happened. And few were ever likely to find out. No electricity

338

means no TVs or radios or newspapers. It means no information.

No electricity means no petrol either. No petrol means you stay put where you are.

Country communities cut themselves off. There were food riots in London. Revolution is only ever three square meals away. The British government was overthrown. The People took control. But what could the People do? Could the People get the power back on? No, the People could not. How can you mend a broken system if you have no way of finding out which part of it is broken? How can you check an electrical system without electricity?

In the country we were luckier. At least we had something to eat. We could live off the land. Like the shufflers of old had done.

Norman and I crept back to Castle Doveston to view the ruins and see what might be salvaged. We went in the daytime and we went with caution for fear of the chimeras.

But all the chimeras were dead.

Those which had not been vaporized in the blast had come to grief in the security ditches I'd had dug. The ones with spikes at the bottoms. The spikes that had been given a coat of Norman's invisible paint.

We marvelled at the ruins. Everything had gone. From the ground up. But from the ground down, things were different. The cellars had survived intact. The trophy room was untouched and so were all the storage rooms. Norman brought his convenient keys into play and we opened them up. Food, glorious food. Enough to last us for years. Enough to last *us*. As long as we didn't share it around. As long as we could hang on to it for ourselves.

Norman opened up the Doveston's armoury and broke out the mini-guns.

And that's where we holed up. For eight long dark years.

From then, until now.

Which brings me to the present and to how the writing of this book came about. The Doveston's biography.

I'd had no intention of ever writing it. What would have been the point now? There were no more books and no more bookshops. People didn't read books any more. Books were for burning. Books were fuel.

It was in the early springtime of this year, 2008, that the man came to visit us. He was alone and unarmed and we let him through our barricades.

The man said that his name was Mr Cradbury and that he was employed by a London publishing house. Things were changing in the big metropolis, he told us. The power was back on there and nearly all the time. There was TV too, but only black and white and only showing public-service broadcasts.

A new government had been installed after the revolution and it was slowly getting things back together. A little at a time. This new government would not be making the same mistakes that the old one had made. We would not be seeing too much in the way of technology. It had brought back conscription and many young men had now joined up with the People's Cavalry.

Things were changing. There was a new world order.

Norman and I listened to what Mr Cradbury had to say. And then I asked Norman whether he thought that Mr Cradbury would taste better fried than boiled.

'Definitely fried,' said Norman.

Mr Cradbury became agitated. He had travelled all the way from London to meet us, he said. He had a proposition he wished to put to me.

'Where have you hidden your horse?' Norman asked.

Mr Cradbury wasn't keen to tell us. He said that he had not even known whether we were alive or dead, or indeed whether, if we were alive, we'd still be living here. But he'd come, all the same, braving the robbers and brigands and highwaymen, because what he had to say to me was important and so could we please not cook him and eat him?

'We can search for his horse,' said Norman. 'I'll get the fire started.'

Mr Cradbury fainted.

Once revived, Mr Cradbury had a great deal more to say. His publishing house, he said, had been asked by the new ministry of culture to publish a book. It would be the first book to be published this century. It was to inspire the young. It was very very important and only I could write this book. Only *I* had all the necessary information in my head. Only *I* knew the whole truth. And, if I would take on this task, I would be most handsomely rewarded.

'Go on then,' I said. 'What is this book that you want me to write?'

'The biography of the Doveston,' said Mr Cradbury.

Mr Cradbury made me an offer I couldn't refuse.

I refused this offer and he upped it a bit.

Electrical power would be restored to the village. I would be made mayor of the village. Being mayor would entitle me to certain privileges. I would draw up a list of these. Norman and I would be supplied with food and drink and fags and pretty much anything else that our little hearts desired. And Norman would receive a box of Meccano. A big box. *The biggest box.*

Mr Cradbury agreed to everything. But then I knew that he would. I knew that I could ask for pretty much anything I wanted, and I knew I'd get it too. Because I'd been expecting the arrival of Mr Cradbury, or someone just like him. I knew that it had only been a matter of time before I was called upon to write the Doveston's biography. I'd had long enough to reason things out, to understand what had really happened, and why, and who was behind it all. So I didn't ask any more questions. I just shook Mr Cradbury's hand.

And so I wrote the book. And that was it. You've read it. So why are there still some pages left to go, you may ask. Wouldn't it just have been better if it had gone out earlier on a chorus of 'Here we go'? Well, perhaps it would.

If you could examine the original manuscript of this book, which, I am told, is to be stored in the New State Archives, you would see that up until this paragraph, it is all hand written. Yet these final chapters are typed.

They are typed upon a 1945 Remington Model 8 manual typewriter.

The Newgate Prison typewriter.

All statements have to be typed up. It's one of the rules. It's the way things are done. There's not much point in arguing.

I wrote the rest of the book in longhand. It took me months. But I do have a photographic memory. I didn't need any notes made in Filofaxes, or access to the Doveston Archive. I had it all in my head. All I had to do was write it down. Tell it the way I saw it. How I remembered it. How it really was.

On the day of my arrest, Norman and I had been fishing. Private access to the trout stream is one of the perks you get, being the mayor.

It was nice to be away from all the noise of the builders I'd had Mr Cradbury bring in to rebuild Castle Doveston. We'd had a splendid afternoon and Norman had caught four large troutish things, which didn't give off too much of a radioactive glow. We were whistling and grinning and pushing each other into bushes as we shuffled home for tea, and I remember thinking at the time that even after all we'd suffered, we still seemed to have come through smiling.

I'd handed the finished manuscript to Mr Cradbury on Edwin's Day last. Which was the day before yesterday. Norman and I had long ago renamed the days of the week. There was Edwin's Day, then Norman's Day, and then we'd got a bit stuck. So we'd had Edwin's Day II and Norman's Day II and so on. But that didn't work, because there were seven days in the week.

So Norman had said, 'Well, poo to it. If we're renaming the days anyway, why bother with a

343

seven-day week? If we had a two-day week instead, it would be far less complicated.

He was right, of course.

The only problem was that certain people, and I will not name them, kept saying it was their day when it wasn't. When it had, in fact, been their day the day before.

So Norman hit upon another idea.

As we had to take it in turns to empty the latrine and this really did have to be done on a daily basis (as it was only a very small latrine and neither of us wanted to dig a bigger one), Norman said that we would easily be able to remember whose day it was if their day coincided with the day they emptied the latrine.

I asked Norman, Why not the other way round?

Norman said that it was the fact that he'd known in advance that I'd ask that question, which had decided the matter for him.

I have still to figure out just what he meant by that.

So, as I say, we were shuffling home from the fishing, whistling and grinning and pushing and whatnot, and I was saying to Norman that hadn't he noticed how we always had good fishing on Edwin's Days? And good hunting and good birds'-nesting? And didn't it seem just the way that Edwin Days were particularly lucky days for that kind of thing? In fact much nicer and sunnier days all round than certain other days I could mention.

And Norman had asked whether I'd noticed how on Edwin's Days the latrine never seemed to get emptied properly? And wasn't that a coincidence? And perhaps we should rename Edwin's Days Old-baldy-fat-bastard-who-never-empties-the-latrine-properly Days.

And I was just telling Norman that even though in my declining years, of failing eyesight and somewhat puffed in the breath department, I could still whip his arse any day. Be it a Norman or an Edwin.

And Norman was singing 'Come over here if you think you're hard enough', when we saw the helicopter.

It wasn't a real helicopter. Not in the way we remember real helicopters to be. Real helicopters used to have engines and lighting-up dashboards and General Electric Mini-guns slung beneath their hulls.

That's how I remember them, anyway.

So this was not what you'd call a *real* helicopter.

This was an open-sided, pedal-driven, three-man affair. It was all pine struts and canvas sails of the Leonardo da Vinci persuasion. Old Leonardo. Which meant *dead* in Brentford rhyming slang, didn't it?

The helicopter was parked close by the building site. There didn't seem to be too much in the way of building going on – a lot of down-tooling and chatting with the helicopter's pedal men, but that was about all.

'I'll bet that some high-muck-a-muck from the publishing company's come to tell them to pack up their gear and go home,' said Norman.

'Why would that happen?' I asked. 'Mr Cradbury promised to have the house rebuilt if I wrote the book.'

'Your faith in Mr Cradbury is very touching,' said Norman. 'Have you ever thought to ask yourself just why his company is being *so* generous?'

'Of course.'

'And what conclusions have you come to?'

I did not reply to this.

A builder chap came shuffling up.

'There's a toff from London to see you, your mayorship. He's come about that book you've been writing. He's waiting for you in the trophy room.'

'Well, there you go then,' said Norman. 'It was great while it lasted. But if you'd listened to me when I told you to take at least five years writing that book, at least we'd have had the house finished.'

'A book only takes as long as it takes,' I said. 'I'd better go and speak to this toff.' I paused and smiled at Norman. 'We have had some laughs, though, haven't we?'

'And then some,' said the ex-shopkeeper.

'It's been good to know you, Norman.'

'Eh?'

'I'm glad to have called you my friend.'

'Have you been drinking?' Norman asked.

I shook my head. 'I'll see you when I see you, then.'

'Er, yes.'

I took Norman's hand and shook it.

And, leaving him with a puzzled look upon his face, I shuffled away.

He had been my friend and companion for almost fifty years.

I would never set eyes on him again.

I shuffled past the builders and the helicopter-pedallers and I shuffled down the worn-down basement steps and along the passageway to the trophy room. And I stood for a moment before I pushed open the door and my hands began to tremble and my eyes began to mist.

346

Because, you see, I knew.

I knew what was coming.

I'd seen it and I'd felt it and I knew that it had to happen.

I did a couple of those up the nose and out of the mouth breathings, but they didn't help. So I pushed open the trophy-room door.

The London toff was standing with his back to me. He wore a long black coat with an astrakhan collar, over which fell lank strands of greasy white hair. He turned slowly, almost painfully, and his head nod-nodded towards me.

He was old, his face a mottled wrinkled thing. But beneath two snowy brows a pair of icy blue eyes were all a-twinkle.

His hands seemed crooked wizened claws. In one he held my manuscript. And in the other, a pistol.

He smiled when he saw me.

And I smiled in return.

'Hello, Edwin,' he said.

'Hello, Doveston,' I replied. 'I've been expecting you.'

28

And now, the end is near and so de da de da de da da.
Da de da de da de, da de da de, da de de dada.

Trad.

'You've had the gardens redone,' he said, as casual as
casual could be.

'I've moved all the trees. I could never be having
with that Gaia logo of yours. I uprooted the trees, one
by one, and repositioned them. It took me nearly eight
years. You can't really appreciate the new pattern from
ground level. Did you see it as you flew in?'

'No.' The Doveston shook his old head. 'I was
sleeping. I sleep a lot nowadays. But not in comfort. I
have dreams.'

'I'll just bet you do.'

'So,' the Doveston said. 'Here we are again. I must
say that you look well. The country life evidently suits
you.'

'Huntin', shootin' and fishin',' I said.

'And you've been expecting me?'

'Oh yes.' I perched my bum on the edge of the
table. 'I knew you'd be along pretty smartish, as soon
as you'd read my manuscript.'

'This?' The Doveston held the wad of papers in his trembling hand. 'This rubbish? This load of old bollocks?'

'Now, I did consider calling it that,' I said. '*A Load of Old Bollocks*. But I settled for *Snuff Fiction*. I felt that *Snuff Fiction* said it all.'

The Doveston hurled the manuscript down. It was an excellent hurl. If I'd been awarding points for hurling, I would have given him at least nine out of ten.

'Well hurled, sir,' I said.

His body rocked. 'It's rubbish.' His voice cracked and quavered. 'It's rubbish. It's bollocks.'

'You don't like it, then?'

'I hate it.'

'And might I ask why?'

The hand that held the pistol twitched. 'That book isn't about *me*. That isn't *my* biography. I come out of it as little more than a peripheral figure. That book is all about *you*. What *you* thought. What *you* felt. How *you* reacted to everything that happened.'

'So you really really hate it?'

'I loathe and detest it.'

'I felt pretty confident you would.' I pulled from my pocket a packet of cigarettes. Doveston's Extra Specials. Mr Cradbury had got them for me. I took one out and I lit it. 'Care for a smoke?' I asked the Doveston.

'No.' The old man's head rocked to and fro. 'I don't any more.'

'Too bad. But tell me this. What did you really expect me to write?'

'The truth. My life story. The truth.'

349

'The truth?' I shook my head, blew out smoke and spoke through it. 'What you wanted from me was a whitewash. A snow-job. That's why you left all your money to *me*. So I would be forever in your debt. So I would think what a wonderful fellow you were. And when the time came for me to write your life story, I would write a hagiography. And to do what? To make you a role model for the young. The shuffler who made it big.'

'And why not?' The Doveston waggled his pistol. 'I am the man, you know. *I* am the man.'

'The man who runs it all?'

'All,' said the Doveston.

I puffed upon my Extra Special. 'I thought that was probably the case. There's one thing I can't figure out though. How did you fake your own death? The head and the hand looked so real. I would have sworn they *were* real.'

'Of course they were real. They were my head and my hand. It was me, lying there in the coffin. I was worried for a moment, when Norman wanted to show you the way my head had been stitched back on. I'm glad you stopped him. You see, I just couldn't resist it. Attending my own funeral in person, hearing all the nice things people had to say. I was somewhat miffed that you didn't get up to say anything. And I didn't think it was funny when that twat from the Dave Clark Five sang 'Bits and Pieces'. Nor the fact that you put someone else's brand of cigarettes in my pocket. Or the way Norman knocked the vicar into the lake.'

'Oh come on,' I said. 'That *was* funny.'

'Well, perhaps a wee bit.'

'And so everyone, including me, thought you were dead. And I would probably have gone on thinking it, if it hadn't been for what happened here on that final night of the last century. When I discovered that all those people were members of the Secret Government. And when you blew them all to buggeration. I knew then. That wasn't a revenge killing. That was a *coup d'état*. You wiped them all out so you could take over.'

'I'm very impressed,' said the Doveston. 'I really didn't think you'd work that out.'

'Sit down,' I told him. 'Please sit down.'

He sank into the single chair. The pistol on his knees. His eyes now rolling wildly.

'But please tell me this,' I said. 'Because I really have to know. What was it all about? Why did you do all the things you did? Was it just to have power? Surely you had enough. You were so wealthy. So successful. Why did you do it all? Why?'

'You never understood and why should you have?' He stroked the barrel of his pistol. 'It was all so wild, you see. So off the world. It was all down to Uncle Jon Peru Joans. He was *my* mentor, you see. Oh yes, *I* had a mentor too. And all those things he told us about. All that wacky stuff. The talking to the trees. The revelation. Armageddon. The mad mutant army marching over the land. It was all true. Every bit of it. Especially the drug.'

'I can vouch for the drug,' I said, 'it helped to fuck up my life.'

'It was only in its first stages of preparation then. It

351

was raw. When it was accidentally administered to the crowd at Brentstock, it was still crude, but I realized then what I had. Something incredible, once it was refined and refined.'

'So all of this is about a drug?'

'Not *a* drug. *The* drug.'

'I don't understand,' I said.

'No.' The Doveston rocked in his chair. 'You don't. A lifetime's work has gone into the refinement of this drug. My lifetime. But why not? After all, what is a lifetime anyway? A drop of water in the ocean of eternity? A fleck of dandruff on the head of time? A nasty brown dingleberry on the arsehole of—'

'All right,' I said. 'I get the picture.'

'Oh no you don't. As I say, you only experienced the drug in its crude and unrefined form. It gave you flashes of the past and the present and the future. But they weren't all altogether accurate, were they?'

'Well—'

'But now it is perfected. After a lifetime of work and a fortune spent in research and development, it is perfected.'

'So the world can soon expect Doveston's Wonder Pills, can it?'

'Oh no. You fail to understand. These pills cannot be mass produced. It has been the work of a single lifetime to perfect *one single pill*.'

'Just the one?'

'I only need the one.'

I shook my head and sighed and I dropped my cigarette butt and ground it out with my heel. 'I don't get it,' I said. 'Everything you did, you did to get your hands on one single pill. What does this pill do?'

'It bestows immortality.'

'Does it bollocks. And even if it did, look at the state of you. You're an old man. Do you want to live for ever in your condition?'

'No no no. You still fail to grasp it. When the pill is placed in the mouth, its effect is instantaneous. It allows you to experience the past, the present and the future simultaneously. All of it. Can you imagine that? Can you possibly imagine that? In the space of a single second, which is all the time the effect of the drug lasts for, you experience everything.

'You are beyond time. Outside time. You wrote something about it in your load of old bollocks. About Christopher Mayhew. When he took mescalin. When he said that there is no absolute time, no absolute space, and when he said that within the span of a few moments he had experienced years and years of heavenly bliss. When I take my pill, I will experience eternity, all in a single second. For me the second in the real world will never pass. I will be immortal. Eternity within a single second.'

'And what if it doesn't work?'

'Oh, it will work.' The Doveston patted at his pocket.

'You have this pill with you?' I asked.

'Of course. In the silver coffin-shaped snuffbox that Professor Merlin gave to me. When my time comes, when I am dying, then I will take the pill.'

'And you're sure that it really will work? That you will experience eternity? Enjoy eternal bliss?'

'There is no doubt in my mind.'

I whistled. 'Do you want me to put that in my book? It might make the end a little bit more exciting.'

'Your book.' The Doveston spat. He spat down upon the scattered pages of my book. 'Your mockery of a book. Your load of old bollocks. That to your book and that again.'

And he spat again.

'That's not very nice,' I said.

'You betrayed me,' he said. 'Writing that rubbish. You betrayed me. Why?'

'To get you here, that's why. If I'd written the whitewash you'd hoped for, you never would have come. But I knew that if I wrote it the way I saw it, the way I felt it, the way it really was, I knew that would *really* piss you off. That you would come tearing around here to fling it in my face. When Mr Cradbury made me all those offers that I couldn't refuse, then I knew for certain that you were alive. That you were commissioning the book. And I just had to see you again. Just the one more time. To say goodbye.'

'Goodbye?'

'But of course, goodbye. If you'd read the book carefully, you'd know what *I'm* talking about. Take this page here, for instance.' I reached down to pick up a sheet of paper. But as I did so, I slipped upon the Doveston's spittle. Or at least pretended that I did. Just for a moment. Just for a second, actually. Sufficient to stumble; to reach forward.

To snatch away his pistol.

'Matters adjust themselves,' I said.

He quivered and shivered.

354

I twirled the pistol on my finger. 'Goodbye,' I said.

'Goodbye?'

'Goodbye to you, of course. In the first chapter of the book, I promised the readers something special. Something different. And I promised how I would write of your terrible end, as I alone could. I wanted the biography that I wrote to be different from any other biography that had ever been written before. And I've come up with a way to achieve this end. This will be the first biography ever written which ends with the subject of the biography being executed by his biographer. Now, is that an original idea for a book, or what?'

'What?' the Doveston cowered. 'Execute *me*? Murder *me*?'

'Absolutely,' I said. 'I've been planning it for years.'

The Doveston's lips trembled. 'Why?' he asked. 'Why? All right, so you went to prison. But didn't I make it up to you? Didn't I leave you all that money?'

'Only so I would praise you in the book. And the money was really nothing but a short-term loan, to ensure the Great Millennial Ball went ahead. And you knew that money would be useless after society collapsed.'

'So I left you all the food in the cellars.'

'Just to keep me alive, so that when you were fully in control, I would write your damn book.'

'So why?' The Doveston's eyes went every which way. 'Why do you want to kill me?'

'Because of something you did many years ago. Something that seemed trivial to you at the time. A bit

355

of a laugh. A joke. You took away something from me. Something that I loved. I mentioned it in the book. But I didn't make a big thing out of it. I didn't want to warn you. I wanted you to come here, so that I could kill you, because of what you did.'

'I don't understand. What did I do? What did I take from you?'

I leaned close to his ear and whispered a single word. A single name.

'No!' His eyes rolled. 'Not that! Not because of that.'

'That,' I said. 'That is why you are about to die.'

'Please . . . please . . .' He wrung his hands together.

I cocked the pistol. 'Goodbye,' I said.

'No, wait. No, wait.' He fumbled in his pockets and drew out the little silver coffin-shaped snuffbox. 'Don't deny me this. Don't deny me my lifetime's work. Let me take the pill before you pull the trigger. It will be but a second for you. But for me it will be an eternity. I will be immortal. Please.'

I nodded thoughtfully.

'No,' I said, snatching the snuffbox from his hand. 'I deny you immortality. I condemn you to death.'

He begged and pleaded and rocked in the chair. But I shook my head. 'It's a pity you were sleeping when the helicopter landed. Had you looked down and seen the pattern of the trees, you would have known what was coming. You would have read the name that the trees spell out. I gave you that chance. A chance to cheat fate. Because when I was under your drug and in my kitchen, I saw the future. This future. This moment. I put it in the book. You didn't read it carefully enough. Goodbye, Doveston.'

I put the snuffbox into my pocket.

I threw aside the pistol.

I put my hands about his throat.

And I killed him.

And now we really have come to the end. And if you are studying this manuscript in the New State Archives, you will notice that the script has changed again. That once more it is written in longhand.

Well, it would be, wouldn't it? They don't let you use the typewriter to whack out your final words while you sit in the new-fangled electric chair, waiting for the arrival of the executioner.

You are given a pen and paper. You are told that you have five minutes.

I must have gone a little mad, I suppose, after I killed him. I realized what I'd done, but I couldn't feel any guilt. I had behaved *very* badly. But I had not killed an innocent man. After I'd strangled him, I picked up the leather bondage teapot. The one with all the spikes, that had once belonged to Chico's aunty, and I smashed his brains out with it.

I must have made a lot of noise. The helicopter-pedallers rushed in. They beat me most severely.

The magistrate was not in the mood for mercy. He was a young fellow and he said that his father had told him all about me. His father had been a magistrate too. His father had once sent me down for fifteen years.

The New World Order had no time for people like me, he said. People like me were a waste of time.

He condemned me to the Chair.

I don't remember too much about the trial. It was held in private and the outcome was a foregone conclusion.

I don't really remember too much about what happened after the pedallers beat me up and dragged me into the helicopter.

Although there is one thing I remember and I will set it down here because it is important.

I remember what the pedallers said to each other as they got their legs pumping and the helicopter into the air.

'Senseless, that,' said one. 'A truly senseless killing.'

And then he said, 'Here, Jack, look down there. I never noticed that when we flew in.'

And Jack said, 'Oh yeah, the trees. The trees are all laid out to spell letters. Huge great letters. What is it they spell?'

And the other pedaller spelled them out. 'B,' he said, 'and I and S and C—'

'BISCUIT,' said Jack. 'They spell BISCUIT.'

Yes, that's what they spelt. Biscuit. My dog, Biscuit. He murdered my dog, so I murdered him.

Was that wrong?

When I wrote that passage about being in prison, the one about bad behaviour and about the bad man who kills. Kills an innocent man. Remember? When I asked whether there really is such a thing as an innocent man?

Well, I still don't know the answer to that.

★

But that is it for me. The man in the black mask is coming to turn on the power. I must put aside my pen and paper.

For it is time for my big aaah-choo!

My goodbye.

Well, almost.

You see, they always allow a dying man to make a final request. It's a tradition, or an old charter, or something. There's no point in trying to come up with something clever. So I just kept it simple.

I just asked whether it would be all right if I kept my silver coffin-shaped snuffbox with me. As a keepsake. And would they mind if, in the final second before they pulled the switch, I just took the one little pill inside.

They said, No, they wouldn't mind. That would be OK.

They said, What harm could that do?

It wasn't as if it was going to let me cheat death.

It wasn't as if it would make me immortal or something.

And here he comes now. The prison chaplain has said his last words. The executioner's hand is moving towards the switch.

I must sign off now.

I must take the pill.

I know that its effect will only last for one single second in real time and then the switch will be pulled and I will die. But for me that single second will be an eternity. And what more can anyone ask for out of life, than eternity?

Not much, in my personal opinion.

P is for pill.
P is for paradise.
I've had a lot of trouble with Ps in the past.
But not this time.

No absolute time.
   No absolute space.
   Years and years of heavenly bliss.

And swallow.

         Here we go, here we go, here we go.
         Here we go, here we go, here we go-oh.
         Here we go, here we go, here we go.
         Here we go-oh, here we go . . .

Here we gone.

And snuff.

SPROUT⟨P⟩LŌRE

The Now Official
RŌBERT RANKIN
Fan Club

Members Will Receive:

Four Fabulous Issues of *The Brentford Mercury*, featuring previously unpublished stories by Robert Rankin. Also containing News, Reviews, Fiction and Fun.

A coveted Sproutlore Badge.

'Amazing Stuff!' – Robert Rankin.

Annual Membership Costs £5 **(Ireland)**, £7 **(UK)** or £11 **(Rest of the World)**. Send a Cheque/PO to: **Sproutlore, 211 Blackhorse Avenue, Dublin 7, Ireland.**
Email: jshields@iol.ie. WWW: http://www.iol.ie/ -jshields/fanclub.html

Sproutlore exists thanks to the permission of Robert Rankin and his publishers.

APOCALYPSO
by Robert Rankin

The Ministry of Serendipity at Mornington Crescent runs everything. And that means everything. When the Ministry learns of a spacecraft that crashed four thousand years ago into the Pacific Ocean it sends an élite team of paranormal investigators to recover it. A mad alien thaws out, there is hell and horror all around and thousands flee in terror.

Porrig has inherited a planet, or it might be a bookshop, or it might be a gateway into another world. And Porrig is worried, because he has learned a terrible secret. But if he told people, would they listen? No.

But perhaps they should, because a mad alien has thawed out, there is hell and horror all around and thousands are fleeing in terror. And there is every likelihood of there being a bloody big explosion at the end. Will Porrig manage to do anything about it at all?

0 552 14589 0

THE DANCE OF THE VOODOO HANDBAG
by Robert Rankin

'This is Rankin at his comic best. He does for England what Spike Milligan does for Ireland. There can be no higher praise'
John Clute, *Mail on Sunday*

Henry Doors is the world's richest man. His company, Necrosoft, doesn't just market computer software, it sells immortality.

Billy Barnes is the world's most ruthless individual. When Billy isn't feeding bits of his granny to the voodoo handbag, he's furthering his ambitions: to control Necrosoft and run the planet. His way.

Lazlo Woodbine is the world's greatest private eye. And Lazlo's on the case. Or he will be, as soon as he can persuade the doctor to release him from his straitjacket.

Barry is the world's most famous sprout. He lives in Lazlo's head and he is confused by all of the above.

'We read Rankin for his exuberant salmagundi of old jokes, myths urban and otherwise, catchphrases, liberatingly crazy ideas, running gags, recurring characters and locations, unreliable autobiographical anecdotes ... He becomes funnier the more you read him'
Mat Coward, *Independent*

0 552 14580 7

THE BRENTFORD CHAINSTORE MASSACRE
by Robert Rankin

*'Jim took himself to his favourite bench before the Memorial Library.
It was here, on this almost sacred spot, that Jim did most of his really
heavyweight thinking. Here where he dreamed his dreams and made
his plans…'*

There is nothing more powerful than a bad idea whose time
has come. And there can be few ideas less bad or more
potentially apocalyptic than that hatched by genetic scientist
Dr Steven Malone. Using DNA strands extracted from the
dried blood on the Turin Shroud, Dr Malone is cloning
Jesus. And not just a single Jesus, he's going for a full half-
dozen so that each of the world's major religions can have
one. It's a really bad idea.

In Brentford they've had a really good idea. They're holding
the Millennial celebrations two years early to avoid the rush
and it promises to be the party of this, or any other, century.
Unless, of course, something REALLY BAD were to
happen…

'Stark raving genius … alarming and deformed brilliance'
Observer

The fifth novel in the now legendary *Brentford Trilogy*

0 552 14357 X

SPROUT MASK REPLICA
by Robert Rankin

The epic tale of a family of fervent God-botherers.

His great-great-grandfather died at the Battle of Little Big Horn. He wasn't with Custer though. He was holding a sprout-bake and tent meeting and went over to complain. His great-grandfather (also a sprout farmer and man of the cloth) always wore weighted shoes while in the pulpit to avoid any embarrassing levitations during moments of extreme rapture. His grandfather (lay preacher, taste for sprouts) spoke only in rhyming couplets and owned a pig called Belshazzar. His father (an elder in the Sacred Order of the Golden Sprout) practised body-modification in an attempt to win a bet with his brother (a monk). And then there was him.

Can this be Robert Rankin's autobiography? He swears that it isn't, but as a self-confessed teller of tall tales, whoever is going to believe him?

0 552 14356 1

NOSTRADAMUS ATE MY HAMSTER
by Robert Rankin

BE CONFUSED. BE VERY CONFUSED.

They're making a movie in Brentford. It's unlike any movie that's ever been made before. All the Hollywood Greats are in it. All the *dead ones* anyway. They've got this *Cyberstar* equipment, you see. A computer system that can generate life-sized moving holograms of famous film stars. The big question is, where did they get it from? Or should the question be WHEN?

Russell's producing the movie. Not that he really knows how to, but he's prepared to give it a go. He's a very nice chap, is Russell, perhaps a bit too nice. He works too hard and he cares too much, and people take advantage of him.

Morgan takes advantage. He tells Russell stories. In fact, if Morgan had never told Russell about Pooley and Omally, Russell would never have spent his lunch-time trying to locate the real Flying Swan. And if he'd never done that, Russell would never have found out about the alien technology in the Second World War, seen the flying saucer, met Adolf Hitler, heard the voices of God, helped make a movie that would change the future of the entire human race and come within a gnat's testicle of selling his spine to Satan.

AND THAT AIN'T THE HALF OF IT!

0 552 14355 3

A SELECTED LIST OF FANTASY NOVELS AVAILABLE FROM CORGI AND BLACK SWAN

13017 6	MALLOREON 1: GUARDIANS OF THE WEST	David Eddings	£5.99
12284 X	BELGARIAD 1: PAWN OF PROPHECY	David Eddings	£5.99
14255 7	ECHOES OF THE GREAT SONG	David Gemmell	£5.99
14256 5	SWORD IN THE STORM	David Gemmell	£5.99
14274 3	THE MASTERHARPER OF PERN	Anne McCaffrey	£5.99
13728 6	PEGASUS IN FLIGHT	Anne McCaffrey	£5.99
14478 9	AUTOMATED ALICE	Jeff Noon	£6.99
14479 7	NYMPHOMATION	Jeff Noon	£6.99
14598 X	JINGO	Terry Pratchett	£5.99
14614 5	THE LAST CONTINENT	Terry Pratchett	£5.99
13681 6	ARMAGEDDON THE MUSICAL	Robert Rankin	£5.99
13832 0	THEY CAME AND ATE US, ARMAGEDDON II: THE B-MOVIE	Robert Rankin	£5.99
13923 8	THE SUBURBAN BOOK OF THE DEAD, ARMAGEDDON III: THE REMAKE	Robert Rankin	£5.99
13841 8	THE ANTIPOPE	Robert Rankin	£5.99
13842 8	THE BRENTFORD TRIANGLE	Robert Rankin	£5.99
13843 6	EAST OF EALING	Robert Rankin	£5.99
13844 4	THE SPROUTS OF WRATH	Robert Rankin	£5.99
14357 X	THE BRENTFORD CHAINSTORE MASSACRE	Robert Rankin	£5.99
13922 X	THE BOOK OF ULTIMATE TRUTHS	Robert Rankin	£5.99
13833 9	RAIDERS OF THE LOST CAR PARK	Robert Rankin	£5.99
13924 6	THE GREATEST SHOW OFF EARTH	Robert Rankin	£5.99
14211 5	THE MOST AMAZING MAN WHO EVER LIVED	Robert Rankin	£5.99
14212 3	THE GARDEN OF UNEARTHLY DELIGHTS	Robert Rankin	£5.99
14213 1	A DOG CALLED DEMOLITION	Robert Rankin	£5.99
14355 3	NOSTRADAMUS ATE MY HAMSTER	Robert Rankin	£5.99
14356 1	SPROUT MASK REPLICA	Robert Rankin	£5.99
14580 7	THE DANCE OF THE VOODOO HANDBAG	Robert Rankin	£5.99
14589 0	APOCALYPSO	Robert Rankin	£5.99
99777 3	THE SPARROW	Mary Doria Russell	£6.99
99811 7	CHILDREN OF GOD	Mary Doria Russell	£6.99